You've Got the Marquess's Mail

The Brelsford Brothers, Book 2

Michelle McLean

ARE YOU SIGNED UP FOR DRAGONBLADE'S BLOG?

You'll get the latest news and information on exclusive giveaways, exclusive excerpts, coming releases, sales, free books, cover reveals and more.

Check out our complete list of authors, too!

No spam, no junk. That's a promise!

Sign Up Here

www.dragonbladepublishing.com

Dearest Reader;

Thank you for your support of a small press. At Dragonblade Publishing, we strive to bring you the highest quality Historical Romance from some of the best authors in the business. Without your support, there is no 'us', so we sincerely hope you adore these stories and find some new favorite authors along the way.

Happy Reading!

CEO, Dragonblade Publishing

**Additional Dragonblade books by
Author Michelle McLean**

The Brelsford Brothers Series
The Marquess Married a Murderess (Book 1)
You've Got the Marquess's Mail (Book 2)

CHAPTER ONE

Six Months Ago

LORD HUGO BRELSFORD took another healthy gulp of the brandy sloshing in his cup and raised a brow at his younger brother, Arthur, who had just wagered a very large sum of money on a rather silly prediction.

"I am telling you, Hugo, Edward will never marry. He is too happily confirmed in his bachelorhood. Which means it will fall to *you*, dear brother, to carry on our family line."

Hugo just shook his head. "You are far too unobservant, Arthur. And it will lose you your wager."

Arthur frowned. "Explain yourself."

"Have you not noticed how besotted our brother is with one Mrs. Selena MacLaren?"

Arthur's frown deepened and Hugo snorted. "He has spoken of nothing else since the day they met. He ensures he is at every event she may possibly attend and mopes about if she does not. And his spirits are impossibly high when he does encounter her, no matter how inconsequential or disastrous the interaction. Mark my words, they will be engaged within a fortnight."

"Bah," Arthur scoffed. "Even if that were true, there are far too many unsavory rumors about the woman for our father to ever agree to the match, even if the lady herself were to agree. Our brother may be besotted, but that does not mean the lady shares his affections. By all accounts, it is the opposite. Did she not literally run from him at the art gallery only a few weeks ago?"

Now Hugo frowned, his confidence in his assertation foundering. "Yes. But that does not mean—"

"If she doesn't find a husband," a slurred voice rumbled from across the room, "I will be responsible for her upkeep for the rest of her life. And who wants that responsibility? She's a handful. Enough to drive a man mad. Likely why she is still unwed. This is a situation that must be remedied, post haste."

Hugo and Arthur glanced over to see who was causing the ruckus. Hugo groaned when he recognized him.

"Henry Girard," Arthur muttered. "That blowhard. What's he blathering about now?"

"His unwed sister apparently." Hugo chuckled. "He has been focused on little else but finding a suitable match for her since their father died. Though the lady, by all accounts, has been resisting his efforts. It seems as though we have a similar problem."

"Eh?" Henry said, having wandered closer. They must not have been as circumspect about their whispering as they'd thought. "Similar problem? I thought your sisters were all married. Do you have another one somewhere who will be a spinster haunting your house for the rest of your days?"

Hugo frowned. He didn't remember if he had ever seen Miss Girard. If he had, it hadn't been memorable. Still, the way her brother spoke of her did not sit well with him. "That seems rather uncharitable of you. I'm sure your sister is a fine woman."

Henry's eyes narrowed. "She is. She is intelligent and relatively attractive, I suppose. But she is also stubborn and opinionated and…outspoken." He grimaced. "She's rejected every suitor I've suggested, and for the most ridiculous reasons."

He sat down—without being invited—but Arthur and Hugo just glanced at each other without saying anything. The man was too drunk and focused on his own grievances to likely listen, in any case.

"One was too old. Another too ugly." Henry snorted. "As if such things matter at all. They were both wealthy, landed gentlemen. Fine matches that would have offered security." He took another drink and shook his head. "The good Lord save me from obstinate women."

"Yes," Hugo said, cocking a brow. "The nerve of them wishing to have an attractive spouse of their own age who will not repulse them at every turn instead of simply settling for a comfortable bank account."

"Exactly," Henry said, jabbing his finger at him…and obviously not registering the thick layer of sarcasm with which Hugo spoke.

"*Do* you have any unmarried sisters left?" Henry said, leaning forward with sudden intensity. "I am looking for a wife myself." He sat back and drained the rest of his glass before raising it and waving it about a bit, apparently attempting to flag someone down to refill it for him.

"Are you now?" Hugo asked, his lips twitching.

"I am not nearly so picky as my sister," Henry continued. "I do not care about her looks or age. As long as she is still young enough to bear an heir and comes with a healthy dowry, that is." He chortled while Hugo and Arthur gave him twin looks of horror.

No sister of theirs would ever go near this man. Luckily, none were available.

"No, I'm afraid not," Hugo finally answered.

Henry's face fell. "Then to whom were you referring?"

"Our eldest brother," Arthur reluctantly said.

Hugo could see the moment the possibilities registered in Henry's mind. Henry paused, a sudden gleam in his eyes. "Ah yes. Lord Edward. Well now, perhaps, as we *do* share a common problem after all, we could be of help to each other."

Hugo and Arthur glanced at each other. The cheek of the man! He didn't need to utter another word for Hugo to know exactly what he was angling for. He should put a stop to any notions Henry might harbor along those lines. Then again, it could be so much more amusing to play along.

"How so?" he asked, glancing at Arthur from the side of his eye when his brother's head jerked in his direction.

"Well, obviously, I have a sister in need of a husband. You have a brother in need of a wife. My sister is a spinster, true, but not so old as all of that. Barely five and twenty, and healthy as a horse."

Arthur's eyebrows hit his hairline, so surprised was he. "And it is your contention that an untitled, outspoken, opinionated spinster of five and twenty is an appropriate match for the heir to the Duke of Haltham?"

Henry slammed his glass down on the table. "My sister may not be titled, but our family is wealthy and well-respected. I have been assured of my father's seat in Parliament, a seat members of my family have now held for four generations. We may not be as noble as the Duke of Haltham, but my sister would not muddy your bloodline, Lord Arthur. It is an insult to suggest otherwise."

"Of course, I assure you he meant no offense," Hugo said, keeping his voice level, not only to keep from upsetting the man further, but also because he sincerely did regret the insult which Arthur had just levied. The Girards were, indeed, a respectable and wealthy family. Just not quite as highborn as the Duke and Duchess of Haltham may be aiming for their heir. The other women who had been suggested were all titled daughters of nobility. Still, Miss Girard was respectable. On the other hand, Henry's entire tone and demeanor were off-putting, if not downright offensive. He was all but offering his sister up for sale, based solely on the Brelsford's bloodline and status.

Though, to be fair, that was the Marriage Mart in a nutshell. Most people had the grace to not be so blatant about it, however.

Henry puffed out his chest. "Then you surely have no objection to a possible match between my sister and your brother."

Hugo raised his brows. The man must be more drunk than he thought. Even if he, Hugo, had no objection—and frankly, he did, based solely on Henry himself—he had no say over who his elder brother married. His parents, who *did* have a large say, had been unable to persuade the man to marry for years.

But considering the amount of brandy Henry had consumed, he likely wouldn't remember much of this evening by the next day. And Hugo never let a chance to amuse himself slip by. No harm in having a little fun with the man.

"Of course not," Hugo said. "In fact, Edward has such confidence in our judgement that he has tasked us specifically with finding him a suitable match. Your sister seems as if she could be quite compatible with him. In fact, I grow more certain by the minute that a match between them could be arranged."

Henry clapped. "Wonderful news! I am glad to hear it." He pushed away from the table and staggered to his feet. "I shall look forward to speaking with you further on this matter."

He gave them an unsteady bow and swayed back to his table where his raucous friends awaited. "I am in the mood to celebrate!" he shouted before being swallowed up by his group.

Hugo chuckled, but Arthur stared at him, nonplussed. Yes, perhaps he had gone a bit too far. His own brain was more than a bit befuddled by drink.

"Are you mad?" Arthur asked.

"Quite possibly," Hugo said, blowing out a breath. "Oh, do not be so serious, Arthur. There's no harm in having a little fun. I offered nothing of real substance. Any rational person would understand I have no authority to arrange a match for my elder brother. Henry may be too drunk to realize that now, but once he sobers, he will. If he even remembers any of this, which is highly doubtful."

Arthur just shook his head. "You had better hope so. He seems the sort to see insult where none is meant. I have no doubt he will cause trouble if he takes any of this seriously."

Well, that was true enough. Perhaps he should have kept his mouth shut.

Hugo drained the last bit of brandy in his glass and stood.

"Let us depart then, before I get us into more trouble. We shall just hope Mr. Girard has forgotten all about this conversation by morning."

CHAPTER TWO

Three Days Later

MISS ADALINE GIRARD descended from her carriage and nodded to a group of women who were walking past. The Misses Gracely's she knew, though not the other woman with them. They glanced at her and hurriedly looked away, covering their mouths to hide their giggles.

Adaline raised her brows. Good heavens. What had brought that on?

She pushed open the door to her cousin Lucy's hat shop, already putting the strange incident behind her. Today was ribbon day. And she was eager to see what gorgeous new creations Lucy had come up with. Lucy had also informed her she was expecting a new shipment of velvet ribbon in a beautiful sapphire blue, and Adaline was hoping to procure some to wear in her hair with her new ballgown.

As she entered, Mrs. Boyles and her daughter were just leaving. Adaline smiled at them. They froze for a second before returning her smile. Odd.

"My lady," Miss Boyles said with a quick bob of a curtsy, before she burst into giggles.

Her mother hissed at her and hurried her out the door.

"Whatever was that about?" she asked aloud.

"Adaline," Lucy said, hurrying toward her. "Thank goodness you are here."

She grabbed Adaline's hand and dragged her to the back of the store, glancing out once more at the empty salon before rounding on Adaline.

"Is it true?"

Adaline simply stared at her, baffled. "Is *what* true?"

"What everyone is saying?" Lucy said, throwing up her hands.

Adaline cocked a brow. "My dear Lucy, I have no idea what anyone is saying. We've only just returned last night. You know how Mother prefers to be in the country since Father passed. It is a miracle I convinced her to return as early as we have. But there are several balls coming up that I simply couldn't miss and—what on earth is it?" she exclaimed at the growing look of horror on Lucy's face.

"Oh…oh dear." Lucy let out a deep breath and then reached out to grasp her hands, tugging her over to plop down on the overstuffed sofa she kept in the back room. "There…have been rumors."

"Rumors?" Adaline asked slowly.

Lucy nodded. "About you."

"Me?"

"Yes."

Adaline waited, but Lucy hesitated.

"Oh, for the love of Heaven, out with it. It cannot be as dire as all that," Adaline said with a chuckle. "I haven't even been in town for weeks."

Lucy pressed a hand to her face and then nodded again. "Very well. Henry has been prattling all over town that he has procured a match for you. With Lord Edward Brelsford."

"Lord Edwar—the Marquess of Lockhaven?" Adaline's jaw dropped. "But…I have never even met the man. Surely Henry would have spoken to me first. I cannot believe—"

"That is not the worst of it, dearest," Lucy said gently.

"Not the worst? My brother has supposedly betrothed me to a man I do not know. How can it be worse?"

At least the man was handsome, she supposed. And not too much older than she. Still—

"Apparently, the marquess was unaware of any such match," Lucy said, closing her eyes briefly.

Adaline blinked at her. "If he was unaware, then how did Henry…"

"I do not know," Lucy said. "Only that two days ago, Henry began spreading it about that he had procured this match for you. And that not only had you been informed, but you were delighted. So delighted that you had already begun ordering your trousseau, and new calling cards with your new title emblazoned upon them. And…"

She hesitated again, and Adaline blew out a breath. "Just say it," she murmured. It couldn't be much worse than she'd already heard.

"He said you'd already begun choosing names for your children. The first, of course, being Edward, after his father."

"He *what*?" Adaline shouted, lurching to her feet. "How could he say such things, in public, without even speaking with me first?"

"Oh, darling girl, it is even worse than that," Lucy said, her gaze full of sympathy.

Adaline's knees went weak with dread, and she dropped back to the couch. "How much worse?" she asked faintly.

"Yesterday in church, the first banns were read…for Lord Edward Brelsford, the Marquess of Lockhaven, and his soon-to-be bride, the widowed Mrs. Selena MacLaren."

Adaline's head spun. "So…so…Henry has been telling the entire world that not only am I engaged to Lockhaven, but am thrilled about the prospect, to the point of naming our future children, when all the while Lockhaven is actually engaged to be married to another?"

"I'm afraid so," Lucy said, gripping her hand.

Adaline let out a sound that might have been a squeak, but her throat was so tight with horrified emotion, no sound escaped.

"I...I need to go," she said, rising stiffly and moving to the door.

"Are you all right, dearest?" Lucy said, following her.

"Yes," she answered faintly.

In all truth, no, no she was not. But there was nothing poor Lucy could do about the situation.

"I will tell anyone I hear uttering a word of this nonsense the truth of the matter."

"Thank you," Adaline said with a vague smile.

But what was the truth of the matter? How had such a rumor been started?

Well...she knew the how of it. Henry.

"I will come to visit you this evening," Lucy said, watching from the door as Adaline hurried into her carriage. She waved to her cousin before instructing the driver to take her home.

Her numbness was beginning to wear off and was replaced by a burning anger toward the apparent instigator of this humiliation.

Henry.

Oh, they would have words.

The door had barely closed behind her when she was shouting for her brother.

"Miss Girard," Bartlett, their butler, stopped in front of her, his face lined with concern. "I am afraid I must inform you that the Misses Chomleys and Lady Bennett have sent their regrets for this afternoon. They will not be able to attend your soiree after all as they have taken ill."

She stared at him, aghast. "They have taken ill? *All* of them?"

Bartlett frowned with both confusion and insult on her behalf. Dear man. "So it would seem, Miss."

She rounded on her heels, aiming her voice at her father's...well, her brother's now... study. "Henry!" she yelled again with no care for decorum.

He popped his head out of the door to his study, his startled face glancing about until he saw her. And then the coward ducked back in, closing the door behind him.

She snorted and stomped over, not bothering to knock before she threw the door open.

He made a distinctly ungentlemanly squeak as he dropped into his seat. "This is my private office," he sputtered. "You cannot just—"

"I can, and I shall," she retorted, marching toward him.

He remained sitting, keeping his desk between them. "Well then, what has you in such an upset?"

She stared at him, open-mouthed with surprise. "Do you really need to ask?"

She could see in his face that he knew exactly to what she referred. His jaw worked a few times, his teeth visibly grinding. "I do not—"

"Henry," she snapped. "How could you? The whole of London is laughing at me."

He let out a sigh. "I merely sought to find you the most advantageous match. I would have thought you'd be pleased to be the Marchioness of Lockhaven."

She threw her hands up. "Perhaps. If I had ever met the marquess. Or, indeed, if he had any notion whatsoever that I even existed!" She planted her hands on the desk, leaning as close to Henry as she could get without actually climbing over the furniture. "Why would you spread it about that we are betrothed when, apparently, not only did the man never offer for my hand, but he is already engaged to someone else?"

"I had been assured by his own brother that the match was all but set. Lord Hugo was very clear—"

"Lord Hugo is *not* Lord Edward. He has no say over who his elder brother weds. Perhaps if you had spoken to the duke, you might have had cause to hope. But even *then*, you should not have said a word until the contracts were signed and the banns were read. Instead, not only have you have bandied it about that a match was made, but you made it seem that I had not only agreed but done so eagerly. So eagerly that I was already ordering stationary and naming my children! Are you mad?" she shouted.

He had the grace to look a little sheepish, but that stubborn streak of his would just not allow him to admit he was in the wrong. "I am only trying to secure your future."

"Yet all you have done is destroy it," she lamented.

Henry rolled his eyes. "Well, that seems a bit dramatic."

Adaline threw her hands up again. "No, Henry. It isn't."

"What is all this ruckus about?" their mother said, entering the study.

This time Henry threw up his hands. "Does no one knock?"

"No," both Adaline and their mother said.

"Now, explain yourselves, both of you. I can hear your voices all the way in my salon. If my guest hadn't had to cancel at the last minute—"

"Oh no, Mother. Not you too," Adaline said.

"What do you mean?" she asked.

"I mean, Henry has apparently destroyed the reputation of not only myself but the entire family. He's made us a laughingstock." Then she went on to tell her mother about what had happened.

"I did no such thing," he said, slamming his hands on the desk as he rose. "Lord Hugo Brelsford is at fault. *He* is the one who assured me of this match. *He* is the one who has humiliated our family for his own sport. If you want to blame someone, blame *him*."

"I shall blame you both," Adaline said. "The next time you wish to play games with someone's life, I suggest you stick to your own."

With that, she spun around and marched straight to her room, leaving their mother to chastise Henry further.

She had a bleak future to contemplate.

Even Lucy visiting her later that evening did not lift her spirits as they usually did. Her dear cousin had been her companion for three years when her own parents had died. Her father had been a vicar. A good man, but not wealthy enough to leave his daughter more than a pittance to survive on once he'd passed, let alone a dowry. Luckily, Adaline's father had welcomed his cousin's child into his family, and she and Lucy had been fast friends ever since. And they continued to be close, even after Lucy had married Mr. Darrow and used the small dowry the Girards had provided for her to start the millinery.

To call Lucy Darrow honest was an understatement unworthy of the title. She took the virtue to militant and brutal levels. But she could at least always be counted upon to tell Adaline exactly what was on her mind. She was also wise beyond her years with an uncanny ability to predict the outcomes of whatever circumstance came their way. Though perhaps that wasn't too difficult, as Adaline had a penchant for finding trouble. Or diving into it when it found her. So Adaline typically heeded her advice.

But at this moment, even Lucy's sage wisdom failed to comfort her.

"It will blow over soon enough," Lucy assured her. "There is always some new gossip or scandal brewing."

"But what if it doesn't?" Adaline asked. "Mother and I have both had our invitations go unanswered, or had our guests plead illness and send their regrets. If this morning is any indication, I will be greeted with laughter and hateful remarks wherever I go. How will I ever find a husband if I cannot get anyone to stop laughing at me long enough to court me?"

Lucy raised a brow. "I didn't think you were so eager for marriage."

"I wasn't," Adaline said, letting out a long sigh. "But now that Father is gone and Henry is in charge of the household, I would give anything to be the mistress of my own domain. I certainly cannot trust him to secure my future."

"Hmm, no, I shouldn't think so," Lucy agreed. Then she took Adaline's hands, giving them a gentle squeeze. "Don't you worry. People will forget. And as horrible as this is right now, you are not ruined. Embarrassed, yes. But that will fade. Let us just hope that Henry keeps his matchmaking schemes to himself from now on."

Adaline chuckled, feeling slightly better. Lucy was right. She may be the joke of the town at the moment, but she wasn't in ruined disgrace. As long as she kept a low profile for a few weeks—and Henry didn't do anything else to worsen the situation—with any luck, she would be back to dancing at balls and walking down the street without being laughed at in no time.

⌇⌇⌇⌇⌇

CHAPTER THREE

H UGO BREATHED A sigh of relief when a sharp knock at the door interrupted his brother's tirade. Edward had been chastising him for no less than three quarters of an hour over his role in the current scandal involving Miss Girard and Edward and their non-existent engagement. He couldn't deny he deserved some censure for his ill-advised prank. But at this point, Edward had more than conveyed his feelings on the matter.

"My lord," Timothy, a brawny young footman said, addressing Edward upon entering. "Mr. Henry Girard is waiting for an audience. Shall I tell him you are not at home?"

Hugo swore under his breath and Arthur turned a shade paler.

Edward sighed and rubbed his finger against his temple. "No. Show him in. Might as well get this over with," he muttered once Timothy left. "But we are not finished," he said, pointing at Hugo and Arthur.

Henry Girard entered the study with his chin in the air and his chest puffed out. That did not bode well for civil conversation.

"My lord," he said, addressing Edward and ignoring Hugo and Arthur entirely. "I demand retribution for the insult that has been dealt to my family."

Edward's eyes narrowed, his demeanor changing from one of placation to tightly reined anger as he leaned back against his desk, his arms folded across his chest.

"I beg your pardon," he said.

Henry faltered slightly at the icy tone of Edward's voice, but he pressed on. "My sister's reputation is in ruins, and our family is now a laughingstock. You are at fault. I demand satisfaction."

Hugo stood. "If you are to blame anyone, Mr. Girard, it is I who am at fault, not my brother. I am the one who—"

"The offer was for Lockhaven's hand, Lord Hugo, not yours. Therefore, he is responsible," Girard insisted.

Edward's brows rose. "You hold me responsible for an offer that was made in jest whilst I was I not even in the room?"

Girard hesitated, shifting his weight from one foot to the other before he puffed out his chest and tried again.

"Regardless of who made the offer, it was made in your name. My sister is now humiliated. After all the effort I have put forth to find her a husband, her prospects, such as they were, have all disappeared. She will be left a spinster with no support. If ought happens to me, she will be alone in this world. That is on your head, my lord."

"And just what do you propose I do to rectify the matter?" Edward asked, his voice dangerously low.

Girard, however, was too stupid or conceited to register the danger he was in. Instead, his face turned smug. "In addition to a public apology, it is not unheard of in such situations for a small sum to be paid to the aggrieved woman. As compensation for her lost prospects and security for her future."

"Did I hear you correctly?" Arthur asked, astonished. "Are you truly trying to extort money from my family in payment for a situation you, yourself, caused?"

"I?" Girard asked, mouth agape.

"Yes," Edward responded. "You."

"I will take responsibility for my part in this," Hugo said. "I made an ill-advised joke and assumed you were astute enough to recognize my sarcasm. I apparently was wrong. But it was you and your sister who spread the tale about town. If your sister has been humiliated, it is through no fault of ours."

Girard bristled. "You…you brigand! Scoundrel! You dare besmirch our name so? I will have satisfaction, sir! Rapiers at dawn!"

"That is enough." Edward pushed away from his desk. "In case you have forgotten, Mr. Girard, duels are illegal. And one would only result in further humiliation on your part. My brother is a champion fencer, as you well know. And you, if I recall correctly, are not. Pistols would go even worse for you."

"Now," he continued, before a deflated Henry could speak again. "My brother has apologized for his part in this mess. And our family does truly regret any embarrassment this has caused Miss Girard. However," he said, his voice raising slightly as Girard looked ready to argue again. "Had you kept the matter between our families until the offer you thought you had in hand was verified, the embarrassment would have gone no further. If your sister or your family has suffered any humiliation, it is your own doing. Worsened all the more by your coming here and demanding monetary retribution, of all things. You should be ashamed, sir."

He marched to the door of the study and opened it. "You may convey our apologies to your sister, and our assurances that the scandal will pass. Provided you allow it. Any further damage to her reputation going forward will be squarely on *your* shoulders. Neither I nor anyone in my family will entertain another word on the matter. It is at an end."

Timothy stood in the doorway holding Henry's hat and coat. "Good day, Mr. Girard," Edward said.

Henry gathered what dignity he had left and stomped out the door, his jaw working around words he didn't dare release.

As soon as he left, Hugo rubbed a hand over his face with a groan. "I apologize, sincerely," he said to Edward who simply snorted.

"You should. Though the situation is not entirely your fault," he said with a glaring glance at Arthur.

"True. But I am the elder between Arthur and I. I should have known better."

"I won't argue that," Edward said, his lips twitching.

"I suppose a duel was the least I could have expected. And as I am a lousy shot, and not nearly as handy with a rapier as you insinuated, I am indeed grateful for your…diplomacy."

"Yes, well…let us not test my diplomatic skills again, shall we?"

"I…" Hugo hesitated, not really wanting to offer what he was about to offer, but ready to suffer the consequences of his actions all the same. He stood and clasped his hands behind his back, ready to fall on the proverbial sword for his family's honor. "Perhaps the gentleman and his sister would be appeased if I were to marry her in your stead."

Arthur snorted. "You?"

"Why not?" Hugo retorted, his brother's derision stinging more than he expected.

"Because she wanted to be a duchess. Not cast off to a younger son," Arthur said.

Edward waved them away. "The point is moot. Father and I already discussed it."

Panic-tinged shock jolted Hugo, despite the fact that he'd offered only seconds ago. It was one thing to offer oneself up on a platter. It was an entirely different thing to know you'd already been offered up without your knowledge or consent. Which only served to further illustrate Edward's feelings on the matter. A fact that Hugo did not appreciate in the slightest as it did nothing but amplify his guilt.

"However," Edward continued, "Father seems to be much of the same mind as you, Arthur. He refused to consider it, for which I am now glad. Mr. Girard could not have been more insulting if he tried, and that is quite a feat. Demanding payment." Edward scoffed. "The utter gall of the man. Father would never willingly accept Miss Girard now, and I wholeheartedly agree. I am sorry for whatever embarrassment this has caused her, but if they were willing to try and extort money from us… Well, Arthur, perhaps you spoke the truth, and the entire situation was a scheme to force my hand."

He let out a long sigh. "In any case, Mr. Girard is angry enough that I really can't be certain the man wouldn't do you harm, Hugo. Gain his sister the prestige of our name and then avenge the family honor and leave her a happy widow."

Hugo dropped back into his chair, his forehead creasing in a deep frown. It was quite humbling to realize that he had misstepped so spectacularly this time that someone wished his death. He understood being angry, but…the Girards seemed to be taking it rather farther than was warranted.

"Well, then, what can I do—" he started, but again, Edward waved his words away.

"Do not dwell further upon the matter. It is handled. Though I would suggest steering clear of the Girards in the future."

Hugo snorted softly. *That*, he could do.

Edward let out another long sigh, pinned both of his brothers with yet another disappointed look that fairly screamed exasperation, and turned to go.

Hugo jumped up from his seat and followed his brother to the door, Arthur on their heels.

"Once Selena and I are wed, we will be traveling for quite some time," Edward said. "We will likely travel to Wales to visit her parents for a time after spending a few weeks in Brighton. She hasn't seen them much over the last few years."

He spun, bringing Hugo and Arthur to a crashing halt. "I trust Father and I will not have to step in again, and you will be able to handle my affairs while I'm gone with more care than you have shown so far."

"Of course," Hugo said. The chastisement smarted. He understood the reasoning behind it, and appreciated his brother's restraint, all things told. But it stung, nonetheless. And forced a closer look at his shortcomings that he didn't enjoy. Acknowledging them meant doing something about them. And he'd been avoiding that since he'd been old enough to recognize his own failings.

Still. This was the first time that his mischievousness had caused grievous harm to another. It added a layer to his guilt that he would prefer not to experience again. Perhaps it was time that he grew a bit more serious. A bit. At the very least, he'd limit any more late-night drinking sessions with Arthur. As an extra precaution. Because he had every intention of ensuring that his older brother needn't have any worries whilst he and his new bride were traveling.

Then again, Hell, as they said, is paved with good intentions. He could but hope his own were not part of them.

❧ ⁓ ❧ ⁓ ❧ ⁓ ❧

CHAPTER FOUR

3 months later

ADALINE DESCENDED FROM her carriage, keeping her eyes down as she hurried toward Lucy's shop. It had been several weeks since anyone had laughed when they saw her, but she still got more than enough amused or pitying looks that she found it easiest to just avoid eye contact altogether. Which helped most of the time, though she did grow tired of staring at the ground.

She had nearly reached the door when a blur with a shock of red hair barreled around the corner…and directly into her.

"Oof," she said, grabbing her middle as the young page scurried about, retrieving the packages he'd dropped.

"I'm right sorry, miss," the boy said, juggling his packages back into his arms before darting back down the street.

"Wait!" she called after him, stooping down to pick up a letter he'd dropped. "You forgot one!"

But the boy must not have heard her. Within moments, he was out of sight.

Adaline let out a sigh and turned back to the shop. The little bell tinkled overhead and she entered, drawing the attention of the patrons who milled about inside. Several glanced at her before looking away. Lady Burrows gave her a brief smile before returning to her browsing. And no one laughed or pointed.

Well, perhaps her notoriety was finally behind her. There had been an unfortunate (for her) dearth of scandal this season, making her salacious moment of humiliation last far longer than she'd hoped. As of yet, the universe had not complied with her wishes and sunk Lord Hugo Brelsford—the architect of her misfortune—into the bottom of some abandoned well. But she would settle for London society forgetting that she existed.

She made her way into the back of the shop where Lucy bustled about selecting beribboned and feathered bonnets and headpieces to show her patrons.

"Adaline," she said, flashing her cousin a brilliant smile. "I am just packaging this gorgeous beauty for Lady Burrows," she said, showing her a beautiful turban artfully bedecked in velvet ribbon and festooned with brightly dyed ostrich feathers.

"It's lovely," Adaline said with genuine appreciation. Lucy was a master at her craft.

"Have a seat, I am almost finished."

Adaline sat, then looked at the letter she still held. The paper was good quality and was sealed with red wax stamped with the image of a peacock feather. She didn't recognize the emblem. Hmm.

Upon turning it over, she discovered no address. Merely the word *Grandmother*, written in a strong masculine scrawl across the front.

"What do you have there?" Lucy asked.

"A letter. A page bumped into me outside the shop and must have dropped it. I wasn't able to stop him before he ran off. Might you know him? He has a mop of bright red hair and freckles across his cheeks."

Lucy shook her head. "Doesn't sound familiar. What will you do with it?"

Adaline gave her a mischievous grin and then broke the seal before Lucy could protest. Though she did anyway.

"Ada! That was not meant for you."

"True, but perhaps we can discover who it was meant for by reading it," she said.

Lucy shook her head, though there was great deal of affection in the exasperated look she threw Adaline's way.

"You are incorrigible." She headed toward the front of the shop, hat box under her arm. "I will return shortly."

Adaline nodded, her attention already absorbed in the letter. It was…unexpectedly sweet. Whoever had written it obviously loved his grandmother very much. And he had a wonderful sense of humor. He seemed very much like someone she could be friends with. And she could use a friend now. More than ever.

She spent most of that day and evening thinking about the letter and what to do with it before she finally made up her mind. She would write back to the anonymous author. And hope that she could find the page who had dropped it so that he could deliver both letters to him.

She sat down, thinking for a good long while before she finally threw caution to the wind and began to write. The letter would be anonymous. She would not betray her identity, and she could not know his. It was freeing, this pouring her heart out to a complete stranger. Refreshing. She could only hope that she could find the page again, that he would actually be able to deliver it…and that letter-writer would respond.

Dear Anonymous Sir,

I pray you will forgive both the impertinence and the impropriety of my writing such a letter to you, being that we are perfect strangers. Yet, it is just such a condition that permits me to dare to do so. There is both intrigue and protection in such anonymity, I find. One may do as one pleases without risk of consequence as no one will be the wiser. Such a delicious temptation I could not resist. And I could not do other than to write even t'were that not the case, so that I may return such a sweet missive as the one which you had intended for your dear grand-mother, which I have enclosed with this letter. It is my dearest wish that she may yet receive it. For such an affectionate note penned by such a dutiful grandson must surely raise an old woman's spirits.

If you wonder—and how could you not—how I came to be in possession of your letter, I had a bit of a mishap with your page in front of Harrow's Hats and Millinery Confections. Neither Mrs. Harrow nor I knew for whom the boy worked. Therefore, I must bow to the mercy of the Fates that I will come upon him again so that I might deliver this letter to you. A roundabout and not at all assured method of correspondence, I'll admit. But one which shall have to do.

Truthfully, even if I did know your identity, I would choose secrecy over revelation. My brother, through whom all my correspondence must necessarily pass, would never condone such an improper endeavor as the one upon which I now embark. Writing to a man un-known to me or my family? Unheard of, I dare say. Yet I must confess I am rather reveling in the brazenness of it all. I do hope you will not judge me too harshly for my momentary lapse in propriety. I simply cannot resist the temptation to step outside societal and familial con-straints, even if only for a moment.

I pray this letter finds you, and your grandmother—if it finds you at all—in the best of health and spirits.

Should you choose to write a letter in return, and I sincerely hope you do, have it delivered by page to Mrs. Harrow's shop. She will see that it finds me. But I entreat you to instruct your servant not to betray your identity.

In that way I can remain, Anonymously Yours,
Miss Millinery

It took a week of haunting the streets near Lucy's shop before

Adaline saw that head of red hair again. The boy seemed flustered when she gave him her letter, with the one to the letter-writer's grandmother carefully enclosed, along with explicit instructions to give both to his master. The addition of a shilling in his palm allayed his fears significantly. He ran off with her letter tucked in his pocket.

Two days later, a smiling Lucy handed her a response.

Dear Miss Millinery,

I must inform you, for the sake of honesty, that I do find your boldness in writing to me exceptionally impertinent and highly inappropriate indeed. However, in a fortuitous turn of chance, I quite enjoy impertinent and highly inappropriate activities, and therefore received your letter with immense pleasure. I have not been so thoroughly amused in a very long time. So much so that I have decided to multiply your impertinence and impropriety tenfold and write to you in turn. I do hope you'll forgive me. Something tells me you will.

I thank you for the return of my letter; my grandmother likewise thanks you...or would if she knew of you, which she will not as I have decided, for the sake of propriety, among other things, that our correspondence shall remain my very own closely held secret. The loss of said letter was, unfortunately, the latest in a long line of lifetime mishaps. Truly, I excel in such undertakings. My dear Grandmama often laments that my talents lie solely in the realms of mischief and mayhem. But never has my bumbling brought me such good fortune as the written acquaintance of such a delightful lady.

I confess, I quite enjoy the anonymity as well. It shall

be interesting indeed to correspond with someone with-out sharing any personal details which might inadvertently give us away. What fun! And what a relief to simply be oneself with no worries of judgment or consequences, without the constraints of Society or opinion of others to confine us. It will be a novel, and I daresay welcome experience for us both, I have no doubt.

I thank you for the opportunity to indulge my mischievous side without further vexing my family. However, as the last thing I wish to do is invoke the ire of *your* family, I shall likewise have my correspondence delivered, with strict instructions of anonymity, to the delightful Mrs. Harrow and pray that this letter finds you.

Indebtedly yours,
Mr. Mischief

CHAPTER FIVE

You've Got Mail

Another three months—and dozens of letters—later

Dear Mr. Mischief,

I hope this letter finds you well and reasonably free—or at least sufficiently recovered—from the consequences of your disastrous actions of several months' past. I confess I have been quite concerned since your last letter. And greatly intrigued. I cannot imagine what error you may have committed that would cause you such distress—and whilst I crave to know the specifics of your greatest shame, as you called it, I know divulging such secrets would provide far too many personal details, so I shall have to suffer my curiosity without relief. For your sake, however, I do hope the matter has been resolved to everyone's satisfaction.

I have likewise, in my past, been forced to deal with a particularly unsavory matter. However, at least in my case, the matter has been settled, so I shall put it from my mind. Truthfully, I can do nothing else, or I shall drive myself mad. And that is a state I endeavor to avoid at all costs. Though my efforts to do so are more difficult some days than others, I'll admit.

My mother has finally returned from her travels, a vast relief as I will no longer be graced solely by my brother's presence. He means well, but he takes his position as head of the family a bit too seriously for my tastes. A position made all the more exacerbating by my age...which I will not disclose, of course, as that is far too personal a detail even if we were sharing such things. As we are not, suffice it to say, I am no green maid who needs constant looking after. I am old enough, intelligent enough, and (generally) trustworthy enough to mind my own affairs. Unfortunately, my brother feels otherwise. And until such a time as I can find a man who I can stand the presence of for more than a quarter of an hour to wed—a task I assure you is no small feat—I am for all intents and purposes a prisoner in my brother's household. Such is the plight of women in the world. That is not to say I am not grateful to be so well loved as to merit my family's attentions. However...whilst he means well, can any brother properly care for a sister without being utterly obtuse?

...

Exasperatedly Yours,
Miss Millinery

My dearest Miss Millinery,

Being a brother myself, I cannot say. Though I have little doubt my sisters would agree with your assessment. However, as a brother, I do feel obligated to advocate on *your* brother's behalf and plead for leniency and forgiveness. He likely knows not what he does but surely operates under a great degree of affection.

I speak from experience as that seems to be the driving force behind the vast majority of my errors. And I assure you, your insufficient imagination aside, my errors are grievous indeed. The latest and most egregious misstep has been resolved (thank you for your kind inquiry). Though whether all parties are satisfied with the resolution remains to be seen. For my part, I am simply relieved it is, at the very least, settled, regardless of any satisfaction or lack thereof.

In my defense, there was a good deal of drink involved. A detail that has caused me no small amount of embarrassment as I am certainly old enough to know better. (And never fear, I shall not reveal a more exact age than that—we must follow the rules after all). However, this being the case, and as my most staunch resolutions do tend to evaporate when the spirits are flowing, I have vowed to renounce the wretched stuff once and for all. Or for at least a fortnight. I am repentant, most assuredly, but also realistic. And doomed, it seems to cause mischief and mayhem where'er I go. Though truly, I am attempting to rectify my behavior. I fear it has proven far more difficult than I had anticipated.

In fact, in light of recent events, I feel it only fair to elevate myself. And so I shall sign off...

Mischievously Yours,
Sir Mayhem

CHAPTER SIX

"A RE YOU GOING to read that letter for a fifth time, or do you have one to send in return?" Lucy asked, leveling an exasperatedly amused smile in Adaline's direction while she rearranged her front window display.

Adaline's cheeks flushed, and she quickly refolded the letter from her Mr. Mischief…or Sir Mayhem, as he is now calling himself, and stuffed it into her pocket before pulling out the letter she'd written in return. Lucy took it with another indulgent smile and set it aside.

"Really, I do have other duties aside from playing messenger for the two of you," Lucy said, though her amused demeanor belied her testy words. "Why don't you simply tell each other who you are and write to each other properly?"

"Well, that wouldn't be nearly as entertaining," Adaline retorted. "And it would be highly improper if we actually knew each other's identities."

"It is highly improper regardless," Lucy muttered, moving to straighten the hats in her window display.

"Isn't it though?" Adaline said with a mischievous smile. "That's what makes it so delicious."

"Ada!" Lucy huffed, then pursed her lips, though with a lovingly indulgent expression that warmed Adaline's heart. "Would it be so terrible to fall in love the way regular people do? Perhaps you would have better luck if you were a bit more…conventional."

The warmth that had filled her evaporated. It was not the first time she had been accused of being unconventional. Eccentric. Her mother lamented that fact constantly. It didn't always bother her. After all, who wanted to be the same as everyone else? However…it did hurt at times. Especially to be reminded that she might never find someone who would love everything about her.

It was the rare person who saw her eccentricities as beneficial. And it did mark her as *other*. When despite her differences, she wanted much the same things as any other lady. Security. Freedom. Love. She wanted to belong. To *someone*. Someone who would see all of her, and love everything they saw.

"Oh Ada," Lucy said, reaching out to squeeze her hand. "I did not mean to imply there was something wrong with you. You are wonderful."

Adaline smiled and squeezed her cousin's hand back. "I know, Lucy. Do not fret. I know you worry for me. But you needn't. If I am doomed to spinsterhood, I shall simply move in here and spend all my days entertaining you."

She grabbed a spool of ribbon and spun around, letting the ribbon flutter and wrap around her like a tornado of velvet.

Lucy's laughter peeled out and she hurried to unravel Adaline from her ribbon cocoon.

"You will be the death of me, Ada."

Adaline could do naught but laugh. Lucy was typically as unflappable as they came, so Adaline considered the day well spent if she could shake that stoic air Lucy wrapped around herself like a cloak.

"I still must urge caution, though I know you do not wish to hear it. If your parents knew you were writing to a man who is not a relation or your betrothed…" Lucy started.

Adaline let out a long sigh. "I am well aware. Hence the secrecy."

Lucy snorted. "Hence why I agreed to be your intermediary. I may not agree with your actions, but if you are going to insist upon continuing with this…whatever it is, then I have no choice but to do what I can to minimize the danger to your reputation."

Adaline gave Lucy a fond smile. "I do appreciate you."

"Hmm, I should hope so," she said, though again, her smile softened the tone of her words. "Without me, your reputation would have been in shambles ages ago."

Adaline covered her mouth to hide her giggle. "I am happy for your success," Adaline said, fiddling with the ribbon of a hat on the counter near her, "but I do miss seeing you."

Lucy grabbed a few feathers and a new spool of ribbon and came back around the counter to finish working on the gorgeous bonnet she'd been crafting when Adaline had arrived.

"You see me nearly as much as you did when I lived with you," Lucy pointed out. "You are here practically every day."

"It's not the same," Adaline said with a sigh.

Lucy just laughed again and shook her head. She'd married a handsome but struggling milliner a mere three years ago, and since then had used her savings to move them to a more desirable location and, in short order, had turned his shop into the most popular millinery in London.

Though Adaline was of course happy for Lucy's personal and business success, she missed having her steady presence always at her side.

"Oh dear," Lucy muttered, her eyes creasing in concern as she looked out the window. "Behave yourself, I implore you."

"Whatever do you mean?" Adaline turned her head to look out the window. "Who is it?"

Lucy's expression changed to that of a smiling, welcoming patroness as the door opened, tinkling the bell that hung above it.

Adaline sent a vague smile in the direction of the young woman who came through the door, then froze as her gaze met the storm-gray eyes of the man who entered next. A delicious shiver ran through her, setting her legs to wobbling. The stranger froze as well, his mouth opening with his sharp intake of breath.

A mouth that pulled into a slow half-grin the longer she stood staring at him.

Lord almighty, but the thoughts that sensual smile planted in her mind. She dragged in a breath, trying to beat her more inappropriate thoughts back into submission. Difficult to do with him standing there, towering over her, his coat snug across his broad shoulders that looked more than capable of carrying her off, gazing at her with smoldering eyes that looked as though he wanted to do just that. Despite the fact that they didn't know each other from Adam and had never even spoken a word to each other.

Lucy dropped into a quick curtsy. "Miss Archard, it is a pleasure to see you again. I have your bonnet ready."

"Oh, wonderful," the sweet looking young miss said.

"Mrs. Harrow," the gentleman said. "You grow lovelier by the day."

"Oh," Lucy said, dipping another curtsy beside her and waving him off, though her cheeks pinkened with a pleased flush.

Adaline, on the other hand, remained bolted to the floor, the words he'd just spoken hitting her like a physical jolt to her heart. His voice wasn't quite as deep as she expected it to sound. But it had a melodious quality to it that soothed something in her. She could listen to him speak all day.

"You are too kind, my lord, as always. Please," she said, turning to Adaline with a nervous air that Adaline couldn't decipher. "Allow me to introduce my cousin, Miss Adaline Girard."

His face immediately froze, and Adaline frowned. What ailed him? Had she done something wrong?

"Girard?" he asked, any sign of flirtation evaporating.

"Yes," she said. "Why—"

"Adaline," Lucy said, resignation stamped all over her face. "Allow me to introduce Miss Amelia Archard. And Lord Hugo…Brelsford."

Ada inhaled with a sharp gasp that made Hugo visibly wince.

"Brelsford? Lord Hugo?" Her eyes narrowed. *You,* she said,

her finger jabbing in his direction as she took a step forward.

He held up his hands and took a step backward. "Me?" he asked, halting himself before she could back him any further toward the door.

"Yes, *you*." She stopped advancing, lest she find herself pressed right up against him. That thought oddly tantalized her despite the fury running through her. She shoved that aside and focused on her anger. "It was *you* who arranged for a betrothal between myself and your brother."

He blanched slightly. Nothing more than a slight tightening around his eyes. But she noticed. The sight only fueled her rage.

"I was not the one who suggested it," he said through clenched teeth. "Your brother was the one who came up with the idea."

"You agreed to it!"

"As a jest. How could I guess your brother would take it seriously?"

"Well, I can assure you, nothing about it was remotely funny."

He blew a breath out through his nostrils and leaned toward her slightly. "As it was never a formal offer—though it sounds as if you took it that way—I'll take your opinion of the matter accordingly."

Her jaw dropped. "My opinion of the matter is the only one of any import."

"Oh!" he scoffed. "A very ladylike sentiment indeed."

She glared at him. "This has nothing to do with my genteel qualities—something of which you'd know nothing, you cretin! My opinion is the only which matters in this instance because I alone have suffered harm."

"You alon—" His mouth dropped open. "Madam, I was challenged to a duel, threatened with the utmost bodily harm in such explicit terms that I have scarce been able to sleep a night since. If that is not harm, then I don't know wh—"

"Oh, the two are hardly comparable, sir. A challenge is not

harmful, especially as you refused to even answer it. My reputation, on the other hand, has—"

"Not suffered one whit, as you are well aware, because my family graciously agreed to keep the matter secret. The embarrassment caused by your and your brother's actions and gossip can hardly be laid at my door."

"Oh, it was a good deal more than simple embarrassment, and well you know it. And what else could your family do but keep the matter a secret? Anything else would expose your deplorable natures to all of Society. Despite my humiliation, I would rather have told the world the truth of the matter. It would not only vindicate me but could save countless others. Imagine how many unsuspecting women are likely even now being misled—"

"I assure you, the women of my acquaintance would have a great deal more humor and understanding of the matter and would have recognized it for the innocent frivolity it was. Furthermore, no women I would willingly associate with would have for a moment thought that jest was in any way an actual offer of marriage. The fact that you and your brother did says more about you than—"

"Oh!" Adaline clenched her fists and stomped her foot out of the sheer frustration of being unable to aim it where it was so richly deserved. "I hadn't even heard a word about any offer until I started being laughed at right on the street. I had no knowledge of what my brother had done—or you, as we discovered. You cannot place any of this blame on me. *You* are the cad, sir. The one throwing about offers of marriage, offering assurances that such offers were genuine only to—"

"It would be none the worse for me if the world knew the truth—that you, whether through your brother or not, had accepted such an obviously mock offer. An offer no one with any sense would have for a moment thought was real. And with such insulting alacrity and speed as well!"

"Why you—"

Lucy snatched the spool of ribbon Adaline had been about to throw at his head and pushed between them where they were standing nose-to-nose in full sight of the front window. She glared at them like they were two misbehaving children.

"Unless either of you wish to change the fact that no one else has any idea what has occurred between you, you may want to desist immediately. You are drawing a crowd," she said, her eyes flicking to the window where several passersby had stopped to look inside, eyes wide with interest.

Adaline gasped and stepped back. Hugo frowned, rubbing a finger over his upper lip as he likewise took a step away from her.

Ada forced a smile to her lips which only made him narrow his eyes before he made a visible effort to clear his face of all expression. She snorted derisively. As much as she'd like to strangle the man before her with the velvet ribbon Lucy had thrust into her hand as she dragged her back to the counter, Lucy was right. Her reputation had been salvaged only by a slim margin when the whole debacle had occurred.

Even with her brother's efforts, there had still been enough whispers that Ada's prospects had suffered.

The last thing she needed was a scene with one of the Brelsfords to stoke the flames.

She took a deep breath and steeled her expression into one of bland but polite interest as she stared sightlessly at the display of hats before her while Lucy quickly fetched Miss Archard's hat.

"I am sorry for what my cousins did," Miss Archard said, leaning close enough to Adaline with a contrite smile. "They are incorrigible, but generally harmless."

Adaline gave her a strained smile in return. "I must disagree with the harmless part," she said, her smile turning into a grimace. "But I do appreciate the sentiment. Thank you."

Miss Archard nodded, accepted her parcel from Lucy, and marched to the door. "Come along, Hugo. Before you cause anymore disasters."

The only betrayal he made that her words affected him was a

slight curl of his nose before he nodded sharply to Lucy and tipped his hat. Those stormy gray eyes focused briefly on Adaline, stealing all the breath from her lungs, before he turned on his heel and followed his cousin out the door.

Ada sagged against the counter, all the energy that had been fueling her seemingly sucked out the door with him.

"Well," Lucy said with a sigh. "I suppose that was bound to happen at some point. Best that it was somewhat contained, with blessedly few witnesses."

Adaline frowned. Her cousin wasn't wrong. Truthfully, it was perhaps odd they had not crossed paths before.

And now that she had met the infuriating man in the flesh...she couldn't help but wonder—with a disturbing amount of anticipation—what would happen when they next met.

CHAPTER SEVEN

You've Got Mail

Dear Sir Mayhem,

If you are indeed such a grievous agent of chaos as you believe, then perhaps you should be elevated even further. A simple sir is not exalted enough. Shall I call you the Count of Chaos? Hmm, no. Still not grand enough. Duke of Disaster, perhaps? Prince of Pandemonium? No, that is far too grand. Ah! You shall henceforth be known as the Marquess of Mayhem. That has a nice alliterative ring to it.

...

Signed, as always,
Miss Millinery

My dear Miss Millinery,

Oh, I am indeed a decided and dedicated scoundrel, the likes of which you have likely never seen. The newly exalted moniker is warranted, I assure you. I have tried, upon occasion, to rein in my natural chaotic tendencies. Most recently, in fact, as I disclosed in my last letter.

Unfortunately, I find life to be so interminably boring when attempting to behave that it is hardly worth living. Much to my mother's chagrin, I have no doubt. She suggested a wife might do me good. Perish the thought! Though she is probably correct. Mother usually is. Grandmother agrees with her, which means I'll likely find myself wed within a fortnight. I cannot fight them both.

I did worry, perhaps, that is too personal a detail to share. However, as the women in my family seem determined to change my status from dedicated bachelor to respectable married man, the true state of my current matrimonial condition can remain blessedly obscure.

All that said, I do truly intend to become a better man. I must simply find a way to become the well-behaved gentleman Society would have me be, whilst adhering to my favorite words from the wise Roman Horace who coined the phrase *carpe diem*. There is truly no better way to suffer through a day than to seize it for all it is worth, in my humble opinion. Live life as though each day might be your last. And have a little fun doing it. Otherwise, what is the point?

Can one be an upstanding member of society and still find joy in drawing breath every day? I can only pray such a miracle is possible. For my own sake. And for those forced into my company.

…

By the by, I have decided if I am to rise to the illustrious station of marquess, then I shall elevate you as well. And as you are a lover of the alliterate, you shall henceforth be known as the Marchioness of Millinery. T'is only fair.

…

Your partner in mischief,
The Marquess of Mayhem

CHAPTER EIGHT

Hugo escorted his dance partner back to her chaperone and left her with a polite bow before returning to his grandmother, who looked at him with exasperation. Fond exasperation, but exasperation nonetheless.

"And what was wrong with that one?" she asked with a huff.

He glanced down at her, eyebrows raised. "Nothing at all."

"And yet you spoke hardly a word to her whilst you danced and quit her company almost before the last note was played. You'll have a difficult time finding a wife if you refuse to spend more than three minutes with a woman."

She glanced at him with that look of hers that pierced straight through to his soul. He could never hide anything from her.

He sighed. "She was perfectly fine, Grandmother."

"And?"

He didn't look at her when he answered. "I want more than perfectly fine."

He wanted intelligent, humorous, witty, adventurous, fearless, passionate. Something he already had. In a manner of speaking. Though in reality… He sighed again. He may have already found what he wanted. But in someone he could not have. Someone whose name he did not even know. Whose face he had never seen. Would never see.

"Ah. I see. And you have yet to meet such a woman, I take

it?"

He gave her a sharp nod but again didn't meet her eyes. He didn't dare to. Not that it helped. He couldn't hide from her.

The hint of a smile on her lips implied knowledge he knew she didn't have. She had always seen right through him, though. Always knew his secrets, his mind, sometimes even before he did himself.

But this secret, he could not risk her learning. She would never approve. Although...of everyone in his family, his grandmother might be the one to ignore the unconventional relationship between him and his millinery marchioness. He craved her advice on that matter, for he was well and truly flummoxed.

With every letter he received, he grew more and more enchanted with his mystery lady. And he grew more determined to meet her in person. Yet what purpose would it serve? They could not be together. He didn't even know if she would wish a relationship with him were he able to offer one. Their current relationship was one of friendship, camaraderie. A bit flirtatious, yes. He wasn't sure he even knew how to converse without being at least marginally playful. But responding in kind in an anonymous letter did not mean she would welcome more decisive advances.

And what if she did? What if she proved to be the daughter of a stable hand? Or worse, the daughter of some high-born noble who would not consider a mere second son—even of a duke—as a suitable match for his daughter. For his part, he would not care who she was, what station of life she was born into. His brother was the heir. The one who'd had to worry about bloodlines and family legacy. Hugo had a bit more freedom in that regard. But that did not mean his marchioness did. He was not ashamed to admit—at least to himself—that he feared he would not measure up to her expectations.

"You are thinking rather hard for a man who insists he has no thoughts on the matter," his grandmother said with a sly smile.

"Care to share what's putting that frown on your face?"

He blinked at her and opened his mouth…but then shut it again with a smile. "Perhaps later." When he'd figured out what it was he actually wanted. Or had any right to ask for.

His grandmother pursed her lips together, squinting at him while she weighed her response. He let out a small sigh of relief when she did naught but nod and then turned her attention back to the crowd. Searching, no doubt, for his next dance partner.

"It's a shame about that poor girl," she finally said, tilting her head toward the refreshment table where none other than Miss Adaline Girard stood nursing a glass of ratafia.

His eyes immediately narrowed, and his grandmother slapped at him with her fan. "Remove that sour pucker from your face, my boy. And go ask her to dance."

He turned to stare at his grandmother, open-mouthed with surprise. "Surely you jest."

Her delicate, white eyebrows raised. "I do nothing of the sort. It is partly your fault the poor thing is being ignored. The least you can do is dance with her."

"She is not being ignored, Grandmother."

"Oh no?" she asked, her eyes narrowing before she tilted her head back in Miss Girard's direction. "Then what would you call that, hm?"

He looked toward the lady again, his frown deepening as Miss Girard gave a hesitant smile to two passing gentlemen, who barely glanced at her let alone paused long enough to speak. Which set off the whispers and titters scarcely concealed behind fans of more than a few women in the vicinity.

"And before you argue that it isn't your fault," his grandmother said, interrupting him before he could do exactly that. "There have been enough rumors of what may have happened betwixt our families, rumors that have only worsened since your display at Harrow's the other day, I'll point out. Because of that, most of the ton are giving her a wide berth. And like it or not, my dear boy, that is indeed your fault."

He grimaced against the pang of guilt that hit him in the gut.

"Go ask her to dance. She has only danced twice this evening with a pair of odious men that her brother badgered into offering. Both are too old and too ugly to grace her presence."

Hugo's brows raised in surprise. "How do you know that?"

"I'm observant, boy. Now, go on with you. If you cannot completely mend the peace with the poor thing, at least it will help calm some of the rumors."

Hugo took a deep breath and let it out slowly. "Very well," he muttered.

He shook his head, rolled his shoulders back, then straightened his jacket—girding his loins, so to speak, for the battle ahead.

He took one step forward, then turned and snatched the glass of champagne from his grandmother's hand and downed it in one gulp, before handing her back the empty glass.

"Cheeky boy," she said, giving him an amused glare. "On with you."

Easy for her to say. She didn't almost get stabbed with a hat pin the last time she was in Miss Girard's presence.

He made his way across the ballroom, ignoring the stares that began to follow him the nearer he came to the woman who was now watching him with a wary glare. He came to a stop right in front of her with a slight bow, though he kept his eyes on her.

She raised one brow, her entire body radiating tension.

"Miss Girard," he said.

Her eyes narrowed. "Lord Hugo." Her gaze raked over him, starting at his feet and coming back to meet his own. The hint of disdain in her large hazel eyes seemed to find him sadly lacking.

He bristled at the judgement, but straightened his spine, aware that all eyes in the ballroom were now on them.

"To what do I owe the displeasure?" she asked.

His lips twitched into a faint half-grin. "I thought perhaps you might care to dance."

Her eyes widened. She blinked, then stared...then blinked

some more.

Perhaps she was hard of hearing? Had he sent her into an apoplexy? Should he ask again? He frowned slightly. "I am sorry, Miss Girard, but are you well?"

Those big eyes of hers blinked once more and then she gave a slight shake of her head. "I apologize. But it sounded as though you asked me to dance," she said with a little laugh.

His brow creased in a frown. "I did."

"Why?" she asked, her eyes immediately narrowing with suspicion.

"Why?"

"Yes, why?"

He was quite certain his expression resembled a cocker spaniel trying to understand Latin, but he couldn't hide his confusion. "We are at a ball. People are dancing. You are not. I thought perhaps you would like to remedy that state of affairs. Hence the invitation."

Her lips pursed in a grimace. "I don't understand."

"I…" This time he blinked, his confusion at *her* confusion momentarily striking him mute. "I'm sorry. This doesn't seem a difficult concept but perhaps I am mistaken. You see, at a ball—"

She rolled her eyes. "I understand the concept of a ball, Lord Hugo."

"Oh good."

She scowled but continued, "What I fail to understand is why me?"

Ah. Finally, the crux of the matter. He couldn't tell her the truth without risking insulting her further, so he shrugged. "Why not you?"

"You hate me," she stated, very matter-of-factly. As if such a possibility didn't bother her in the least. How would that feel? He hated that he cared so deeply about whether or not he was liked.

However, while his feelings for her were definitely complicated and did skew toward the unpleasant, he did not *hate* her. He frowned. "I do not."

She scoffed. "You seem to."

Of all the cheek… "I beg your pardon, but it is *you* who seems to hate *me*."

One silk clad shoulder rose in a delicate shrug. "*I* have cause."

Aha! He grinned in triumph though it almost instantly faded. Wait…why did her admitting that make him happy? He hated it when someone didn't like him. "Then you admit it. You *do* hate me."

"I didn't say that."

"You didn't not say it. And you certainly implied it."

Her eyes narrowed. "You of all people should know that an implication is *not* an actual declaration."

He opened his mouth to argue, but damn it all if she didn't have a valid point.

She pursed her lips again. "Why do you care if I hate you or not?"

"I don't." He did, actually. Curious, despite his general inclinations on the matter. With her it was all but a foregone conclusion, so not only should he not mind but it should not have come as a surprise. Though that was hardly the point at hand.

Her eyes narrowed again, but this time a small smile played on her lips. As if she had caught him in a secret. "I think you do."

Do not. "Why do you care if I care?"

"I don't."

He grinned. Now he'd caught her. "I think you do."

Her smile disappeared. "Go away."

"I think we should dance."

She let out an exasperated huff. "Why?"

He let out a sigh of his own. "Because people are watching. They were watching you stand here with no dance partners aside from those your brother dragged your way whilst I have danced with nearly every eligible young woman here. Then they watched us watch each other, and now they are watching us argue. Yet again. I would prefer they watch us dance, as that is the least entertaining thing that we could do, and I would very much like for people to stop watching me."

Her mouth dropped open. "I…" She let out a deep sigh that he felt in his bones. "My head is beginning to ache."

He grinned again. "I do seem to have that effect on people. Though if you'd rather not dance with me, I believe your brother is towing another octogenarian in this direction."

She blinked, startled, and glanced in the direction he indicated to see that her glowering brother had indeed coerced another ancient widower to share her company for a dance.

Hugo raised a brow in question. "So…" He held out his hand. "Shall we?"

She hesitated a few more moments, her gaze flicking around the room. He had been telling the truth. The entire ballroom seemed riveted on the scene playing out between them. "Oh, very well." She put her hand in his, and he turned to lead her onto the dance floor.

He gave her fingers a slight squeeze and aimed his most charming smile at her. "Do try and look a little less murderous. We are trying to stop the attention. Not attract it."

❧⟫⟪❧

ADALINE HADN'T BEEN aware she looked murderous, though judging by the chaos roiling through her gut, she'd believe it. Still, she was usually better at hiding her feelings than this. There was something about this man that drove her to all distraction. She hated that he amused her. Oh, he was aggravating, arrogant, self-centered, and self-serving. But he *was* amusing. Damn him.

She made a concerted effort to appear politely aloof. Because despite what she'd said, she *had* been very much aware of the glances and the whispers. It had been hard to miss when the only men who asked her to dance were the two Henry had obviously harried into an introduction. Just when she had begun to think everyone had moved on to something else. Apparently, they hadn't forgotten after all.

Thankfully no one actually seemed to *know* any details of what had transpired between the Brelsfords and the Girards. But enough had been hinted that everyone seemed to know the issue revolved around the marriageable children in each family. And that was all it took. It didn't matter what the issue might be. The female member of the party would always be the most scrutinized, the most to blame.

In Society's mind, if the families had had a falling out over their children, then it must stand to reason that Adaline was the cause. Her suitors had dried up almost overnight. Invitations still came for their family, thankfully. But not because anyone was trying to be kind, she was certain. It was more likely because they hoped other juicy tidbits would come of the families both being in attendance. But any personal attention Adaline had previously enjoyed had virtually disappeared.

So, Lord Hugo's invitation to dance was actually—not that she'd admit it to him—a good idea. Perhaps it would serve to prime the pump, so to speak. If one gentleman asked her to dance, it stood to reason that more might follow. And hopefully, his outward show of interest might put some of the whispers to rest. After all, if they were sharing an amicable dance at the Turlington's ball, there couldn't be much truth to any feud rumors.

It was the amicable part she struggled with.

He led her onto the floor as the notes of a waltz began.

"A waltz?"

Of *course*, he would choose a waltz. As if there wasn't enough gossip.

He grimaced slightly. "My apologies. I neglected to ascertain which dance was next before…"

"Embarking on this folly?" she asked with a smile.

He raised a brow. "Asking you to dance."

"Hm," she mumbled, taking his hand and steeling her spine as he placed his own on her back.

It belatedly occurred to her that by dancing together, they were considerably narrowing down the members of the family who were involved in their little brouhaha. Though that was likely a moot point as she was the only unmarried daughter in her household and there were only two unmarried sons in the Brelsford's, which already narrowed things down considerably.

Well, it was too late to back out now. That would only set more tongues wagging.

"Do try to smile, Miss Girard," he murmured as he swept her around the floor. "You look as though you'd like to scratch out my eyes."

My, my, wasn't he perceptive?

She gave him the sweetest smile she could muster, hoping it appeared more natural than it felt. "Well, I have spent the last several weeks dreaming of just such an occasion. I confess it is altogether disconcerting to now be taking a turn on the dance floor with you instead of indulging in something far more vicious."

His eyes widened, though his lips twitched with amusement rather than anger. "That seems a bit of an overreaction."

"Is it?" She blinked innocently. "It seemed rather understated to me."

He chuckled, his grip on her tightening slightly as they spun, her skirts swishing gently behind her. She resisted the urge to squirm beneath his hold, and resisted even more, examining the reason for her discomposure. For despite her expectation that she'd find his touch repugnant, she instead found it quite…comfortable. Warm. Comforting even, which baffled her to distraction. This man had turned her life on end, cruelly and carelessly so. And yet, with him holding her, she felt more shielded and protected from the unkind stares of their peers than when she stood surrounded by proven allies. More than she had since the entire fiasco had occurred.

There was something so wrong about how right it felt to be held by him.

The realization made her stiffen in his arms, her smile freezing until her face felt like stone.

"Miss Girard?" he asked. "Is there ought amiss?"

"Aside from the fact that I am dancing with the man who made me a laughingstock in front of the whole of London? No. Why do you ask?"

Hugo's jaw visibly clenched. "Look around, Miss Girard. No one is laughing. No one even knows the truth of what occurred."

"No. Instead, they speculate. Embellish. Whisper. I'm not sure which is worse."

He let out a tired sigh. "On that, at least, we can agree." He gave her a faint smile. "I have apologized for my role in that unfortunate incident more times than I can count, Miss Girard. I realize it may never be enough for you to forgive me, but you shall just have to try as there is little else I can do to rectify the matter short of marrying you myself. And that is a solution I am sure you find as horrifying as I do."

She blanched, unable to hide the reaction. He would not be her first choice of husband, no. And she wouldn't have expected that she would be his first choice either, especially considering their interactions to date. But that didn't stop the sharp bolt of pain from stabbing through her all the same. Most of the men in London had made it abundantly clear they had no interest in her. But they'd had the decency not to say so to her face. And certainly none had elaborated so much as to call the prospect horrifying.

"Well. Isn't that just what every woman wishes to hear? True or not, you could have at least had the decency not to say so." She bit off her words before the embarrassment and anger that choked her became too apparent in her wavering voice. She would never let him know how much his admission hurt.

Even more so when she realized she hadn't hidden it from him nearly as well as she'd hoped.

He gazed down at her with genuine surprise. "I…apologize if I was perhaps too vehement. Sincerely. I assumed, based on your obvious abhorrence of my presence, that you shared my sentiments. I certainly did not intend any insult. If you—"

"Rest assured, Lord Hugo, I am just as horrified to be forced into your company as you have made clear you are to be in mine. Let us hope your sacrifice has not gone in vain and this interminable dance has done at least a measure of good in quieting the wagging tongues."

His jaw popped again, and his hand tightened almost imperceptibly on her back. "I am afraid any good it might have done is being promptly undone by the sour expression on your face. Really, has no one ever taught you to hide your thoughts better? Every person in here can read you like an open book."

She gave up all pretense of civility and glared at him. "Do you sit around at night thinking of ways to insult me? Or is it just a natural talent?"

He did have the grace to look chagrined, though that did not make her feel any better.

"Again, I meant no insult—"

"You apparently never do. And no, to answer your question. My apologies that I am not as adept at deceit as you."

"It is not deceit," he ground out, doing his best to look as though they were enjoying themselves. Though all he was achieving was a sort of pained smile that actually brought her some comfort to see. At least she wasn't the only one suffering.

"It is a matter of privacy," he continued. "Something which you appear to neither care for nor understand."

"So you also find my manners, and intelligence, lacking. I'll add that to the list."

He let out a sigh. "That is not what I said."

"It most assuredly was."

He gave her a strained grin. "People are beginning to stare, Miss Girard."

"People have *been* staring, Lord Hugo."

"Exactly my point, Miss Girard. This dance was supposed to alleviate the issue. Not exacerbate it."

Adaline knew he was right, though it made her hate him all the more. Even more so because she knew she was being purposely obstinate. He really wasn't saying anything that didn't make sense. She even agreed with him for the most part. There was just something about him that seemed to draw out the worst in her. Or at least the competitive nature in her...

She pasted a sickly-sweet smile on her lips. "Is this better?" she asked through gritted teeth.

He stared at her, eyes wide with bemusement—or perhaps horror. It was difficult to tell. "Not in the slightest."

"I'm afraid that's the best I can do in current company."

"Are you this argumentative with everyone?"

She actually stopped to think about it for a moment. Truth be told, she did enjoy a good argument now and then. But... "As a general rule, no."

He snorted. "So it is only me, then?"

This time she gave him a true smile. "You are a source of much inspiration, I'll admit."

"Ah, *there*. That smile right there," he said, his voice laced with triumph. "You *are* capable of a genuine smile."

"Of course I am. In the right circumstances."

"Ah. And I take it those circumstances are not any that involve me."

"That isn't strictly true. I've genuinely smiled several times whilst in your presence."

"Hmm, yes. Mostly when you're insulting me."

She pursed her lips. "That isn't the only time."

"Oh? So you will be smiling again?"

"Of course. Just as soon as the music is ended."

He kept his own smile in place, but when he spoke it was through gritted teeth. "You must be the most infuriating, frustrating, cantankerous nuisance I have ever met."

This time she did beam a genuine smile at him. "That is perhaps the nicest thing you have ever said about me. Thank you."

He stopped, dumbstruck, in the middle of the dance floor as

he stared down at her. Luckily, the music ended half a beat later, so she wasn't forced to drag him about like a rag doll. Had she broken him?

"Are you incapable of normal human interaction, Miss Girard?"

Adaline froze. Then dropped her hands, taking a step back from him before bobbing a slight curtsy.

"Wait," he said. "I didn't mean—"

"I shall see myself back to my brother. Have a pleasant evening, Lord Hugo. I do hope I shan't see you again."

She turned and left before he could respond. And before he could see the emotion that tightened her throat and made her vision swim.

Oh, she truly had been delighted that he found her so aggravating. A man who had shown such disdain for her presence and her very being did not deserve to experience the sweet side of her. Nor any part of her true self. But that didn't mean his words hadn't also hurt.

Did anyone truly enjoy being told their very existence was a blight on society? Granted, his words hadn't been quite so severe. But the implication was there. The man seemed incapable of doing anything but insulting her at every turn. Though to be fair to him, she didn't think he intended to be malicious. He apparently just couldn't help it. And so, she would do naught but treat him in kind.

And save her tears for when she was alone in her room, with no one to see them.

CHAPTER NINE

You've Got Mail

Dear Marquess of Mayhem,

I must confess that I am not always the most dignified of ladies. I do try, but my tendencies lean a bit more toward the exuberant. Still, I do endeavor to treat those around me with kindness. Or at least polite respect, until provoked into doing otherwise. So I do find it both distressing and confusing when I am not treated in kind. Why are people so heartless? A man of my acquaintance seems to delight in being cruel, and I cannot understand why. We have distinctly different personalities, I'll grant him that. So perhaps we simply misunderstand one another. Though for a man who hardly knows me, he does seem to know exactly what to say to wound me the most.

…

Confusedly and heartbrokenly yours,
The Marchioness of Millinery

My Dearest Marchioness,
Men, in my experience, often know not what they do.

And those that are more aware, and behave poorly any-way, are deserving of your ire. I fear far too many people have more than a small streak of cruelty in them. I am only sorry you have had to encounter such a person. Sorrier still that I was not there to champion you.

Shall I challenge him to a duel? It would be my hon-or. Simply point my pistol or sword in the right direction and I shall happily die defending my fair maiden. I find myself feeling inordinately protective of you—an emo-tion I realize I have not yet earned where you are concerned. Nor is it warranted, I am sure, knowing what I do of you. You are more than capable of holding your own against any foe. Never forget that.

And before you protest that I do not, in fact, know you, I refute that unreservedly. Whilst we may not know each other's true names or appearances, this intriguing experiment of ours seems to have lent itself to a more intensive lesson in familiarity than I have ever previously experienced. I know you, my dear marchioness. I know your strength, your decency, and genuine kindness. Whoever this man is, he is beneath contempt and unwor-thy of your attention. I pray you spend not a moment more on his sorry existence.

In any case, I heartedly apologize for the failings of my sex. I hope you were not too grievously wounded. If so, please inform me as to how I might remedy the situa-tion. I am at your disposal and wish for nothing but to restore your good spirits.

…

Always at your disposal,
The Marquess of Mayhem

My Lord Marquess,

I fear you are correct. A great many people are cruel indeed. Though I must decline your kind offer of a duel. While I am flattered and cheered by your willingness to die for my honor, I could never live with myself. No misspoken words are worth your life. Though I appreciate the gesture all the same. Besides, wounded though I may be, it would be unjust to punish this man in so severely a manner (as I have no doubt you would win). For I myself am no saint, I assure you.

As for our experiment, I am much of the same mind as you. As I find more and more often with every letter we write. It is as though I am able to be my true self for the first time. Without the demands of societal rules and the awkwardness of personal interactions, there is no need for anything between us but the strictest honesty. One might think a friendship which exists only on paper might be necessarily restrictive. However, on the contrary, it is as though we have finally been granted a freedom that has, thus far, been denied. Though I cannot help but wonder if I should frighten you away should you be faced with me in real life.

I do feel as if I know you intimately. Though that hardly seems possible considering the entirety of our relationship has been with pen and paper as intermediaries. Still, I know you, my dear marquess. I have experienced firsthand your intelligence, your humor, and most of all your kindness. Your words, though they are but written, have the power to mend any ills in my life it seems.

And for that, I shall always be most gratefully yours,
The Marchioness of Millinery

Postscript—that name still seems far too grand for me. I am simply…

Your Very Plain and Ordinary Miss Millinery

My Dear Marchioness,

Nothing you could ever tell me would frighten me away. Of that, I can assure you. As always, your letter has left a smile upon my face that rivals that of the cat in the cream. I am delighted, though not surprised, to find we are yet again of the same mind. As for the rest, you are *my* Miss Marchioness of Millinery. And that is no simple, plain, or ordinary thing. Though it is a mouthful. I believe I shall shorten it to Millie.

Assuredly still and always yours,
Marquess of Mayhem

My Stubborn but Most Appreciated Marquess,

I can only hope I give you no cause to regret your faith in me. I can make no promises, though I *can* assure you my intentions will always be genuine. As for my new name, I find it quite charming. However, as you know, my dear Marquess of Mayhem, turnabout is fair play, yet your name does not as easily lend itself to a pet name. Shall I now call you Mark? Or perhaps simply Mayhem?

…

Your Millie

My Dearest Millie,

You may address me as you like, so long as you *do* address me. My powers of mischief and chaos shall always be at your disposal.

...

Your Mayhem

CHAPTER TEN

THE LATE MORNING sun filtered softly through the gray London sky, casting a light haze over the cobblestone streets. Hugo leaned against a stone wall on the corner of the shop-lined street. His gaze flicked continuously toward the hat shop across the lane, while Arthur's gaze grew more and more amused.

Tucked cozily between a bookseller and plumassier, the millinery beckoned customers with its windows piled high in velvet bonnets and feathered caps. But hats were the furthest thing from Hugo's mind.

Arthur nudged Hugo with a conspiratorial grin. "There he is, Hugo. And he looks to be triumphant."

He nodded at the young boy who had just exited the shop and was hastening in their direction. Hugo ignored his brother and moved toward the boy who greeted him with a grin.

"Did they have it?" Hugo asked.

"Aye, milord. I did just as you said and asked did they have the marquess's mail. The missus gave me this."

He handed Hugo the letter, its wax seal with its simple leaf motif sending a thrill through his chest.

"Thank you," he said, flipping a coin to the boy. "Be here this time next week and I'll have another for you."

"Aye, sir. Thank 'ee!"

Hugo stared at the letter for a second before slipping it into his inner pocket.

Arthur just shook his head, his grin grating on Hugo's nerves. "You've that look again, Hugo. The one you wear when you have a secret tucked under your arm. Another missive from your mysterious lady, I'd wager?"

Hugo tried for nonchalance but failed. "It is merely a letter," he replied, though the warmth in his cheeks betrayed him. "A friendly exchange. Miss Millinery is…well, someone with whom I can be candid. It is freeing, Arthur, to speak honestly, with no fear of consequence."

"Or so you hope," Arthur teased, eyebrows raised. "You have no true idea with whom you correspond. What if she's the baker's daughter, or a bored countess, or a clever maid with an eye for mischief?"

Hugo smiled, the memory of Miss Millinery's last letter flickering in his thoughts—her wit, her insight, her gentle rebukes. "What if she is? It is no matter. We are…" He struggled to find the words. Finally, he shrugged. "We are friends. Our letters are a refuge, for us both. I can say things to this lady I would never dare say in other circles. And there is no judgement in response. In fact, oftentimes she agrees with me."

"Ah, a woman whose presence you never have to suffer, who agrees with everything you say without judgement. I now see the appeal."

Hugo rolled his eyes. "No, it's not like that. She doesn't agree with everything I say. In fact, she argues quite frequently. But…she never thinks the less of me for the disagreement."

Arthur nodded. "And do you return the favor?" Arthur countered. "Does she divulge secrets for which you do not judge? Or are you simply enamored with the idea of being understood?"

Hugo considered this. "Both. Is it so wrong to crave genuine conversation?"

Arthur's grin softened. "Not wrong, Hugo. Only dangerous. You grow too enamored of this woman, I fear. And hearts are tender and fickle things. Never safe, especially when the object of its affection is hidden behind ink and paper."

With a gentle shake of his head, Hugo let the subject drop. He could not explain it better than he already had and was tired of trying. His correspondence with his Miss Millinery was something he treasured. And in the end, it did not matter if anyone but he understood it.

They had wandered toward a bustling section of the marketplace where multiple vendors hawked their wares. And there, at a stall overflowing with fragrant meat pies, a familiar figure stood rigid, her face pale with embarrassment—Adaline Girard, her chestnut hair pulled back in a neat chignon and her blue pelisse fitted perfectly at the waist. She argued softly with a merchant whose patience was fraying. Miss Girard's gloved hands turned out her pocket, which remained stubbornly empty.

"Miss, I assure you, if you had coin, it is now gone," the merchant said, his lips pursed in disapproval. "I warned you not to feed that urchin, but you didn't listen. He took the pies *and* your coin and now you want to leave me here with no compensation—"

"No, no, not at all," Miss Girard insisted. "I can fetch the money, but I cannot do that if I remain here. I give you my word, I will return promptly. Or if my maid would—"

"Not likely, miss," her maid said, her arms folded and feet firmly planted behind her. "I'll not leave you here on your own, nor will I stay behind and allow you to travel back home on your own. What would your mother say? Anything could happen and you here unaccompanied." She shook her head firmly. "No, miss. My place is with you. I'll not leave your side."

Miss Girard closed her eyes and heaved a mighty sigh. Hugo could not help but smile. He knew the sentiment behind that sigh.

"Go ahead without me, Arthur," he said, his gaze remaining on Miss Girard.

Arthur glanced back and forth between them. "Is that wise?

The last time you met, you nearly came to blows."

"That is a severe over-exaggeration," he said with a scoff.

Well, perhaps not severe…

"She may not even accept your help. The woman despises you."

Hugo snorted. "With good reason." Then he shrugged. "Regardless, I cannot leave a lady in need of help. Even one who hates me."

"Very well. But I do believe I shall stay and watch."

Hugo's eyes narrowed, and Arthur shrugged. "I have no doubt that woman would gladly challenge you to a duel. You may need a second. Or an alibi."

Hugo hesitated only a moment longer before crossing the narrow lane, Arthur following at a slight distance.

"Miss Girard," Hugo said softly as he approached, careful not to startle her. The merchant's gaze flickered between them, calculating.

Adaline's eyes widened, her cheeks blooming pink. "My lord," she managed, voice taut.

"I see you are in a difficulty," Hugo replied, his tone gentle.

Her lips pinched together before she gave a sharp shake of her head. "I am quite all right."

"No, she isn't," the merchant jumped in, wagging a finger. "She—"

Hugo held up a hand to stop him. "Permit me to settle the account."

She protested again. "That isn't necess—"

"Yes it is!" the merchant interrupted.

Before Miss Girard could protest further, Hugo withdrew his pocketbook and handed the merchant several coins. More than enough to pay for whatever pies Miss Girard had tried to purchase. The man's demeanor changed at once. He bowed, offering profuse thanks.

Miss Girard's lips pressed into a thin line. "You needn't have interfered, my lord. He would have relented eventually and allowed me to return—"

"But this way the matter is settled, and you may leave the marketplace. With your chaperone," he said with a gallant nod at her maid. At least *she* was smiling at him gratefully. Miss Girard, on the other hand, looked as though she was about to toss him into the Thames.

Arthur, damn him, leaned against a nearby stall, his face alight with amusement.

Miss Girard's gaze followed his, and Arthur stepped forward, bowing with easy charm.

"Miss Girard. We have not yet met. I am Lord Arthur Brelsford. Delighted to make your acquaintance."

Her eyes narrowed. "Are you?"

Arthur didn't even blink, obviously not surprised by her coolness. He merely gave her a gracious smile. "Of course. Even under less than ideal circumstances." He flashed Hugo a wink, then tipped his hat. "Alas, I must leave you in my brother's capable hands. Hugo, try not to provoke further disaster."

Miss Girard gave a curt nod, her eyes wary. "Thank you, Lord Arthur."

Arthur disappeared into the crowd with a final wave, leaving Hugo and Miss Girard standing in tense silence.

Hugo cleared his throat. "May I walk you to your carriage? It seems your footman is elsewhere, and you have already had enough trouble for one day."

Miss Girard's gaze flicked to the bustling street, searching for any sign of her absent attendant. She hesitated, pride warring with practicality. "If you wish," she said quietly, "though I assure you, it is not my custom to accept aid."

"Consider it penance," Hugo replied, lips twitching with humor. "For past offenses, if nothing else."

Miss Girard bit back a smile, the tension in her shoulders easing ever so slightly. "I appreciate the sentiment, my lord. But it will take a great deal more than a few coins and an escort to my carriage to atone for all your sins."

Hugo chuckled at that. "Of that I am painfully aware, Miss Girard. Let us consider this a start."

Together, they set off along the winding path toward the upper square, where carriages lined the curb in neat ranks, their drivers exchanging gossip and news. The crowd parted just enough for them to walk side by side, a breath of air keeping their shoulders from brushing together with every step.

For several moments, silence reigned, broken only by the clatter of hooves and the distant laughter of children. Miss Girard adjusted her gloves, her gaze fixed on a passing flower seller whose baskets overflowed with violets.

"I did not wish to embarrass you," Hugo finally said. "Only to help. I do sincerely apologize if my assistance caused you any discomfort."

Miss Girard's shoulders lifted in a small shrug. "You have a talent for finding me in awkward situations, my lord."

He winced. "I do seem to be cursed in that respect. I hope you forgive me for asking but... Was it truly a pickpocket? The market is rife with them," he hurried to explain. "I have twice lost my own coin purse to their nimble fingers. In fact, not three years ago, in this very square, my brother Arthur fell prey to the same scoundrels."

He launched into what he thought was the amusing tale, only to stop a few minutes later when he belatedly noticed that Miss Girard had not only remained silent during the last several minutes—a novelty for her in his limited experience—but had stopped walking and was staring at him in baffled bemusement.

"You do enjoy the sound of your own voice, do you not, Lord Hugo?"

He blinked, then flashed a delighted smile at her. The woman had spirit. And she wasn't wrong, though few had called him on it. "Indeed, I do, Miss Girard. Though I had thought you might be interested in the anecdote as it is similar to your own misadventure. And, truth be told, I've always been one to want to fill the silence."

"I suppose I cannot fault you there," she said, though her expression suggested she would very much like to. She turned and began walking again. "I occasionally have the same tendencies myself. However, one should never mistake impatience for interest."

"I shall endeavor to be more careful in the future." Far from being insulted, he was instead charmed. Intrigued. How refreshing to have someone say exactly what they are thinking. "And what are you so impatient for then?"

Miss Girard sighed, then pursed her lips. "To get home and put this horrid day behind me, for the most part. It was quite an unpleasant experience all around. And yes," she said, before he could speak again, "it was most likely a pickpocket, to answer your previous question, considering I did have money when I arrived at the vendor and did not when it came time to pay. I am not usually so trusting. I do know how to protect myself from pickpockets. But sometimes, they just look so hungry. So when they come begging…"

Her lips pursed again, and she blinked, swallowing hard. "In any case, the urchin got the pies I purchased, along with the coin I needed to purchase them with."

Hugo searched for words, mindful of their past. "It is unfortunate. You should not be punished for having a kind heart."

She looked at him in surprise.

"I *am* capable of compliments. In the right circumstances," he said with a half-smile.

"I shall remember that for the future," she said, her lips twitching. Then she let out a sigh. "I am accustomed to keeping better watch and having better judgment. But today I…couldn't just walk away without trying to help. And then the merchant was so stubborn. It is infuriating, to be at the mercy of strangers."

"And yet you accepted my help," Hugo said softly.

Miss Girard's eyes met his, glinting with challenge. "Reluctantly," she allowed. "But I am not so proud as to refuse rescue when truly in need. Though I cannot promise to be happy about it."

Hugo laughed, the sound genuine and free. "You are braver than I. I once tried to refuse help from Arthur after a riding accident and ended up with a sprained ankle *and* battered pride."

Miss Girard laughed quietly, her smile transforming her face. "Brothers are relentless in their assistance, are they not?"

"Have experience of your own, do you?"

"One overly persistent brother, yes."

Hugo sighed. "I envy you. I have two. And three sisters."

Miss Girard laughed again. "You are blessed indeed."

"Blessed and cursed. For more reasons than my siblings," he said with a chuckle that brought an answering smile from Miss Girard.

"That is something I can wholeheartedly understand," she said.

He glanced at her again as they slowly made their way through the marketplace. She was quite pretty when she wasn't yelling at him. Then again, he tended to prefer most people when they weren't yelling at him.

"What is it?" she asked, her eyes narrowing when she caught him watching her.

He cleared his throat, not about to explain what he had been thinking. The last thing he wanted to do was insult her again. And while most women wouldn't find a compliment to their beauty an insult, *this* woman, when the compliment was coming from *him*, most certainly would.

"I…was simply enjoying the fact that we are apparently capable of civil conversation without it devolving into a yelling match."

She snorted lightly. "If civil conversation is something you enjoy, it is a shame that it is likely not something you experience often. Given what I know of your temperament."

Her lips twitched at her jest, but she kept her gaze on the path before them.

Hugo chuckled. "I assure you, madam, my temperament

around most people is quite jovial."

"Ah, it is only I who brings out the worst in you then."

Hugo's head jerked toward her. "No. That is not what I meant."

"That is what you implied."

"No, but it's—"

He stopped when he noticed the small smile playing at her lips and aimed a mock glare at her. Which only made her chuckle quietly.

"Forgive me, my lord. I could not help but needle you. Though, to be fair, you *did* say it, and you *did* mean it. However," she said, holding up her hand to stop his protests, "you seem to bring out the worst in me, as well. I cannot say that I have always been proud of my behavior in your vicinity."

"Well then," he said with a slight bow of his head to acknowledge her admission. "Perhaps we can agree to at least attempt to behave in a slightly more civilized manner toward one another."

Her eyes narrowed, but she finally gave him a sharp nod. "It will be a great effort," she said, narrowing her eyes at him. "But I will agree to try."

"As will I," he said turning toward her with a bow.

She gave him a faint smile and then nodded at a carriage a few feet away. "That one is mine."

"Oh miss," a young footman said, running toward her. "I'm sorry, miss. I tried to chase that ruffian what stole your purse, but I lost him, and then when I returned to the stall you were gone and the merchant chased me off so I looked for ye at Mrs. Harrow's but ye weren't there so I thought I best come back to the carriage because ye'd have to come back here to get home but I'm right sorry, miss, I didn't mean to run off, I just wanted to get back yer purse and—"

"All is well, Thomas," Miss Girard said with a laugh. "Breathe. As you can see, Thompson and I am unharmed," she said, nodding behind her to her maid who had been following faithfully a respectful distance behind them. "Though I daresay we are very tired and should like to return home now."

The boy broke into a grin. "Right away, miss."

He reached out to take the small parcels Thompson held and stowed them in the carriage. Miss Girard turned to Hugo with a strained smile.

"Well then, Lord Hugo. I...do thank you, for your assistance today."

Hugo cocked an eyebrow. "That was very pleasant and nearly convincing, Miss Girard. Well done."

She rolled her lips between her teeth to keep from smiling, which only made him smile more. In more usual circumstances, he tried to avoid poking at a woman who had her dander up. But in Miss Girard's case, he couldn't help but do the opposite. Though, truthfully, he would bet good money that she enjoyed their sparring as much as he.

"I did say I would try, my lord."

"That you did." Hugo grinned again and offered her another bow, along with a polite nod to Thompson who watched him warily from inside the carriage.

He offered Miss Girard his hand to help her up, grinning when she took it with obvious reluctance.

"Well then. Now that you are safely delivered to your carriage, I shall bid you goodbye. Have a pleasant afternoon, Miss Girard."

"I am about to be quit of your company, my lord," she said, settling back against the plush cushions. "So I have no doubt it will be very pleasant indeed."

That drew a hearty laugh from him, and she bit her lip against her own smile again.

"I believe you may need to redouble your efforts, Miss Girard."

This time she let a small smile through. "Perhaps. Though I believe I have put forth enough effort today."

Hugo laughed again and shook his head as he closed the

carriage door. "That you have, Miss Girard. That you have."

He stepped back and watched as the carriage pulled into the busy lane, joining the rest of the carriages, horses, conveyances, and pedestrians all out enjoying the weak afternoon sun.

Well, he supposed he couldn't expect miracles, after all. They would just have to take it a few small steps at a time. He was very much surprised to find that he had rather enjoyed his short sojourn with Miss Girard this afternoon.

And was even more surprised to find he hoped to do so again in the near future.

CHAPTER ELEVEN

You've Got Mail

Dearest Mayhem,

I find myself rather perplexed this evening, not able to make heads nor tales of anything anymore. Somehow, a simple afternoon outing turned into one of the most aggravating, then confusing, then somehow, almost pleasant afternoons I have experienced in some time. People continue to surprise me. One, whom I naively assumed to be a trustworthy innocent, instead proved most villainous. And another, to whom I have never attributed anything but villainy, instead proved to be most noble. Even if begrudgingly so. As I was likewise pleasant despite my best intentions to be otherwise. I do have a tendency to be obtuse when the mood strikes me. Often creatively so. Consider yourself forewarned. However, I confess, I no longer know what to think.

Have you ever found yourself similarly confused by the actions of others? Or even of yourself? I certainly did not behave as I would have previously assumed I would have done on such an occasion. Have you ever had an instance in which you have behaved in a manner wholey surprising to you? For the good or ill? Especially for the ill, as that would be much more intriguing. Have you ever done anything truly evil?

Overwhelmed with curiosity,
Millie

My Curious Millie,

I find myself uncertain how to respond to your kind in-quiry. Truly evil is such a subjective term, after all. What might seem truly evil to one might seem acceptable and even necessary to another. Is a squirrel who steals the nuts of a dormouse evil? To the dormouse, most certain-ly. But to the squirrel's family, he is a savior. I fear such a question is far too nuanced to answer definitively.

...

Your (likely not evil though that may depend upon whom you ask) Champion of Squirrels, Dormice, and Anonymous ladies,
Mayhem

My Lord Champion,

I suppose I must concede to your point. Evilness is, ap-parently, subjective. Poor little dormouse. Though I would argue that there are varying degrees within such subjectivity that bears further discussion. I suppose if one is stealing to feed one's family, that is perhaps not so evil. Though the dormouse might disagree. However, being cruel for the amusement of oneself or others, I would argue, is vastly more evil.

Very well, then. As evilness is far too subjective a topic, tell me then, what actions of yours have made you feel the most ashamed? I shall tell you mine, if it will help loosen your tongue. Several years ago a dear friend of mine made a decision with which I did not agree. I was overly harsh and unforgiving in my treatment of her and it damaged our friendship. I was thinking only of myself and how her decision would affect me. Though she has forgiven me, I have never forgiven myself for the hurt I caused her. While I have done many, many things in my life of which I'm ashamed, this is the one which I most regret. I do try to be more careful with my advice now. And my judgement. Though I fear I am not always successful.

There. I have now shared my greatest shame with you. I pray you do not think less of me now.

Hopefully yours,
Millie

My dearest Millie,

That you are aware of how your actions affected others and are not only remorseful but have taken steps to rectify your actions speaks volumes of your character. Most with whom I am acquainted do not bother. Far from thinking less of you, such an admission only makes me admire you more. I hesitate to reveal my own shame with you for fear you will not feel the same. However, as you have been brave enough to share with me, I cannot do less.

As you no doubt have surmised from our letters, I am a consummate jokester. Or at least I have been in the past. On one unfortunate occasion, a joke went regrettably astray and an innocent bystander was lamentably hurt. It is my greatest shame. Even more so because my actions could not be reversed. The damage could not be undone. And apologies did far too little to assuage the wounds I caused.

Such an outcome was one I had never predicted, though I should have. I have oft, in my past, been far too blasé, far too quick to act for a laugh rather than think for a moment about how my actions could misfire. The only good thing to come from this incident is that I now take far greater care with my words and actions. I have made a concerted effort to gain some maturity. Some measure of responsibility. Thoughtfulness. I cannot say I always succeed, but I do try to think before I act which is a far sight better than before.

It has also made me a bit more charitable toward my enemies and those who would wish me harm than I might have in the past. For I cannot know the truth of the motives behind their actions. In truth, it has been far more difficult than I ever anticipated. But I do at least try, which is far more than I could have said for myself even a few months ago.

In a few instances, my overtures have been pleasant-ly, and surprisingly, returned. Which I daresay encourages me to continue my quest toward emotional maturity. The journey will no doubt be long and fraught with more failures than successes. But it is the effort, I find, that is important.

I do hope you will not think less of me now, my dear marchioness. For I remain, as always,
Your Mayhem

My dearest Marquess of Mayhem,

Well, you did earn your name for a reason, I suppose. But do not fear. As you most charitably said to me, I find that your actions speak volumes of your character. To your advantage. Far from thinking less of you, I find it admirable that you can learn from your mistakes and endeavor to improve upon yourself. Few do, I fear. Particularly men. I commend you for attempting to remedy the characteristics that caused such pain in your past. Knowing that you are doing so gives me the courage and strength to continue to do the same. Perhaps I shall even try being more charitable toward my own enemies. A daunting task to be sure. But one in which I have good company.

Keep me appraised of your progress, my dear Mayhem. And I shall do the same.

Yours in remorse and gratitude,
Millie

Chapter Twelve

ADALINE TILTED HER face to the sun, welcoming its warmth on her skin. She had spent the afternoon visiting with several would-be suitors her brother had rounded up. They hadn't been terrible, truth be told. But the necessity of remaining polite and feigning interest in every word they uttered had completely exhausted her.

Her choices, after all, had been much reduced since the mystery surrounding the falling out between the Girards and the Brelsfords had made its rounds. But time had finally helped calm those rumors to a degree. There was always something new and juicy for the ton to splash about, after all.

Still, Adaline did wish she were able to choose a match that truly suited her. Not just settle for one because she had no other choice. And the longer she remained under her brother's roof, the more she wished to find a good match. She was ready for her own household and the freedom that would afford. Oh, she'd have a husband to contend with. But surely it would be better than being subject to her family's rules and supervision.

Her mother likely only agreed to let her escape to Hyde Park to promenade with Lucy in a further attempt to garner suitor attention.

"It is an agreeable afternoon, is it not, Adaline?" Lucy asked, her eyes bright as she surveyed the passing crowd, ever eager for new gossip or acquaintances to enliven her day.

Adaline nodded. "Indeed. Any afternoon in which I can escape my brother's machinations is agreeable, dear cousin."

"Oh," Lucy laughed, looping her arm through Adaline's. "You are incorrigible. You know your brother is only trying to ensure you have the best future possible. Which, under the circumstances, may be rather more difficult than he'd have hoped."

"It is his own fault. Still, his plotting has served to make me more eager for marriage, I will give him that."

"Truly?" Lucy asked.

"Hmm," Adaline nodded. "It is the only way I will escape him."

Lucy laughed again. "Have some patience. Perhaps he will actually find someone whose presence you can tolerate for more than three minutes."

Adaline arched an eyebrow, but before she could reply, her attention was caught by a burst of childish laughter from the nearby square. Her eyes shifted, seeking its source, and came to rest on a group of children in bright jackets and bonnets, tumbling about the green with wild abandon. At their center, laughing heartily as he lifted a small girl into the air, was a figure Adaline recognized with a jolt.

She stopped short, her gloved hand tightening on Lucy's arm. "Good heavens. Is that—"

Lucy followed her gaze. "Why, it's Lord Hugo."

"Hm." Adaline watched him for a moment, bemused. "I had not thought him so… domesticated."

Lucy's lips twitched with reluctant amusement. "Nor I," she confessed.

"I was under the impression he was always to be found at a club or in some gaming hell. Not engaged in such an innocent pastime as this. Whoever would let him so near their children?"

Lucy's eyes sparkled. "Perhaps he has reformed. Though surely the children are some relation to him. Unless he often takes it upon himself to play with random children he comes upon in the park."

Adaline did not reply, her thoughts too tangled to unravel. Seeing Hugo so unguarded, his dark hair askew and his coat grass-stained, was at odds with every recollection she harbored. Though, in all fairness, the last time their paths had crossed he *had* come to her rescue with unexpected gallantry. And their conversation had been surprisingly pleasant.

Still, she would be a fool to let one simple act of kindness erase the insult he had served her and her family with his irresponsible scheming. An insult that had provided ample fodder for whispered speculation about her reputation. She had expected never to speak civilly to Lord Hugo Brelsford again.

Yet their last meeting had changed that. And she had, mere days before, vowed to emulate Mayhem's example and at least attempt to be more charitable toward her enemies. If she had truly meant it…here was her chance.

Lord Hugo, her greatest enemy, stood there before her, his laughter ringing through the air as he spun a child around. Most men of her acquaintance couldn't be bothered with children. Her own father, though she knew he loved her, would never have engaged in such activity. But there Hugo was, by all appearances genuinely enjoying himself.

Adaline could not help but stare, her curiosity piqued against her will.

As if sensing her attention, Hugo glanced up. His brown eyes widened in surprise. A moment later, the wooden hoop the children had been rolling escaped them and rolled across the grass, coming to rest at Adaline's feet.

"Send it back, miss! Send it back!" called a little boy, breathless with excitement.

Adaline retrieved the hoop and sent it rolling back toward the children with a graceful flick of her wrist. The children shrieked with glee, and she couldn't help but laugh in return. Especially when they rolled it right back to her, trying to entice her into their game.

Her smile faded as Lord Hugo—after being goaded in the back with his grandmother's walking stick—approached, a hesitant smile on his lips, his coat askew and an errant blade of grass caught in his hair. For a moment, they both hesitated, awkward under the weight of their past grievances. Still, their recent civility—and Mayhem's words—kept Adaline from running off.

Lord Hugo bowed, his manner impeccably polite despite his dishevelment. "Miss Girard, Mrs. Harrow. What a wonderful surprise."

Lucy inclined her head, but Adaline regarded him with narrowed eyes. "A surprise indeed, my lord. I confess I did not think to find you enjoying such domestic amusements. I had thought you reserved your energies for more, shall we say, adult pursuits."

Lord Hugo's lips curved in a rueful smile. "And why should children have all the fun? Besides, I am at the mercy of my family this morning." He nodded toward the cluster behind him. "My sisters' broods. They are relentless."

Adaline's eyes danced. "You, at anyone's mercy? That is a sight I had not thought to see. Do they know you are the devil incarnate?"

That drew a laugh out of him. "That is a closely guarded secret. Known only by the two of us."

"Oh," she scoffed, "I'm certain more people are aware of your devious nature."

His eyes flashed with amusement. "I'm touched by your concern for my family, considering the last time our families crossed paths there was almost a duel. With me on the wrong end of the pistol."

"True. But the fault for that lays firmly at *your* feet."

"To my everlasting shame," he said. His words were accompanied by a gentle smile. But there was something about his eyes, something in his demeanor and countenance that conveyed his sincerity. He seemed…genuinely remorseful.

Adaline swallowed hard past the sudden lump in her throat. She hadn't expected remorse from him. Hadn't expected kindness. Friendliness. Even jolliness. It seemed he did nothing but surprise her each time they crossed paths, and she wasn't quite sure how to react.

Then he reached out to take the hoop from her, surprising Adaline again with the jolt of awareness that tingled through her when their hands brushed.

"You may add it to your repertoire of sordid tales of me, Miss Girard. Though I did hope after our last encounter I had earned myself a little kindness."

She arched her brow, feigning innocence. "I am always kindness itself, my lord. It is not my fault if you so often provide the ton with fodder for the gossip mills."

Lucy stifled a laugh, and Lord Hugo's eyes sparkled with something perilously close to genuine amusement. "And here I thought myself safely dull these days. Shall I endeavor to scandalize you further, or may I hope for your approval at last?"

"Approval is a high bar, my lord. I am not so easily impressed by feats of athleticism with a child's toy."

"Then I must try harder. Next time, perhaps, I shall juggle three at once."

Adaline's lips twitched as she fought a smile. "I dare you to try, my lord."

He inclined his head, mock-serious in his reply. "A challenge I cannot refuse. Prepare yourself for astonishment, Miss Girard."

Lucy, delighted by their repartee, clapped her hands. "I do believe you have met your match, Adaline."

Lord Hugo glanced at Lucy with a conspiratorial wink. "Your cousin's wit is famous, Mrs. Harrow. I live in hope she will one day use it for my benefit rather than my undoing."

Adaline's cheeks flushed, but she held his gaze. "Be careful what you wish for, Lord Hugo."

Before he could reply, the children, impatient with the delay in their game, clamored at Lord Hugo's side. "Uncle Hugo! The hoop! You promised to play!"

He turned with a sigh of mock resignation. "Familial duty beckons. If you will excuse me," he said with a gallant bow.

"Of course." Adaline bowed her head in return. "Meeting you today was… surprisingly not dreadful."

His laughter rang out. "I share your sentiments completely, Miss Girard." He bowed his head again to her and then to Lucy. "Mrs. Harrow."

Then, with one last parting glance at Adaline, a look more thoughtful than teasing, he rejoined his charges, the children enveloping him with shouts of glee. In moments, he was lost to the laughter and chaos of little hands tugging him back into their game.

Lucy and Adaline stood in silence, watching them for a moment. Lucy was the first to break the quiet. "That was not at all what I expected of Lord Hugo. He seemed almost… likable."

Adaline harumphed. "Unexpected indeed," Adaline replied, her tone softer than she intended. "Even more unexpected that I might have actually enjoyed his company. For a second time."

Lucy grinned. "He has changed, I think. Or perhaps you have. It is difficult to hold on to old resentments when the subject engages in chivalrous rescues and plays at hoops and sticks with children."

"Hmm," Adaline muttered, not wishing to voice her agreement out loud. Though Lucy was correct. It was becoming more difficult to hold onto the anger that used to burn in her chest whenever the name of Lord Hugo Brelsford was mentioned.

They resumed their walk, but Adaline found herself glancing back, watching Hugo as he darted past a tree, a little girl shrieking with delight as he scooped her into the air. The image unsettled her. It was so at odds with the irresponsible villain she had always thought him. Memories of their last meeting plagued her. The initial tension, the cautious words, followed by the realization that perhaps she did not know him at all. Nor he, her.

"Do you suppose people can truly change, Lucy?" Adaline asked quietly as they moved away from the green, the sunshine casting long shadows at their feet.

"I suppose they can surprise us," Lucy replied. "Perhaps you and Lord Hugo are not so very different after all."

"Who are you not so different than?" Henry asked, sauntering to a stop beside them. He'd been visiting with his tailor.

"Me," Lucy said, looping her arm through Adaline's with a smile. "We are very much alike."

Henry raised his brows. "Yes, we are all aware," he said drolly. "Was that Brelsford I saw you speaking with?" he asked, his forehead creasing in a frown. "I specifically told you to keep your distance from that man. He has caused this family enough trouble."

Adaline let out a sigh. "We only spoke for a moment, Henry. He was quite civil."

"I do not like it," he blustered. "He cannot be trusted. I have told you—"

"Yes, yes, do not worry so, Henry."

He continued to grumble but thankfully moved on to other topics. Namely what eligible gentleman he thought he might be able to entice to call upon her.

Adaline pursed her lips, trying to ignore him. Instead, despite her assurances to her brother, her thoughts lingered on Hugo's laughter and the warmth in his eyes. A warmth she had not expected to ever find there. For the first time since Hugo had set their feud in motion, Adaline wondered if she had been too hasty in her judgments. The morning's encounter had left her oddly unsettled. And, strangely, a little bit hopeful.

As they turned down a quieter lane, the sounds of children's laughter fading behind them, Adaline realized she was already looking forward to the next time her and Hugo's paths might cross. Mayhem would be so proud.

Adaline nearly stumbled at the sudden awareness that she was anticipating her next encounter with Lord Hugo nearly as much as she did her next letter from Mayhem.

When had that happened? And what did it mean?

She wasn't sure she was ready to find out.

CHAPTER THIRTEEN

You've Got Mail

Dearest Marquess,

Recently, I followed your advice and tempered my ire when dealing with a particular enemy when we crossed paths. And the encounter was surprisingly cordial. Enjoyable even. I confess, I do not know what to think. I have spent so much time wishing this person ill, that no longer doing so feels…odd, to say the least. Though unexpectedly refreshing. The weight of my anger has been lifted, and I have found myself focusing on more pleasurable pursuits.

As with so many other things, I again owe you my thanks, my dear Mayhem.

Much more happily yours,
Millie

Dearest Marchioness,

I read your letter (as always) with a great happiness that increased with every word upon the page. While I cannot take credit for your actions (those are yours to own regardless of whatever poor advice I might have given), I read your news with exceeding delight. Though I have no doubt any poor sod who had the temerity to become your enemy deserves all the misfortune that befalls them in this world. Should you find yourself desiring delayed restitution for any lingering ill feelings, please consider me at your disposal. In that way, you may keep your newfound relief while the villain still receives their just desserts. A happy compromise that allows me the pleasure of ensuring the scoundrel pays for their past trespasses against you.

As for these pleasurable pursuits in which you have now immersed yourself…I am intrigued. Tell me more. I do, as a whole, immensely approve of such past times. In truth, they are the only pursuits that I deem worthy of my own time. Or such was the case in the past. I am trying to expand my horizons somewhat. The journey to doing so is, unfortunately, tedious. Therefore, I find myself infinitely interested in both what you have found worthy of your precious time and, most especially, in what you find pleasurable. Tell me about the passions that bring you joy. You, and your secrets, are ever safe with me.

…

Eagerly awaiting your response (as always),
Mayhem

My Noble Mayhem,

I had thought to be astonished at the sheer impudence of such a request. Though upon further reflection, I find I am neither exceedingly surprised nor particularly offended. Nor should I be, in all fairness, as it was I, not you, who began the conversation.

I have warned you about my obtuse nature. Under normal circumstances, the very act of imploring me to trust you would, in fact, make me distrust you even more. However, you are *you*. My Mayhem. So, very well. I shall trust in you—and our anonymity—at least in this one instance. Now that I have considered it, perhaps it will be fun to reveal a secret of which no one but myself is aware.

Then here it is. I adore books. I read voraciously, far more than is seemly for women, or so I have been told by more than one person in my life. I will read anything and devour every book I can get. I am fond of poetry and histories. I recently read a book on botany by the Duke of Beaubrooke that was surprisingly fascinating.

But my favorite by far are novels. This, in and of itself, is not so scandalous. However, my interests lie specifically—I hardly dare utter it, even to you—in those of a romantic or, on occasion, scandalous nature. I enjoy Austen. I also quite enjoyed The Mysteries of Udolpho.

But most recently—and if you betray my confidence and tell a single soul, I shall deny it to my dying breath—I read two novels that I have not been able to remove from my thoughts. One entitled The Monk, and the other *Les Liaisons Dangereuses*. They were both... disturbing in many ways. Far more descriptive than I had anticipated. Yet exciting. Tantalizing, even. Perhaps more so because had I been discovered, my father would certainly forbid me from ever reading another word. I hid them tucked between the pages of an ancient tome on philosophy.

I can hardly believe I have committed such a confession to paper. If I were wise, I would throw this letter directly into the fire. But then, I have rarely been wise where you are concerned. I suppose it is futile to begin now.

Well. There you have it. The revelation of one of my dearest passions and deepest secrets. I shall await *your* revelations with great anticipation.

Your strangely exhilarated partner in secrecy,
Millie

Dearest and most surprising Millie,

I love that your dearest passion is reading. Though I am saddened at your need to hide any part of what brings you such joy. Rest assured, you will never need to do so with me. As for your choice in reading material…I confess I am a bit surprised. And exceedingly delighted. And in truth, encouraged that such subject matter has tantalized rather than frighten you. I would like to know what exactly you found so tantalizing. I could think of a good many examples. I wonder which of them appealed to you more? The murder? The mayhem? (A personal favorite, as I'm sure you've deduced). Or perhaps it was the passionate scenes. I am not afraid to admit it is my dear hope it is the latter. And if that is the case, it is a subject I should be happy to explore more deeply with you at any time you wish.

As for my own passions, I share your love. Which is no surprise to me as we seem to have much in common. I also draw. I have yet to expand this dabbling into actual painting. But I do enjoy sketching a good deal.

Before you protest that our passions are not at all similar, I must confess, I do not sketch mere landscapes, or birds, or whatever bowl of fruit might happen to be nearby. I sketch my fantasies. The images that dwell in my mind when I close my eyes and plague my thoughts when I wake. You feature quite heavily in these scenes, despite my never having seen your face.

I have told no one about this hobby of mine. And until this moment, no other living being has ever seen one of my sketches. Save you.

I pray that it does not scandalize or offend you. The dream was so vivid and beautiful I simply had to capture it the moment I awoke. I dreamt I had visited the hat shop, hoping they would have a letter for the marquess. Instead, upon entering, I found you, reclining on a chaise, lit by the warmth of the sunbeams streaming in through the window and scarcely covered in unwound spools of soft velvet ribbon. And nothing else. The scene was quite literally breathtaking. I hope you find it so as well. I have included this sketch with my letter.

Always and most passionately yours,
M.

Postscript—if you enjoyed The Monk, I would recommend Rosa Matilda's Zofloya. I think you will find it equally tantalizing.

CHAPTER FOURTEEN

"YOU ARE DAYDREAMING again," Lucy said. "Thinking of a certain marquess?"

Adaline blinked and glanced up, her cheeks growing warm at Lucy's knowing smile.

"I…am afraid I do not know what you mean," Adaline said, turning her attention back to the tassel she had been picking at to get to the gold threads woven within. "My mind always wanders whilst drizzling. It is hard to keep it from doing otherwise."

"Hm, that may be true," Lucy said, extracting another bit of fringe from the drizzling box at her feet that overflowed with braids, bits of tapestry, tassels, and other random textiles waiting to be picked apart for their gold and silver threads. "But I think your mind has been wandering in a certain direction of late."

Adaline opened her mouth to deny it but couldn't. She had been smiling more and more of late. And they both knew why.

"Perhaps it has," she said, not bothering to hide her smile this time.

"I take it his latest letter has something to do with that."

Adaline grinned again. "He is now calling me Millie. *His* Millie. And he calls himself my Mayhem."

She didn't mention their more intimate discussions. And certainly did not reveal the drawing he had sent with his last letter. The one of a naked woman reclining on a chaise surrounded by ribbon…and very little else. He had drawn her with her arm covering her face, though something about her seemed vaguely familiar. The whole scene had such an ethereal, quiet beauty to it. He was supremely talented. And that he was imagining *her* when he drew it…

Adaline covered her face with her hands and shook her head. "I cannot believe I am mooning over a man I have never even met."

"But…" Lucy prompted.

Adaline dropped her hands with a sigh. "But…I find I cannot help myself."

Lucy's chuckled. "Yes, that is often the way of it. When I met my George, I found myself swooning over the most ridiculous things. The way he smiled at me. Or let his gaze linger a moment too long. Simple things I never would have thought twice about before."

"Yes, but you at least had the benefit of seeing Mr. Harrow in the flesh. I have never even met this man. How can I be so…" She waved her hands toward herself. "I am hopeless."

Lucy chuckled again. "Perhaps you are simply hope*ful*."

"Well, that's true enough," Adaline said with a soft snort. "I am ready to be mistress of my own household. My mother and brother mean well but…"

This time Lucy snorted. "Yes, they can be a bit overexuberant in their duties as your family."

"Yes!" Adaline threw her hands up. "I know they love me, but Mother scrutinizes everything I do, every book I read—which she doesn't really approve of, regardless of the topic—and Henry examines every bit of mail that might be sent to me and has scared away every possible suitor I might find interesting with his overprotective bullying. I know they care but…they care a mite too much. And, before you caution me," she said, smiling at her cousin, "I know a husband may be just as controlling as my family. A bit like exchanging one jailor for another."

"Oh, it's not *that* bad," Lucy protested.

Adaline shrugged. "Even so, at least as a married woman I will have my own household. Some measure of freedom. I cannot be the spinster daughter who lives with her mother, or God forbid, under her brother's rule her whole life."

"As long as you are careful whom you choose as husband," Lucy cautioned. "A cruel husband can be far worse than a loving family."

Adaline shuddered at the thought. "That is very true. But Mayhem…" She couldn't help the smile that played on her lips. "He wouldn't be cruel. Or controlling. I am sure of it."

Lucy smiled, though it didn't quite reach her eyes. "*Are* you sure of that, dearest? After all, you do not even know the man's real name. Perhaps he is hiding other things from you as well."

"Perhaps," Adaline mumbled.

She had considered the possibility, of course. She could admit she was more than a little infatuated with her Mayhem, but that didn't mean she had been robbed of all reason. He could be anyone. Someone entirely unsuitable. Perhaps someone who was already married.

She shied away from that thought as one too painful to contemplate.

"I do think he is likely a gentleman," she finally said. "His writing is too meticulous, the parchment too fine. And, let us not forget, that the original letter was found in front of your shop. Only someone who could afford your exorbitant prices would be in your shop."

"Oh," Lucy grumbled. "My prices are *not* exorbitant."

Adaline chuckled and Lucy relented. "I do understand your meaning though. And I hope, for your sake, you are correct. Even still…"

"I know," Adaline said with a sigh. "I do not know who he is or if we will ever meet in person so it would be foolish to pin my hopes on what is, for all intents and purposes, a fantasy."

Lucy's eyebrows rose. "That is very wise." Then her eyes narrowed in suspicion. "I do not trust it."

Adaline's laughter rang out and she tossed her tassel at Lucy. "All will be well, Lucy. Stop worrying so."

"Hmm. And what of the other man in your life? Does he not feature in your daydreams at all?"

Adaline's cheeks were flushing before she could deny knowing of whom Lucy spoke.

"Lord Hugo is hardly in my life." She frowned slightly, knowing that wasn't entirely true. "Well, at least not in the same manner."

"No, that's true. He is tangible, visible, and exists beyond the confines of a letter," Lucy teased.

Adaline grimaced, but she could not deny the stark facts. Lord Hugo was real. Mayhem was, by and large, real only to a point. Despite how much they revealed about themselves in their letters, there was still a large degree of imagination and speculation about their relationship. She had never heard his voice, his laugh, or seen his face. Part of her felt as if she knew him better for all of that. Part of her missed the physical aspect of becoming acquainted with someone. There was much to be said for being able to see the unspoken words that people often unconsciously revealed.

And Lord Hugo was nothing if not real. Larger than life, almost. When she'd hated him, she'd been able to ignore the more physically appealing aspects of his nature. But now that she'd become more familiar with him, she knew he wasn't the devil she'd thought. He was actually quite intelligent. And thoughtful. On occasion. Certainly attractive, if somewhat arrogant, but…amusing and unexpectedly kind. With eyes always full of laughter. That deep voice that seemed to resonate in her chest when he spoke. And he had a handsome face she could not help but think of despite her best intentions.

"Perhaps if his arms did not fill out the confines of his jacket so well, it would not be so difficult."

"Whose arms, dearest?" Lucy asked, her innocent gaze belied by the amused smile tugging at her lips.

Adaline bit down on her lip, mortified she had uttered that aloud, and mumbled something non-committal under her breath. Then she let out a sigh. Thoughts of both men tumbled about in her head. Not warring. Somehow harmonious. Combined, they made her perfect man. One who both challenged her and accepted her. Protected her but allowed her to fight for herself. Tantalized and intrigued her.

She might never have the opportunity to choose between the two. And perhaps that was a good thing. One man, she had never wanted. The other she could never have. Yet both suddenly seemed a possibility.

And how ever could she make such an impossible choice.

THE BLUNTED TIP of Arthur's foil stabbed into Hugo's chest.

"Ow." He grimaced, rubbing at his sternum as his brother planted his foil tip-down against the ground and leaned against it slightly while catching his breath.

"If this was a rapier, you'd be dead right now."

Hugo ran a hand through his damp hair with a scowl. "And then you would be guilty of fratricide."

Arthur snorted. "I would be applauded. And you would deserve your fate. If you cannot keep your mind on the sharp, pointy object in your hand, you should not be fencing."

Hugo waved his foil in his brother's general direction. "As you have so kindly pointed out, this is neither sharp nor pointy."

Arthur's exasperated scowl brought a smile to Hugo's lips.

"My point stands," Arthur said. "Are you still daydreaming about that letter you've been carrying about in your pocket? Or is it the harridan you've been stalking who has stolen your wits?"

"Do not call her that," he grumbled. "And neither."

"Or both," Arthur said, amusement still pulling at his lips.

Rather than acknowledge the truth of that remark, Hugo

turned away to grab a towel, taking far longer than necessary to mop his brow.

Millie was never far from his mind. That had been the case since the moment he'd received her first letter. Each subsequent missive had only cemented her in his thoughts. In his dreams. And in his heart, though he was loath to admit it. He had never before been in love, and he wasn't quite sure what to do with such emotions. Especially when the object of his affections existed only on paper.

And then there was Adaline Girard. An unexpected disturbance in his life who had only served to captivate him more and more. Far from the animosity of their first meeting, each subsequent encounter seemed to be more pleasant than the last and only served to whet his appetite for more of her company. He found himself wanting to share everything with her, just to see her reaction. Would her eyes flash with furious fire? Would she laugh, either with him, or at him? Would that delicate brow of hers rise in sardonic amusement?

He seemed to be counting the minutes until he could match wits with her again and have those piercing golden eyes of hers boring right into his soul.

He sighed. He'd spent his life avoiding feminine entanglements and in the space of a few months had somehow managed to become inextricably enmeshed with two of the most fascinating—and unattainable—members of the fairer sex.

"I only seek to caution you—" Arthur started, but Hugo cut him off.

"You have already done so. Numerous times."

"Yes, but you are not taking my caution into account, so therefore I feel the need to harp on the point."

Hugo snorted. "Your harping is not needed, I assure you." The constant running monologue in his head was far more than adequate.

"Hmm." Arthur rubbed a finger across his upper lip, and Hugo let out a long-suffering sigh.

"Oh, just out with it before you explode."

The grin Arthur aimed at him made Hugo want to remind Arthur who was the elder brother. But he didn't want to draw any more attention than they already had. The last thing he needed was a fresh rumor with him and his love life at the center. Not that continuing this discussion at home would be any better. Their mother had forbidden them to fight in the house, and he certainly didn't want to bring her into their conversation.

However, of the two options, their present location was preferable. They were certainly not alone at Angelo's Fencing Academy, but it was still best to let him have it out here. Arthur's words of caution were an irritant, to be sure. But one that Hugo could quickly handle. And then ignore. At home, there was more danger of his mother overhearing. And she was an entirely different story. She and his father had already made their thoughts on Adaline Girard perfectly clear. There would be no approval of her from their direction. As for his…literary activities, if those were discovered, there would be hell to pay. And he was still floating in the heaven that Millie's letters created.

Oh, devil it. He rubbed a hand over his face, alarmed by his own thoughts. Maybe he did need a good talking to. An intervention of sorts. A stiff drink?

Or…just another letter from Millie. Or an afternoon with Adaline.

"That," Arthur said, pointing at Hugo's face. "That look right there. That is what concerns me so greatly."

"What look?" Hugo asked, though he could imagine all too well. If even half of what he felt was betrayed by his expression, his brother did indeed have cause for concern.

"You know what look."

Yes, yes he did. But he wasn't going to make it that easy for Arthur. "Do I?"

"Look, Brother. I want nothing but your happiness. But I fear that this obvious…infatuation you have over this woman—"

"Which one?" Hugo asked, curious if his brother could perhaps deduce which enticed him more. Because damned if he could determine his own mind on the subject.

Arthur merely scowled. *"Both.* Your infatuation with them both is dangerous."

Unhelpful. Not incorrect. But still, unhelpful in his current predicament.

Arthur continued on, oblivious of Hugo's inner turmoil.

"If anyone were to discover your correspondence, you'd be forced to marry the woman. She'd be just as compromised as if you had been caught kissing behind the garden shrubs. Perhaps even more so, as there is tangible proof of your indiscretion."

Arthur didn't know the half of it. Their last batch of letters alone…their discussion of her reading activities, the drawing he'd sent her…Hugo rubbed another hand over his face. Though regret was the furthest thing from his mind. He wanted nothing more than to continue what he and Millie had started.

"Do you think I haven't considered that?" Hugo turned on his heel to return his foil to the receptacle where they were stored and began to gather his things. "We have been taking the utmost precaution. We do not use our real names or any personal, especially identifying information. Our letters are sent through an intermediary. The threat of discovery is minimal."

"But not non-existent. Are you prepared to deal with the consequences, should they occur?"

Hugo paused, though he didn't truly have to ponder it. He'd been thinking of little else for weeks now.

Arthur sat back, a surprised huff punching from his lungs. "Good God. You have."

Hugo shrugged, still trying to play nonchalant, though his emotions were anything but. The thought of marrying Millie not only didn't concern him, it sent a chorus of thrills ricocheting through his body.

Until thoughts of Adaline intruded. For despite their acrimonious beginnings, the prospect of a match with her sent a similar chorus of thrills through him. Which made him feel like the worst kind of scoundrel.

What an atrociously convoluted mess he had enmeshed himself in.

Arthur followed him through the building, blessedly silent while they nodded to friends and acquaintances as they quickly changed and made their way to their carriage. The reprieve did not last however. As soon as the carriage door had closed behind them, Arthur started in on him again.

"I do not understand the purpose of either your continued correspondence with your mystery lady or with your strange friendship with Miss Girard. Either will likely end in nothing but disaster for you. And them. What are you thinking?"

Hugo threw his hands up. "I am thinking that it is long past time that I married. Mother and Father have been harping on me to do just that since the day after they married off Edward. Grandmother has thrown every eligible woman at me and frankly has pointed out a few that are slightly less than eligible. One young duchess married to an especially ancient duke, in particular. Are either of the women with whom I am currently involved really a worse choice than her? Or any other? I am ready to take on more responsibility, including a wife. Would it truly be so bad if I found one whose company I actually enjoy? A woman I might even grow to love?"

A woman he was already half in love with—and yes, that applied to both of them, God help him. Not that he'd mention either of those points, considering Arthur was already bubbling over with worry.

"No. I suppose not. If you must marry, that is. I, on the other hand, would prefer not to marry at all," Arthur said. "I am far too young."

"You are nearly six and twenty, Arthur. Father was married with three children when he'd reached your age."

Arthur's mouth dropped open, momentarily struck dumb by the reminder of that bit of information. Then he recovered, waving it away. "We are discussing you."

"Yes. And I am telling you that if I must marry, I could do much worse than Adaline Girard. Or Millie."

"Millie?" Arthur asked, perking up.

Hugo's lips pinched together. Damnation. He hadn't meant to let that slip. He waved his hand. "Nothing. It's a pet name. It doesn't matter."

Arthur flashed him a delighted grin. "Oh, but I think it does—"

"Let it go, Arthur," Hugo said, a note of warning in his voice that Arthur, surprisingly, listened to.

He slumped back against his seat, though an amused smile still lingered on his lips. "Be all that as it may," Arthur said, "I do not think you are taking this as seriously as you should, especially when it comes to this Millie of yours. Miss Girard is a problem in and of herself, for a variety of reasons, not the least of which is our family's decided prejudice against her. But this mystery woman…are you really considering—"

Hugo let out a long-suffering sigh. "I do not see how I could take it any more seriously. I am willing to marry the woman if we are discovered. How much more serious should I be?"

"Truly? She could be literally anyone, Hugo. A nursemaid. A seamstress. A…a…an actress!"

Hugo's brows rose higher with every suggestion. And his smile grew wider.

"What if she's a married woman with six screaming children clinging to her skirts?" Arthur continued. "Or…the queen's laundress. She could be the queen herself! I've heard she's fond of a bit of correspondence."

Hugo laughed until his stomach hurt. "Or," he said, still chuckling, "she could be a simple young lady who accidentally discovered a like-minded soul with whom she has formed an unexpected but thoroughly enchanting connection."

Arthur groaned. "And why would a simple lady be sitting around writing to a strange man she has never met? I am appealing to whatever working faculties you might have left, Hugo. Something isn't right. Any normal young lady would be busy with suitors and engagements. Why is she not? She could have a club foot. Or be horribly pockmarked."

Hugo thought on that for less than it took to draw a full breath before he shook his head. "I wouldn't care."

That made Arthur pause. "Truly?"

"Truly," Hugo said, without hesitation. "The woman is witty, kind, adventurous, passionate. She amuses me and intrigues me. I want to know her thoughts on everything and I tell her everything of mine. And none of that requires that she look a certain way."

Arthur stared at him again, his mind obviously churning as he thought of another argument. "What if she is a mere child?"

"What?" Hugo blanched, horrified at the thought. But he immediately dismissed it. "She is not a child. I am certain."

"How can you be sure?"

"Her manner of speaking, her thoughts, the representation of her life—or as much of it as she has shared with me—all indicate she is older. At least old enough to marry, as her family seems to be seeking a match for her as much as ours has for me."

Arthur's eyes widened. "What if she is much older? Ancient even? You could be courting an octogenarian!"

Hugo rubbed his hand over his face again as Arthur laughed until he wheezed.

"Well," Hugo finally said. "If that is the case, then at least I shall marry someone with some experience of the world. Perhaps she can teach me a few things."

That set Arthur off again. Hugo laughed, but he was in earnest. He did not care who this woman was. He was reasonably sure she was of an age with him and likely a lady, simply because of her manner of speaking. Her penmanship. The quality of her quill, ink, and paper. And she was writing to him through the hat shop which suggested it was an establishment she frequented.

He had briefly considered the possibility that its proprietress was his mystery lady but quickly abandoned that thought once he saw her with her husband. Plus, she did not behave as he believed

Millie would. She was kind enough, polite enough, but not nearly as boisterous or venturesome.

As for the identity of the real Millie…he told the truth when he said it did not matter. It did not. Oh, to a point, he supposed. If she were already wed, that would certainly be cause for disappointment. Then again, he knew that was not the case, as she had been under the care of her brother when her parents had been traveling.

So, she was likely a lady, young enough to need a chaperone but old enough to resent it. Given everything he'd gleaned from her letters, he thought her to be in her early twenties. Old enough to know her own mind and tenacious enough to use it. Very similar to Miss Girard, now that he thought on it.

In any case, who she was, what she looked like…none of that mattered. She was Millie. That was enough for him.

Perhaps they should put all this speculation to rest and just meet?

CHAPTER FIFTEEN

You've Got Mail

My Dear Mayhem,

Do you ever feel as if you were the unfortunate Sisyphus, doomed to push a boulder up a hill for eternity? A melodramatic way to begin a letter. I do apologize. But at times I feel as though I am repeating the same day, over and over. Rise. Dress. Accompany Mother to whatever function she has planned for the day. Attend whatever functions she has planned for the evening. Prepare for bed. Sleep. Repeat.

I do wish there were more to my life. I am not ashamed to admit that your letters are the bright spot in my days. Perhaps I should take a cue from your moniker and cause a little more mayhem in my own life. At the very least, it might get me out of yet another afternoon of dreary embroidery. Well, that isn't entirely fair to the embroidery. I do not hate it, as such. On occasion, I find it quite peaceful. And I do admire the finished product. It is reaching that state that sometimes wears on me.

And now that I have thoroughly bored you with talk of sewing and such, I shall apologize. It has been a quiet week. One in which I have not seen my nemesis even once. It has made my days quite dull. I had not realized how much I had grown accustomed to our altercations.

What does it say about me that I await such confrontations with such anticipation?

In my defense, this person has a remarkable ability to appear wherever I seem to be. With no sightings in more than a week, I am not sure what to think. In fact, I am just a little (a very little) bit concerned. Perhaps he has come to a fitting end. Or has moved on to torturing another poor soul.

And now I shall have to spend my afternoon at church, praying for forgiveness for my own wicked soul.

Yours in boredom and appallingly awful behavior,
Millie

My Dearest Millie,

I find your admission neither melodramatic nor cause for apology. In fact, there is no need to beg forgiveness of anyone for any of your thoughts, least of all me. Never me. I want to hear every last one of them, no matter how mundane you feel them.

As for boring me with embroidery, it is not possible. For one, I find everything you tell me—especially when you are letting slip a few tantalizingly personal details—utterly enthralling. And secondly—and I tell you this only because I know I can count on your utmost secrecy—I enjoy a bit of embroidery myself from time to time. My old nurse taught me. As you can imagine, I was a stubborn and willful child, prone to mischief. (If you are wicked, I am the devil incarnate. Which only suggests to me that we shall get along famously, as we have already proven).

And I was also fascinated with sharp, pointy objects.

After one particularly mischievous morning that may or may not have involved divesting my brother of some of his much admired hair, she sat me down, bribing me with my choice of sharp, pointy needles, and she put me to work with a bit of shiny thread and an old shirt. It became her "punishment" of choice whenever I acted too out of hand. Suffice it to say, I became very adept at the skill. I can embroider a flower-laden vine that would bring you to tears.

As for Sisyphus and his boulders, I do understand exactly what you mean. I so look forward to your letters breaking the monotony of my days that I have, at times, considered taking up residence beside the hat shop just to more quickly receive them. I hope it brings you comfort to know that if you are toiling with seemingly eternal boulders, I am right there beside you.

Regarding your nemesis, never fear. Nemesi (is that the plural of nemesis? My tutors would be so ashamed) rarely do one the courtesy of completely disappearing from one's life. They have a terrible habit of reappearing just as one becomes complacent with their absence. I have no doubt yours will make an appearance soon. Also…you have inadvertently revealed he is a he. Intriguing. Who is this man? What did he do to earn your ire? I would challenge him to a duel, happy to die in the service of my marchioness, though you are more than capable of dealing with the scoundrel I have no doubt. However, should you desire, please know that I am available in whatever capacity you should need me. You have but ask.

I cannot help but think that there is a simple solution to our mutually monotonous days. I know that part of the fun of our correspondence is the anonymity. It is truly freeing to be able to be completely myself without any worry of judgement or consequence because we are completely incognito. However...having said that...I must confess that the curiosity over who you are is driving me to distraction.

We enjoy each other's letters so much. Surely I am not the only one who has considered what might occur if we were to ever converse in person.

I do know the risks. Perhaps you would find me a dreadful bore and run away never to be heard from again. And that would be a true tragedy. But...

Do you ever think that we should perhaps meet?

Yours through mischief and monotony,
Mayhem

CHAPTER SIXTEEN

ADALINE'S MIND CONTINUED to spin, though it had been several days since she had received Mayhem's last letter.

Did she ever think about meeting him? Of course she did. She thought of little else. Even when she closed her eyes at night—especially then—she thought of it. Her dreams ranged from wonderful—moments filled with laughter and passion—to nightmarish. Where he'd spend mere seconds in her presence and run screaming from the room. Or worse, looked right through her. Find her too unworthy to spend any more time or attention on. Decide that she was nothing like he thought, that the real her was too much to deal with and turned his back on her.

She could handle the first scenario. It wouldn't be fun to have him run screaming. But it would be preferable to his apathy. Though neither scenario would be her choice.

And then, what if everything was wonderful? What if he was exactly as she hoped? The man in his letters, come to life? That was almost more terrifying than him running.

"Do try not to look so glum, my dear," her mother said. "It is a beautiful day to promenade, and we are here to be seen. Your sour expression will not put any lingering rumors to rest."

"Yes, Mother," she murmured, too soul-weary to argue.

Her mother glanced at her with surprise, then gave her a gentle smile. "Why don't you go for a short walk. I think I spotted a bird's nest just over there."

That did perk Adaline up. She had a small collection of birds' nests she kept in a cabinet in the library. Her mother, who collected bird figurines, often pointed out nests to her. It was one of the few things they shared. Adaline smiled, grateful to have something with which to occupy her mind.

The nest wasn't too far from the ground, but just far enough she couldn't quite reach it. She certainly didn't want to take it if it was still occupied. She reached up on the tips of her toes as far as she could, but she needed another few inches.

She dropped back to her feet with a sigh and blew an errant curl from her eyes.

"Do you need any assistance?"

Adaline sucked in a yip of a breath and slapped her hand over her mouth, twisting to find Lord Hugo Brelsford leaning against the tree.

"What are you doing here?" she demanded, cringing at how irritable her voice sounded.

Hugo raised a brow. "I am out taking the air, enjoying a sunny afternoon, chatting with acquaintances…the typical things one does in the park. I think the more interesting question is what are you doing?"

She scowled at him. "It is not so interesting. I was merely trying to see into the bird's nest."

"Ah." He stretched to his full height and glanced into the nest. "It's empty aside from a few bits of shell."

"There is still shell inside?" she asked, forgetting to show her disdain for him in her excitement.

"Yes. Would you like me to retrieve it for you?"

"I…" Asking for his help was a step more than she was willing to take just yet. "No, thank you. I can manage."

He raised that brow of his again. "You do not have to decline just because it is I who offers."

"That isn't why I declined," she said, though they both knew it absolutely was.

"Well, then…" He moved aside with a little bow and a gesture of his hands. "Please do not let me get in your way."

She gave him a strained smile and moved back beneath the nest, cursing herself for her damned pride. She had no idea how she was going to get the nest. Perhaps if she got a stick and poked it from beneath, though that risked damaging it. Were she younger, and not in full view of half of London, she would hike up her skirts and climb the tree.

Well, she couldn't quite do that. But perhaps she could use the trunk for enough leverage to gain those last few inches she needed.

Adaline gathered her skirts in one hand, lifting them just enough to keep her feet clear, and then placed one foot on the trunk of the tree, trying very hard to ignore Lord Hugo standing there with his arms crossed and his lips already twitching with amusement.

She pushed off with her foot, reaching up as high as she could. Her hand did make contact with the nest. But she neglected to take into account how she would land once she'd pushed off from the tree. Her feet hit the ground harder than she anticipated, and down she went.

There were gasps from several onlookers, a few muffled giggles from a few more. And even worse, the smiling face of Lord Hugo as he squatted beside her, holding her bird's nest.

"Are you hurt?" he asked, his eyes still shining with merriment. She wondered if he would still look like that if it hadn't been apparent she was unharmed.

"Aside from my pride, no," she muttered.

He chuckled and helped her to stand, taking one of her hands in his and wrapping the other about her waist to haul her off the ground. The feel of his arm wrapped around her, his hand holding tight to hers, stole her breath more than the impact of hitting the hard ground had. He kept his arm around her, even after she had regained her feet. Not for more than an extra heartbeat, perhaps two. But long enough for her to glance up and meet his gaze, see the surprised expression in his own eyes that suggested he was also feeling this strange, exhilarating warmth spreading through him at their closeness, at the feel of his hands on her, even through the layers of their gloves and clothing.

What sort of sorcery was this? Her heart sped, her pulse pounding. And still he did not let her go, nor did he pull his gaze from hers.

"Adaline!" her mother called, her voice faint though getting closer.

Adaline took a step back, resisting the impulse to bat his hands away. That would have been churlish, especially in full sight of their onlookers. And besides, whether she liked to admit it or not, she enjoyed his touch. Er...needed his help.

"Thank you," she mumbled, taking another step back. She brushed off her skirts and patted at her hair, trying to make sure everything was where it should be.

"Your nest, my lady," Hugo said, holding it out with a flourish.

She took it from him, eyes squinted in suspicion. "Why are you behaving so..."

"Gentlemanly?" he supplied.

"Yes."

He grinned again. "Well, I am a gentleman, after all."

Her eyes narrowed. "By birth, not by manner. At least, not in regard to me. In general."

"Ah, yes." He shrugged a shoulder. "Well...perhaps I have simply grown weary of our war. Haven't you?"

She snorted softly. "No."

His chuckle threatened to draw an answering smile from her lips, and she rolled them between her teeth to keep it under control.

"I suppose it is amusing," he responded. "But it is far too nice a day for battle."

Adaline let out a sigh. It did consume far more energy to stoke her waning hate for him than she anticipated. It was growing tiresome.

"Adaline, my goodness, are you all right?" her mother said, hurrying to her side.

"Yes, Mother, I am fine. I simply misjudged the height of the nest. Lord Hugo assisted me."

Her mother glanced at Hugo, her lips pinched. But she deigned to give him a tight nod. "Thank you, Lord Hugo. We are…in your debt."

"Not at all," he insisted, his words crisp. His entire body seemed to tense, his easygoing manner evaporating under her mother's glare. But then he turned back to her, his gaze softening. "Though perhaps Miss Girard would do me the honor of accompanying me on a walk?"

She stared at him, completely nonplussed. "I…"

"What an excellent idea," another voice said, and Adaline turned to see the Dowager Duchess Catherine, Hugo's grandmother, beaming at them. "I love to see the young people out promenading, don't you?" she said to Adaline's mother.

"I…yes, of course," Mrs. Girard said, not daring to refute the dowager duchess.

"You two go along. I'll keep your mother company," she said to Adaline. "We'll be just behind you."

Her mother looked as though she'd swallowed a lemon, but she gave Adaline a tight smile and nod.

Adaline and Hugo glanced at each for a moment and then turned to begin their walk along the garden path, both at a loss for words or argument.

"She is formidable, isn't she?" Adaline finally said, and Hugo chuckled.

"My grandmother? That is an understatement," he said with another laugh. "She once bullied the queen into giving up one of her prized pineapples so she could display it at my cousin's wedding. And the queen not only agreed, but thought it was her idea from the start."

Adaline laughed, and Hugo shook his head. "Father likes to

say that if the Duke of Wellington had sent Grandmother to Waterloo, not only would Napoleon have surrendered but he would have done so with a smile on his face, thanking my grandmother for the opportunity."

Adaline snorted softly. "Hmm, is she who I have to thank for our dance the other evening?"

Hugo glanced at her in surprise, and she lifted a shoulder in a shrug. "She not only orchestrated this walk but seems to be entertaining my mother as well," she said with a subtle nod behind them. "A miraculous accomplishment under the best of circumstances, even more so with matters as they stand between our families. It stands to reason."

"What does? That the only reason I'd ask you to dance is if my grandmother was responsible?"

She raised her brows. "Am I mistaken?"

His sheepish grin brought an answering smile to her lips. "I did not say that," he admitted. "But I do protest that you think it is the only reason I would ever ask you to dance."

"You may protest all you'd like. I shan't believe you."

His jaw dropped with exaggerated shock. "You wound me, madam."

"Do I?" She looked up at him, delighted. "Is it fatal?"

His booming laugh drew glances from several startled on-lookers, including her mother. Duchess Catherine merely beamed in grandmotherly approval.

Hugo shook his head. "You are ruthless, Miss Girard. Truly ruthless."

"Hmm." She pressed her lips together, though a smile peeked through anyway. "Only if you are deserving of it, my lord."

He nodded in a brief salute and then turned his attention back to the path. They walked quietly for a few minutes, and the silence was far more comfortable than she would have assumed. She shifted the nest she still held, and he glanced at it.

"May I inquire as to why you risked health and limb for an abandoned nest?"

"You *are* prone to exaggeration, aren't you?" she asked with a raised brow.

He shrugged. "I enjoy…accentuating my words on occasion."

Adaline snorted softly. "You are creative, my lord, I'll give you that."

"And the nest?" he asked, glancing down at it again.

"It is not so interesting. I collect them, is all."

His brow rose again. "You collect nests?"

She bristled at his tone. "It is not so odd. There are those who collect far stranger things. Sir Thomas Lanswater's antiquities, for instance. Or the Duke of Rutland's exotic animal specimens. I've heard he has two stuffed crocodiles and an assortment of rare skins and tusks. A few birds' nests are not so unusual in the face of all that."

"No, of course not. I did not intend to disparage your collection. I was merely curious."

Adaline kept her gaze on the path before her, chastised and a bit embarrassed by her assumption. "My apologies," she mumbled.

He gave her an amused half-smile. "I am beginning to think you will argue with me no matter what I say, just for the sake of arguing."

She rolled her lips between her teeth, hating that he was likely correct. Then she let out a sigh. "I suppose I do have a tendency to assume the worst of you."

He chuckled. "Truth be told, I tend to assume the same of you."

Her eyes widened which only made him laugh harder.

"We are quite the pair, aren't we?" she said.

"I propose a truce," he said. "While I cannot promise not to argue with you—because I do find it inordinately amusing—"

She couldn't hide her smile at that, as she felt much the same.

"I propose," he continued, "that we at least attempt to give each other the benefit of the doubt before we jump to the worst possible conclusion."

Her eyes narrowed as she considered it. Well, there wasn't really anything to consider. It was a fair proposal. Though she also enjoyed a good argument with him. Still, in the interest of peace and their combined sanity… "Very well. I shall endeavor to ask for clarification before I assume you are intent on mortally insulting me."

His laughter rang out again, and Adaline caught a glance of her mother's disapproving face. Though she could not decipher why, exactly, she disapproved. Whether it was due to their laughter drawing attention from others who were promenading, or because it was Lord Hugo Brelsford—a name not generally uttered with fondness in their home—with whom she was laughing, she could not say. Perhaps both.

But she couldn't deny that his company was…diverting. Oh, she still hated him. Or, hated what he had done, at least. Yet despite all that, she couldn't help but look forward to the next time they might meet.

Though that admission brought to mind another possible meeting. Mayhem.

A sharp pang of guilt flashed through her, though she had no cause to feel such a thing. Mayhem was a friend. A dear friend, but one who had no place in her real life. Unless they did finally meet. What would happen then? Would they continue their flirtations? Would it develop into something more? Did she want it to?

A few weeks ago, she would have said a resounding yes. She still would. And yet…

Her waist still tingled from where Lord Hugo had held her. Even now, as they walked, they occasionally stepped a little too close, allowing their shoulders to brush. Was that intentional on his part? Was it on hers? She had certainly made no effort to move farther away to prevent that contact, though she hadn't realized it until just that moment.

What did that mean? What did it mean that she had Mayhem's words constantly in her mind, yet her body seemed to be craving the touch of Lord Hugo? Perhaps if it was only his touch she enjoyed, this would not be such a conundrum for her. But loath as she was to admit it, she did seem to genuinely enjoy the man's company. His wit. Even his wicked teasing.

Was she truly wicked to have her thoughts so occupied by two different men? Who, now that she thought upon it, would be the perfect man if it were somehow possible to combine them.

She let out a sigh, hoping none of her inner turmoil was visible upon her face. She would never recover if Lord Hugo were to discover her thoughts. Mayhem was the only one to whom she felt safe enough to confide those. Though was that merely because of their anonymity? Would that change if they were to meet?

There was only one way to know for sure. But she did not know if she was brave enough to find out.

CHAPTER SEVENTEEN

Hugo gripped the handlebar of his pedestrian curricle and lined the front tire up at the makeshift start line beside Arthur's. He adjusted his stance, making sure the seat was comfortable under his bottom. His feet were planted firmly on either side of the thin frame. Balance steady—a necessary precaution when riding a contraption with one wheel in front and back. He couldn't believe he'd actually let his brother talk him into this, but a challenge was a challenge.

"This is childish," he said, glancing at Arthur, who was rocking back and forth on his own wooden mount, the metal wheels scraping up the dust on the path beneath their feet.

"It is not childish," Arthur insisted, "but it is an excellent form of exercise. Or so I've been told."

Hugo shook his head with a smile. Exercise it might be. And great fun, truth be told, to be able to fly across the ground on the contraption's two wheels. But the new rage of the Season seemed to have two distinct frames of mind. Those who enjoyed the intriguing new contraption, and those who despised them for the havoc they were wreaking on the streets and pathways of London.

He both enjoyed the sheer exhilaration that came with flying over the road and sympathized with those whose peace was being ruined by the hobby horses. Then again, he was part of the group causing the chaos (as he often was). Still, he did feel guilty about it (as he often did).

Several other gentlemen lined up beside them, booted feet wedging into the ground to gain them some leverage when they pushed off. A few of their more astute peers attempting to promenade on this fine afternoon saw what was about to happen and prudently got out of the way. Hopefully, the others would follow suit. They'd chosen a less popular path, but they did need a lane with level enough terrain to accommodate their cumbersome machines.

"Watch for the signal," called Arthur.

Young Lord McKinley stood by the wayside, handkerchief in hand, ready to wave them all forward. A pistol to signal their start had been suggested, but discarded, as too dangerous a tool to use in the presence of so many bystanders.

McKinley raised his arm, and everyone leaned forward, gripping their handles tightly, both feet planted firmly on the ground, ready to push off.

"Go!" McKinley shouted, waving the handkerchief like a madman.

They pushed off, their legs flying over the path, the wheeled contraptions upon which they sat supporting their weight and allowing them to fly down the path. A paved road would have been preferable. The dirt path they were on rattled his bones as he flew down it, running faster as Arthur pulled alongside him. Had they been going down a hill, he would have propped his feet up on the wheel axles and enjoyed the sheer euphoria of speeding down the lane without the necessity of a horse or carriage as one would usually require.

Several walkers in their path gasped and jumped out of their way. He shouted apologies as they flew by, thankful he couldn't hear their grumbled curses. Viscount Finley shouted as the front wheel of his hobby horse hit a stone and sent him flying over the handlebars. Hugo risked a glance back to ensure himself that the man was unharmed. Physically, at least. He sat on the side of the path, his face red though he was smiling.

Arthur took advantage of his distraction to gain a few feet, and Hugo pushed harder, propelling himself faster. Lord Braeswater peeled off with a shouted laugh, the front wheel of his hobby horse wobbling uncontrollably beneath him.

Now only he, Arthur, and Mr. Mortimer remained. And Mr. Mortimer was gaining on them.

He and Arthur glanced at each other, grinned, and sped up until his legs burned. A slight bend loomed before them in the path, and Hugo turned his wheel to make the turn. Only instead of slowing down, as did Arthur and Mr. Mortimer, he propped his feet up and tried to coast through the curve.

And it would have worked, too. If it hadn't been for the small white dog that ran into his path.

He jerked his wheel to avoid the little animal amid a series of feminine screams, angry male shouts, and a possible whimper of his own, and slammed his feet into the ground, though he was unfortunately going too quickly to immediately stop. He tried to dig in his heels, but ended up with them dragging, kicking up an enormous amount of dust until he abandoned that plan and lifted his feet again. His curricle careened around the bend and straight into a hedge of bushes that lined the path.

The bushes at least stopped his runaway machine, which lodged itself firmly in their midst.

He, however, was not so lucky.

Instead, he flew ass over end and landed with a pained grunt on the other side of the hedge.

Right at the feet of a perturbed and disturbingly unsurprised Miss Girard. And her vastly more surprised maid.

"Lord Hugo," Adaline said, arching an eyebrow as she surveyed the carnage. "If your intent was to upend yourself at my feet, you have succeeded most spectacularly."

Hugo, whose pride was more bruised than any portion of his person, disentangled himself from the bush with as much dignity as one could muster when one's face was covered in dirt. He attempted a bow, though he feared the effect was more of a lopsided bob.

"Miss Girard, if I had known I would end up at your feet, I would have chosen softer ground."

Adaline's lips twitched, but her eyes betrayed both exasperation and concern. "You are fortunate not to have broken your neck. Nor anyone else's." She knelt beside him, her manner brisk. Her maid held out a handkerchief.

"Thank you, Thompson," she said, her attention fully on him as her maid stepped back, giving them privacy while keeping a watchful eye. "Let me see your hands. And do not argue. You are bleeding."

"Am I?" He glanced down in surprise, then grimaced at the blood oozing from a shallow scrape along his palm. "It isn't fatal," he said, though he surrendered his hands anyway. He winced as she dabbed at it—more gently than he likely deserved...or expected from her.

"It's a wonder you and your ilk have not managed to maim half of London," Adaline muttered. She removed her handkerchief from her reticule, shoved the soiled one inside, and carefully wrapped his hand.

He raised a brow. "Am I to believe that you would not readily join us if you were able? I thought you were far more adventurous than that."

Her lips twitched again, and she tugged the knot a little tighter than necessary on his binding. He smiled through his slight wince.

"I would not join you, no." Before he could voice his skepticism, she continued. "But I *have* already enjoyed several rides on the Duchess of Beaubrooke's Ladies Walking Machine. And surprisingly managed to thoroughly enjoy myself without disrupting the peace or injuring innocent shrubbery or passersby. Or myself."

She gave a final tug on his bandage and stood.

He chuckled and shook his head. "My apologies for such an

erroneous assumption, Miss Girard. Though I must say, of all the perils I have faced, none compares to your most formidable attentions." He held up his tightly wrapped hand with a half-smile.

She flushed and brushed at her skirts, patting away any remaining dust before looking back at him with a huff. "Come on then," she said, holding out a hand. "If you are restored enough to jest, you are restored enough to stand. Let us ensure you haven't broken anything more than your dignity."

He laughed again and took her proffered hand, though he was perfectly capable of rising on his own. Once on his feet, he found himself strangely reluctant to release her hand. She glanced at him, then softly tugged her hand away, only to lift it, wiping away a remaining bit of dust from his cheek, letting her thumb linger. He reached up and took her hand in his, lightly holding it so she could pull away at any time should she so desire.

She did not. Their eyes met, and for a moment, all the usual japes and sparring faded, leaving just them, bare and exposed. Vulnerable.

Hugo swallowed hard, his pulse thundering in his chest.

"Thank you," he said.

She blinked, breaking the strange spell between them. "It is nothing," she said, pulling her hand away and stepping back. She gazed at him a moment longer and then looked down, clearing her throat. "Well then, if you are quite certain you are recovered, I shall resume my walk. I'm sure Mother is wondering where I have gotten off to."

Hugo hesitated and then regathered his wits about him—and his battered dignity. "May I accompany you, Miss Girard? Provided, of course, you do not find my company too disagreeable."

Adaline blinked again, her surprise evident. Of all the invitations she had ever received, a request to promenade in the park was likely not one she'd ever expected. Nor was it one he'd ever expected to offer. But he found he did not want to quit her company just yet.

"Very well," she finally said. "On the condition that you do so on your own two legs and not on that horrid dandy horse."

He gaped in mock outrage. "Pedestrian curricle."

"Nuisance."

He shrugged. "I've been called worse."

Adaline's lips pinched together, though her shoulders shook with silent laughter. "Whatever term you prefer, you obviously need a few more lessons at Mr. Johnson's school on the Strand."

Hugo chuckled. "That is entirely possible. *You*, I suppose, mastered the skill on your first try."

"Naturally." She beamed at him, a sight that momentarily stole his breath.

"Then, perhaps you would care to ride it with me?"

"*With* you?" She glanced at the walking machine that very obviously had only one seat. "I do not see how that is possible."

Hugo shrugged. "I sit up front, so I can steer, and you sit behind me, side saddle, of course. I'm sure it will be very comfortable."

Adaline looked between him and his pedestrian curricle several times, eyes wide and brows raised. "I'm sure that is simply not done, sir."

"On the contrary, the Prince Regent himself took Mrs. Fitzherbert for a ride in just such a manner only a few weeks ago."

"Did he now?"

Hugo nodded sagely. "The caricaturists have already captured the scene in exquisite detail."

Adaline nearly smiled but bit her lip, trying to force a stern expression through her amusement. "I do not think I'd like to give the caricaturists further fodder for their cartoons."

"Hmm." Hugo scratched his chin. "We could always do the opposite. You can steer and I shall ride side saddle behind you."

That startled a laugh from her, but she shook her head. "That, sir, will assure our chances of being immortalized in the gossip rags. I fear I must politely decline."

"Oh, very well. A walk will have to do. I shall—"

"I will take charge of it, my lord," a young boy said, running up to them. "Lord Arthur sent me to see if you needed assistance," he added, nodding in the direction of Arthur and their friends who stood a short distance off, laughing amongst themselves. At his unfortunate accident, no doubt.

Or… He glanced back at Adaline. Perhaps not so unfortunate.

"Thank you," he said, flipping a coin to the boy. "Tell my brother I will meet him back at home."

"Aye, milord," he said, bobbing a quick bow before hurrying to remove the hobby horse from the bushes.

Hugo turned back to Adaline. "Shall we?" he asked.

She didn't answer but turned and started back up the path, letting him follow. For a few moments, they walked in surprisingly comfortable silence, the only sound the crunch of gravel beneath their feet and occasional laughter from others enjoying the promenade. Hugo stole a glance at Adaline, his eyes drawn to the sunlight glinting off the red gold highlights in her chestnut hair.

When her gaze met his, he gave her a quick smile. "Tell me, Miss Girard, how fares your brother? Is he still contemplating removing me from this earthly coil?"

Adaline giggled softly. "Henry has a tendency toward overprotectiveness, but I believe he has abandoned his quest for your early demise. For now. He spent a week in Bath and declared it the dullest place on earth. Perhaps because he could not find enough diversion to his liking. My mother is despairing of him ever settling down."

"Mothers are apt to despair," Hugo said with a snort. "Mine is convinced I have become too accustomed to my own company to ever end my own bachelorhood. A fate she seems to view as worse than death."

"Surely you exaggerate, Lord Hugo. I know you are not so unsociable as that. Every event I have observed, you attended with apparent enthusiasm."

He grinned. "Apparent is the operative word there, madam. Every event I attend, there is a gaggle of females somewhere within, determined to recommend a daughter, sister, or protégée. I am expected to take advantage and make a favorable match with all due haste."

Adaline let out a sigh. "You have my sympathy, sir. As the only daughter, my family is eager to see me securely settled. My brother, while of course expected to make a good match, is allowed to do as he pleases for the most part, while I must attend every party and ball, guard my reputation and keep my name from the gossips—a task made more difficult of late thanks to a few unexpected circumstances," she said, glaring at him from her peripheral.

His cheeks actually grew warm with shame. The consequences of his ill-fated jest, it seemed, would not fade any time soon. "My apologies again, my lady."

"Hmm," she said before continuing. "I must smile at every gentleman, accept every dance invitation, and never once betray my aversion or boredom."

"And do you ever falter?" he asked, amused but truly interested.

"Of course not. Mother would faint. I reserve my true opinion for select company," she said with another sidelong glance.

"Ah, and am I to infer that I am party to that select company?"

She turned her head to look at him more fully. "I suppose you have not thus far proven yourself entirely unworthy of my confidences."

Hugo chuckled. "Not entirely unworthy, eh? Well, I shall have to hope that one day I might be promoted to the rank of somewhat tolerable."

Adaline's laughter rang out, bright and melodic.

He gave her a conspiratorial smile. "Yet despite my less than pure worthiness, you have deigned to walk with me. Curious, is it not?"

She tilted her head to regard him. "Perhaps, Lord Hugo, I am simply ensuring you do no further harm to the innocent shrubbery in the park."

He stopped, turning to face her, warmth filling him when she turned to him with a smile. "Or perhaps," he said, his teasing tone mixed with what sounded disturbingly like hope, "you find my company less disagreeable than you pretend."

Adaline's lips pursed and her eyes narrowed, though he didn't miss the flush in her cheeks.

"I have tolerated your presence for a mere quarter hour, Lord Hugo. Do not become overly confident."

His laughter echoed in his chest, and he gave her a slight bow, his hand over his heart. "Well, Miss Girard, at the risk of sounding too confident, I will confess that this afternoon has been...shall we say, unexpectedly pleasant."

"Then perhaps I will confess that I have found it the same," she said with obvious reluctance. But a small smile played about her lips. "Good day, Lord Hugo."

He returned her smile, and she turned to walk away, but paused when he spoke again, the words erupting before he'd consciously decided to say them.

"Does that mean that I may seek you out should our paths cross again without fear of threatened duels or other bodily harm?"

She called back over her shoulder. "We shall see, Lord Hugo. We shall see."

CHAPTER EIGHTEEN

You've Got Mail

My Most Chaotic Mayhem,

As you are, as you have so frequently stated, an agent of chaos and mischief, perhaps you could explain to me how it is that a person can change so thoroughly as to be almost unrecognizable. For I am at a loss.

My nemesis, of whom I have spoken frequently, is a person who thus far, for the most part, has been a constant source of aggravation and grief in my life. As you well know. But of late, he has become someone I not only tolerate but whose company I am quickly coming to enjoy. Even seek out. How can someone who was once the source of my greatest grief now often be the source of my greatest comfort? Is this some strange cosmic jest? Divine intervention? Perhaps an illness from which one or both of us suffer?

Is there aught I can do about it? Or should do? Do I give in and accept this new dynamic? Or proceed with caution? Can someone change so vastly? Or perhaps I am the one who has changed. I truly do not know. All I know for certain is that I grow more and more fond of this person and am surprised, confused, and frankly terrified by this change of events.

...

Confusedly yours,
Millie

Postscript—I have thought what it would be like to meet in person. In truth, I both long to speak to you in person, but fear that doing so might change the very nature of our current relationship.

For better, or ill? Once discovered, it would be too late to reverse course. Still, yes...I do think upon it frequently.

My Dearest Millinery Marchioness,

I cannot say what has occurred with your nemesis, whether it be you or they who has changed. But I do not think it is a cosmic jest. I have recently discovered myself that people do, apparently, change, even after a lifetime of certain behaviors. In fact, I have found myself recently behaving slightly less chaotic and slightly more responsible.

I know. It came as a shock to me as well.

However, I have discovered, to my surprise, that I rather like having someone in my life to steady me. To call me out when I have gone a step (or three) too far. No one is more surprised than I that I not only enjoy this turn of events, but have, of late, actively sought it out. Embraced it, even. A felicitous set of circumstances to be sure, as I have vowed to become a little more responsible. Though I would hate to lose my roguishness entirely.

All that to say, yes, people can change. As for how you should proceed, I'm afraid only you can answer that question. Is this change something you can live with? You did say you are enjoying it, at least in part. And change is often unsettling, so it is not unusual to fear the unknown.

Though as this person has been the source of such grief for you, I would urge caution. I don't believe anyone is beyond redemption. But that does not mean one needs to expose themselves to further heartache.

Whatever you decide, I am certain it will be the correct choice. You have ever been my voice of reason. I have no doubt you will discover the best course in due time. And I am always here should you need to someone to listen to your woes.

And never fear. I may have become slightly more dependable of late, but am and always will be…

Your Mayhem

Postscript—I am glad that you have given thought to meeting in person. I do understand your misgivings. And I share them. But like you, I cannot help but dwell upon speaking to you face to face.

CHAPTER NINETEEN

ADALINE FIDGETED IN her seat before her vanity as Thompson clasped a delicate pearl necklace around her throat and ensured every curl was artfully arranged.

"You look beautiful," Lucy said. "Stop worrying so."

Thompson adjusted one last ribbon and then bobbed a curtsy and took her leave.

"I am not worried," Adaline insisted once she and Lucy were alone. She brushed her hands down the pale pink skirts of her gown. "Just…"

"Anxious? Nervous? Excited?"

Lucy grinned at Adaline's startled glance. "It stands to reason, my dear cousin," Lucy said. "After all, a very handsome, eligible gentleman all but promised he would seek you out at the next opportunity. And as most of Society will be attending the theater tonight, there is an excellent chance you shall see him this evening. Lord Hugo would cause any girl to be a little distracted."

"Yes. I mean no, that's not quite…it's not exactly that, it's…"

Adaline sighed. She didn't know what it was. The evening promised delight and dread in equal measure. Yes, she was strangely anticipating seeing Hugo again. Why, she hadn't quite worked out in her mind yet. The man was incorrigible, irresponsible, reckless, and had nearly ruined her with his childish prank. And yet…the more time she spent with him, the more she saw his kindness, humor, love of life. Their recent friendship both confused and exhilarated her.

And sparked a thread of guilt as well. Because there was another presence in her heart and mind. Mayhem. Her mysterious correspondent whose witty letters had become both a source of comfort and torment. Not unlike how Lord Hugo Brelsford's presence affected her. How could one heart entertain such divided affections? And did it even matter? Unless one or the other of them declared any sort of intentions toward her—and the chances of that were slim at best—she would never need to choose between them.

That thought startled her enough that she gasped quietly. What was she thinking? Choosing between them? Between a man who was an abstract fantasy and a man she should want nothing to do with?

Perhaps her mother was right, and it was time to settle down with a nice suitable man who would provide security and respectability. One who was *real*. Who she could trust. Who was…stable, and predictable. And did not fill her mind with shockingly inappropriate thoughts she would be a fool to act upon. That is what she needed.

She would not dwell on what she *wanted*.

Her other choices were too fanciful and unsettling for a variety of reasons that made her head ache to think of them.

"You look lovely," Lucy said again. "Whomever you may see tonight will be delighted with the vision you present, I have no doubt."

Adaline gave Lucy a grateful smile. "I confess, I do find myself eager to see Lord Hugo again, though I know the folly in that."

"Is it folly?"

"Is it not?" Adaline frowned. "The man insulted me and our family enough that Henry was ready to challenge him to a duel. I am still the butt of far too many jokes. How can I spend even a moment contemplating a possible match with him?"

Lucy shrugged. "Regardless of what happened in your past,

you enjoy his company now, in the present. He has apologized for what really amounts to a youthful mistake. One in which he did not bear sole responsibility. I know your family still harbors ill feelings toward him, and with good cause, but..." She shrugged again. "I'm sure they'll come around if he is who you truly want."

Adaline nodded slowly. "And Mayhem?"

Lucy's lips pursed. "I know you have genuine feelings for him. And understandably so. But...you do not know who Mayhem truly is. He could be entirely unsuitable. If he ever even agrees to reveal his identity. Lord Hugo, on the other hand, is charming, respectable, and in my opinion, clearly taken with you. Do you not feel something when you are together?"

A flush crept into Adaline's cheeks. "I do. But it is different. With Hugo, I feel seen. He watches me when he thinks I am unaware, and when we converse, I feel I can truly speak my mind. Even if I say things I ought not. But Mayhem knows the real me and has never judged. In fact, we seem to be of the same mind on almost all matters. I...have grown very fond of him."

"Through his letters?" Lucy asked, her crossed arms and pursed lips showing exactly what she thought of the likelihood of that.

"Yes, through his letters. I will admit, I never would have thought it an efficient way to become acquainted with someone. But I was mistaken. It is perhaps the best way."

"How so?"

"Because there is nothing else interfering," Adaline said with a soft smile. "None of the nervousness one often feels in the presence of a new person. Especially a person with such potential future importance. None of the airs one often gives oneself to appear more important or intelligent or interesting. And perhaps most importantly, no physical attraction, or lack thereof, masking our true emotions with desire. Or...lack thereof." An issue she had definitely encountered on more than one occasion with gentlemen who were otherwise acceptable enough.

"With the letters," she continued, "I, at least, can say what I really feel. It provides a distance that allows us to communicate as the people we truly are. And I am certain it has been the same for him. We have grown close through our letters. He is perhaps the only person I feel I truly know. Who truly knows me."

Lucy gazed at her thoughtfully for a moment. "Perhaps that is because you have never given anyone else the opportunity to truly know you."

Adaline opened her mouth to argue, then shut it again with a sheepish grin. "Perhaps you are right in that."

"Might that be something you could change this evening?"

"I…shall try," she said with another smile.

"Good." Lucy stood and smoothed out her skirts. "And consider…who can truly offer you happiness? A secret correspondent whom you may never meet? Or a gentleman who, despite all reason and opposition, has sought you out?"

Adaline nodded thoughtfully and then looped her arm through her cousin's.

They met her parents in the foyer, her mother's critical eyes appraising her appearance with a final nod of approval. They rode in relative silence to the theater, and did not linger in the foyer upon arrival, much to Adaline's dismay.

Inside, the theater blossomed with color and sound. Gentlemen in crisp cravats and ladies in shimmering gowns filled the marble foyer, their laughter and conversation mingling with the strains of a distant quartet. From above, the chandelier spilled its brilliance across the velvet-draped boxes and gilded balconies.

Adaline pressed a hand to her stomach to calm the riot of butterflies in her stomach as her family took their seats in their box. Adaline settled her skirts, hands folded tight, eyes restless. Lucy joined her, and together they surveyed the crowd. Lucy's constant commentary on the theater-goers helped calm Adaline to a point. But she remained distracted, her eyes constantly on the search for Hugo; her mind reeling with thoughts of Mayhem.

Finally, the orchestra struck the notes of tonight's opening presentation, a short melodrama that would precede the main performance of a comedic opera. The audience seemed to enjoy the performance, but Adaline hardly noticed. To be fair, she was not the only one whose attention was on the crowd rather than the performance. It seemed few people attended the theater to actually watch the stage.

By the time the main performance had begun, Adaline still had not spotted Hugo. He was not with his family in their box, nor had she seen him with any of his usual friends. Perhaps he had not attended this evening. She tried to ignore the crushing disappointment that thought lent her. Even if he had not sought her out, as he'd implied, she had been looking forward to seeing him again. Strange as that thought was.

Lucy leaned in close. "You are distracted, Ada. The performance is quite good tonight."

Adaline laughed quietly, though her fingers continued to restlessly fold and unfold her fan. "You may be the only one in attendance actually watching the actors."

Lucy grinned. "True. But then I have already made my love match. I suppose you can be excused if your attention is reserved for a particular gentleman rather than the show."

Lucy's eyes shifted to one of the grand boxes near the stage, and Adaline's gaze followed. She stilled, though whether her body was frozen from excitement or an attack of nerves, she could not say. Hugo stood with his brother Arthur near the back of their box, laughing at something the gentleman with them had said. He turned his head, his eyes scanning the audience.

He stopped, his gaze locked on hers. For half a heartbeat, he did nothing. And then he slowly smiled, his eyes never leaving hers.

The audience erupted in applause as the rich, velvet curtains dropped to the stage, signaling an intermission before the main performance commenced.

Adaline's brother left to obtain some refreshments as her mother was already parched. Adaline rose as well.

"I believe Lucy and I will walk a bit, if that is all right, Mother.

I feel the need for a bit of exercise, or I shall be asleep in my seat."

"Hmm," her mother murmured, her eyes narrowing slightly. "Very well. Do not go far and don't linger."

"I shan't. We won't be gone long."

Her mother nodded absently and turned back to her conversation with Mrs. Litner, who had wandered over to their box for a visit.

Lucy's brow rose as Adaline glanced at her, but she followed nonetheless. The likelihood of Hugo being in the foyer instead of one of the boxes was slim. But the likelihood of him visiting her box was non-existent. That she wanted to increase the likelihood of chancing upon him was something she did not wish to examine too closely just then. She'd chalk it up to needing a distraction and leave it at that. And if nothing else, Lord Hugo Brelsford was an excellent distraction.

Adaline stepped into the corridor with Lucy and they made their way toward the grand staircase leading to the foyer, her nerves on edge.

She did not need to wait long, however. Lord Hugo stood near one of the balustrades, leaning against the polished wood while he laughed at something an acquaintance said. The golden light illuminated the sharp line of his jaw and the seams of his jacket strained ever so slightly when he crossed his arms and looked around.

Then he glanced her way and smiled. He leaned toward his friend, saying something though his eyes didn't leave hers. The friend nodded, and Lord Hugo walked toward her.

"Go on, Ada," Lucy said.

Adaline hesitated, glancing behind her toward the entrance near their box. Her mother stood just outside the archway, a drink in hand, conversing with several acquaintances. But she watched her, and Hugo's approach, with thinly veiled disapproval. But at this point, with Lord Hugo obviously headed in her direction, doing anything but turning to greet him would result in more scandalous gossip. And as that aligned with her wishes, she moved toward him, crossing the corridor with measured and careful steps.

"Good evening, Miss Girard," Lord Hugo said, his voice warm and low.

"Lord Hugo," she said with a small curtsy.

"I confess I had hoped to see you tonight."

"Did you?" she asked, both delighted and surprised.

"Of course. You brighten the room considerably." He leaned toward her with a conspiratorial smile. "And I have no doubt my prospects for entertainment are much improved with you in the vicinity."

"You mean your prospects for surviving whatever form of recklessness you deem entertainment are much improved with me in the vicinity."

His laughter rang out, and she could not help but smile.

"There, you see. My enjoyment of the evening has already improved a hundred-fold." His smile sent her heart racing. "Though I would argue that you cannot accuse me of recklessness without also accusing yourself. It was not I, after all, who nearly died trying to capture a bird's nest."

Adaline let out an exaggerated sigh. "You are being creative again, my lord."

"Am I?" he asked, his brows raised in mock surprise. "That hardly seems in my nature."

Adaline stared at him, her face void of all expression as she blinked at him, and Hugo's laughter rang out again.

"Oh very well, I shall attempt to rein in my embellishments."

"Hmm, is that even possible?" Adaline asked, cocking an eyebrow.

"Ah, I did say *attempt*, Miss Girard. Not succeed."

She laughed despite herself. "So you did."

His smile sent a tingling warmth through her, especially when his gaze lingered on her. To her mortification, her cheeks flushed, and she quickly looked away, hoping he didn't notice. Though, judging by the amused twinkle in his eyes, he had.

"I do hope you have been enjoying your evening," he said.

"I have," she answered, grateful he had the grace to not mention her obvious reaction to him. "Though I confess, I have been much distracted."

"Hmm" he murmured, the suddenly deeper timber of his voice sending a delicious tingle down her spine. "Well, if I have been the cause of that distraction, I cannot say I am sorry."

She swallowed past her suddenly dry throat and shook her head, though she could not help but smile. "You have a very high opinion of yourself, my lord."

He nodded. "This is true." He leaned in closer, close enough she could feel the warmth of his breath upon her cheek. "Though I must confess, I hope that your own opinion of me might be similarly as high. Someday."

Adaline breath caught in her throat, and she raised startled eyes to meet his. Eyes that gazed down at her in perfect sincerity.

"I…" she said, her voice hardly more than a whisper.

"My apologies for interrupting," Lucy said, stepping closer. Lord Hugo's eyes widened at the sight of Lucy, but his smile was genuine when he gave her a gallant bow.

"Mrs. Harrow, what a delight to see you here."

"Thank you," she said, her smile slightly strained. "I am fortunate that my cousin enjoys my company."

"Hmm, yes, Lord Hugo is also fortunate that *his* cousin enjoys his company as much as she does, or he would be left alone and bereft, I have no doubt," a feminine voice said.

They turned to find Miss Archard approaching with Lord Hugo's mother, the Duchess of Haltham. Miss Archard smiled warmly at Adaline. But the duchess was decidedly less amiable.

"Miss Girard, how lovely to see you again," Miss Archard said.

"Thank you, Miss Archard. Your Grace," she said, turning to bob another curtsy.

The duchess nodded, though her expression remained cool and distant. Lord Hugo's forehead furrowed as he looked at his mother, but before anyone could say anything else, Lucy spoke again.

"I do apologize, but your brother sent me for you, Adaline."

"Yes, Hugo, the next performance should begin shortly. I wonder if you could fetch me some champagne before it does," the duchess said.

"Of course, Mother." He bowed his head toward her, then turned back to Adaline. "Miss Girard, Mrs. Harrow, I do hope you will enjoy the rest of your evening."

He bowed to them and took his leave. Once he was gone, the duchess didn't bother staying, though she at least gave Adaline the courtesy of a nod, icy though it was, before turning her back. Had she given Adaline the cut direct, she never would have recovered what little reputation she had left.

Lucy, however, was incensed and made no secret of it. But Adaline just sighed.

"I can hardly blame her, I suppose. My family is no better when it comes to the Brelsfords." She herself had been no better mere weeks ago. "As you can see for yourself," she muttered, watching an infuriated Henry storm to her side.

"Adaline," Henry said, coming to her side. "I sent Lucy for you ages ago. Why are you dawdling about here? Speaking to those whom I have already deemed wholly inappropriate?"

He cast a glare behind her and Adaline turned to see Hugo speaking with another gentleman a few feet away.

"Keep your voice down," Adaline hissed. "Besides, you did not deem him, or at least his brother, so inappropriate a few months ago. I should think you would encouragement my attachment to someone as well situated as a Brelsford."

"Are you saying that your friendship with him might result in a match?" Henry said, his tone suddenly more calculating than offended.

Adaline snorted and looped her arm through Lucy's, pulling her away from her exasperating brother.

"Adaline," he said, hurrying after her. "I forbid it."

She raised a brow. "Just a moment ago, you seemed intrigued by the possibility."

"I was surprised. How you can so casually converse with a man who all but ruined you, I will never understand."

Adaline let out a long-suffering sigh. "You bear just as much, if not more responsibility for our recent fall from grace as he, Henry. The only difference is, Lord Hugo has had the maturity to admit his faults."

Henry's lips pinched together. "Just keep your distance from him," he said before marching away.

Adaline glanced at Lucy and rolled her eyes, laughing with her as they made their way back into the theater. They settled back into their seats to find that the rest of their box had been filled with several members of a new party. They typically shared the box with the Dresdens, friends of Adaline's parents. But the Dresdens did occasionally rent out their seats when they wouldn't be attending.

Adaline blinked in surprise to find herself beside Lady Markham. Lady Markham was a stunningly beautiful woman. And a notorious one. She had been the mistress of more than one high profile man, men who had made her very wealthy before leaving her. And then one day, she had disappeared for a few weeks, only to reappear married to the reclusive Lord Markham.

No one knew the particulars of their union, though it was rumored it had been an arranged match. Though who would arrange such a marriage, no one knew. Certainly not Lord Markham's family. He was the son of the Earl of Rothendale. Gloriously wealthy, but only a third son for all that. And horribly disfigured from a childhood accident. Though Adaline had always thought he was still handsome, if one looked closely enough. Though he gave few the opportunity.

In any case, the two had been the talk of the ton for months. And they still caused a stir when they appeared in public, which they rarely did. So to find herself sitting beside Lady Markham was unexpected indeed. Her husband was not with her, though that was not so unusual. Lord Markham preferred to stay out of the public eye.

"Good evening, Miss Girard," Lady Markham said. "I do hope you do not mind sharing your box with me this evening."

"Not at all, Lady Markham. I will be happy for your company. I hope you are enjoying your evening."

"Oh, yes, my dear. I always enjoy myself. But I would much rather talk about you. Your mother tells me it is past time for you to find a match."

Adaline's eyes widened, flicking quickly to her mother, who was doing her level best to pretend she was engrossed in the performance taking place below them on stage. Adaline smelled an ambush.

"I…would like to marry one day, yes. Should the right man come along."

"Oh, my dear. They never simply come along. Not willingly anyway," Lady Markham said with a chuckle. "Most of them need a little help. The theater is a veritable garden of prospects this evening, I must say. Take young Lord Calendish there," she said, nodding toward where a tall, gangly fellow stood conversing with a few older gentlemen. "He is newly returned from Oxford and looking for a wife. His mother assures me he is both amiable and well-mannered, and certainly wealthy.

"Sir Reginald Beckswith," she added, nodding in another direction at a rather rotund gentleman with a receding hairline, but a kind enough face. "He is perhaps too somber for a girl of your nature, but he is, nevertheless, a most eligible match. Heir to his grandfather's title and fortune, though that man might very well outlive the entire line of Beckswiths. He is already seen eight decades and is hale and hearty enough to see at least one more, I'd wager."

Adaline couldn't help but chuckle at the woman's increasingly outlandish commentary on the eligible bachelors at hand. And, she had to admit, the information *was* useful. If she didn't already have two prospects lodged firmly in her head. And…her heart.

Lady Markham leaned closer with a conspiratorial whisper. "I have it on good authority that one of our most eligible bachelors has been quite besotted of late."

"Oh?" Adaline asked with a smile. A good bit of gossip was always diverting, provided it wasn't about her, of course.

"Oh yes. Lord Hugo Brelsford has, by some accounts, been most unlike himself. They say he has been attending every event possible in the hopes of encountering a certain young lady."

Lady Markham's eyes twinkled, and Adaline's heart skipped a few beats.

"Is...is that so?" she asked, her mouth suddenly dry. *She* couldn't be the one he sought, could she? And if she was...did she want to be? Their families would never approve. And it wasn't so long ago that she would have rather chopped off his hand than accept it in marriage. But now...

Lady Markham glanced about, cataloging the parade of theatergoers with a practiced eye. "I am merely an observer at heart, you know. And I adore a good romance." She winked at Adaline. "But I do advise caution, Miss Girard. Love is rarely a simple affair. And most hearts are rife with secrets."

Well, Adaline knew the truth of that well enough. Her own heart harbored too many of them. And she couldn't help but wonder what secrets Lord Hugo's might hold. Or Mayhem's, for that matter.

She let out a small sigh. While she appreciated Lady Markham's insight and advice, their conversation had left her even more confused than before. The lady continued to regale Adaline with the latest gossip and tales of romantic intrigues. Adaline listened with amusement, though her gaze drifted again and again to the Duke of Haltham's box, where Lord Hugo sat surrounded by his friends and family.

And when finally their gazes met, and held, she offered him a tentative smile.

Only he did not return it.

He did give her a brief nod, at least not subjecting her to a public rebuff. But her heart sank at the stony expression on his usually jovial face. His gaze held hers a moment longer, with no hint of the warmth or flirtatious merriment he had exuded only a short time before, before flicking away, leaving her reeling with hurt and confusion.

What had transpired in the last hour that had changed his demeanor toward her so thoroughly? Even when he had not been seeking her out, when they had been all but enemies, he had still shown some emotion toward her, negative though it had been. But that was far preferable to the distant indifference he had just shown. As if she were a stranger he had no desire to meet.

Though she wanted to make her escape right then, she refused to give him the satisfaction of knowing he had wounded her. So she remained, stoic and determined, until the performance had ended before taking her leave. She did not look at him again. Would not give him another opportunity to hurt and humiliate her.

She should have known better from the start. He had shown her who he was from the beginning, from the moment he had goaded Henry into believing he could arrange a match to his elder brother. He might have played the charming rogue since then, but something must have changed. Or perhaps he could simply no longer hold his façade in place.

Either way, it seemed she had the answer she had sought.

CHAPTER TWENTY

HUGO HAD ENDURED no less than a quarter hour lecture from his mother the moment they returned to their box. A lecture that had not relented, even when the curtains rose and the performance resumed. And then she had turned it over to his father to continue. Finding him speaking with Adaline Girard with apparent interest had sent both of them into an apoplexy. They didn't outright accuse Adaline of being a fortune hunter, but they said everything but.

"I do not like to speak ill of anyone," his mother had said. "But what else am I to think when this woman ignored a grave insult in order to accept the proposal she thought had come from Edward only to then turn her sights to you. She acted as though she hated you for months—as she rightly should. Only now we find you in the foyer with her, mooning over you like some besotted fool. If you turn her down, will she then turn to Arthur?"

Hugo had scoffed at that, of course. But…she was not mistaken. At least according to the gossips, who had taken their tales straight from Henry Girard. In his version of the story, Adaline *had* agreed to marry Edward. Eagerly. And she *had* hated Hugo for his part in the deception. And now…it seemed she did not, perhaps, hate him so much after all. But her brother's words kept ringing through his head. *"Are you saying that your friendship with him might result in a match?"* Obviously they had not meant for him to overhear. But he couldn't help wondering…was their friendship just another attempt for the Girards to align themselves with his family?

It was enough to cause him to pause, his mind spinning.

The one thing he had never detected in his encounters with Adaline was deception. If anything, it was very much the opposite. The woman had no qualms about telling him exactly what she thought of him, at all times. So he had difficulty believing that she was involved in some sort of grand matchmaking scheme designed to make her a part of the Brelsford family. Just the thought of it was ridic—

A ripple of movement in one of the lower boxes across the theater drew Hugo's attention. Adaline. She sat, the golden glow of a thousand candles catching the coppery undertones in her brown hair as she laughed with the woman beside her. He smiled faintly. He enjoyed being her adversary. Her sharp barbs prompting his even sharper retorts. Their exchanges had always been exhilarating, even when they had been filled with acrimony. But now, there was an extra layer to them that he couldn't quite decipher, but that left him breathless more often than not.

And yet, the memory of his family's grim warnings, and Henry's words in the lobby just now, shadowed every word, every glance.

He continued to watch her, ignoring the chattering his family continued to aim at him.

Adaline sat, a smile playing about her lips as the lady beside her whispered conspiratorially in her ear, occasionally pointing or nodding at various people around the theater.

Lord Calendish. Sir Reginald. A few others scattered about. All eligible men who had been making the rounds of the marriage mart.

Hugo's breath froze in his lungs as he finally recognized with lady with whom Adaline conversed. Lady Markham, a woman notorious for her scandalous attachments to wealthy gentlemen. One who had herself made a very surprising match with an extremely affluent and titled man far above her own station. Why would Adaline be speaking so closely with one such as Lady Markham? Could she be seeking advice on procuring her own match?

The doubts he had barely suppressed surged anew. Had she sought him out tonight simply to test the waters, to see if he might yet be persuaded into proposing? Or was she as adrift as he, simply searching for someone with whom to forge a connection?

Hugo swallowed, his throat tight. As the curtain rose, Adaline's gaze swept the theater again. Searching for him? Or some other eligible bachelor for she and Lady Markham to target. For a heartbeat, Adaline's eyes found his. Their gazes held. And then she smiled. Hesitant, shy even, though that wasn't a word he would have ever applied to her before. Hopeful.

He did not smile back.

The moment stretched, fragile as spun glass. Adaline's smile faltered, and she looked away, her composure slipping for just an instant. Lady Markham whispered something, and Adaline's shoulders stiffened, her mask settling once more.

A pang of regret lanced through Hugo. He sucked in a deep breath, filled with guilt. And confusion. He continued to stare at her, willing her to look his way again. But he could not remedy his momentary lapse. Her eyes did not return to him.

The drama played out on the stage below, but Hugo's thoughts wandered, circling hopelessly back to the women who divided his heart. Millie's gentle wit and the solace she offered in every letter would be very welcome right now. Though, so would Adaline's. They both challenged him, excited him, comforted him. He was beginning to look forward to his meetings with Adaline as much as he looked forward to letters from Millie. For very similar reasons. In fact, they were very similar in many regards. Which made his inner turmoil all the more perplexing.

"Are you even listening, Hugo?" Arthur asked, his face clouded with concern rather than his usual mischief.

He leaned forward, elbows braced on his knees, the epitome of a younger brother who would rather be anywhere but here. Still, he'd always stood by Hugo, even now, when their family seemed firmly against him.

Oh, Arthur agreed with them, of that he'd made no doubt. But he did at least try to see things from Hugo's point of view. Tried to be sympathetic to his feelings and desires. And so Hugo attempted to focus on what Arthur was saying.

"I am," he replied, though his gaze drifted to the stage, where the stage hands adjusted the scenery.

"Are you?" Arthur persisted, his voice softer now, full of sympathy. It made Hugo twitch. "You've scarcely said a word since we left your Miss Girard in the foyer."

"I've hardly had the opportunity," Hugo said wryly.

Arthur chuckled. "They are persistent." He glanced at their surrounding family with a fond exasperation. "And what passed between you and your lady to dampen your spirits so?"

"The only thing to dampen my spirits is the constant berating of my family every time I deign to speak to a woman they have no cause to hate."

Arthur pursed his lips. "I wouldn't say no cause. We do have cause for concern, Hugo. Considering her brother's actions."

"Actions we instigated," Hugo reminded him. "Besides, now that I've become better acquainted with her, I wonder if the stories about her have any merit. She does not seem the type of woman who would act in the way she's being accused."

"Perhaps. But do you truly trust that she and her brother are not aligned in their desire for revenge? It is clear that he is holding a grudge against us."

Hugo snorted. "Because showing an interest in me obviously smacks of depravity."

Arthur chuckled. "Your words, brother. Not mine." He sat back, though remained close enough the others would not hear them. "So, what did you speak of then."

Hugo sighed. "Nothing of import. We spoke of trivialities, as one does."

Arthur arched a brow. "Trivialities do sound like you. But I do not believe it."

"No?"

"No. You've been mooning about ever since you got that first letter from…your lady. And it has only grown worse since you've struck up this…" He waved his hand, searching for the correct word to use. Hugo chuckled inwardly. Good luck with that.

"Friendship," Arthur finally said, "with Miss Girard. Leave it to you to fall in love with two women who could not be more unsuitable."

Hugo gaped at him. "I am not in love."

Was he?

"So says you. But your attentions to Miss Girard have not gone unnoticed. Regardless of the current state of your affections for either an imaginary woman or a physical one, you, dear brother, are going to have to make a choice. Soon. Before the whole of London does it for you."

The line of Hugo's jaw hardened. "You sound like Father."

"Perhaps because I have the same fears." Arthur's tone was gentle, but his words struck with precision. "Adaline Girard is a lady with a cloud of rumors over her head."

Shame burned Hugo's cheeks. The scandal had been partly his doing, yet Adaline had borne the brunt of society's censure.

"Rumors we had a hand in creating," Hugo reminded him.

"We made the offer. But Girard ran with it, incriminating his sister at the same time. So, you surely understand why her apparent interest in you is understandably confusing and concerning to most people."

"Perhaps after becoming more acquainted with me, she has realized I am not the devil and has forgiven me."

Arthur's smiled, though his skepticism was palpable. "Perhaps. Though I am not sure you will convince our parents of that. Especially as her brother is still in search of a match for her. Given the history between you, a friendship is…odd, at best. It is not so unreasonable that our family might have concerns."

"I know."

And he truly did not know what to do about it. He had tried to get over his fascination with Miss Girard and could not. Nor could he forget the other…

His hand moved to the interior pocket of his coat, where a bundle of folded letters pressed close to his heart. Millie. The name itself was a comfort. A mystery, to be certain. But one which he could not relinquish. He'd never seen her face, but still knew her as he did few others. Though, sometimes he wondered if she, too, was an invention he had conjured by his longing for a connection.

"Then there is Millie," Arthur continued, as if reading his thoughts. "You write to a woman whose name may not even be her own. What if she *is* Adaline, playing at some revenge game? Or someone worse? You are not a boy, Hugo. The time for illusions is past."

The world spun a little. Could it be? Adaline did remind him of Millie. And their letters were delivered through her cousin's shop.

But…no, it could not be. Surely, she would have revealed something during their encounters that would have betrayed her identity as the author of the letters if they were one and the same. No. They must be two different women.

Women who both haunted him, left him restless.

And he could not have both.

"What would you have me do?" Hugo asked quietly.

Arthur's mouth curved in a half-smile. "Decide. That is all. You owe it to yourself. And to them."

Hugo fell silent, his mind a tumult of longing and guilt. The orchestra's tuning faded, replaced by the distant laughter of ladies dripping in diamonds, the clatter of gentlemen's boots on marble. All around him, the theater blossomed with color and intrigue, but his world had narrowed to two faces, two sets of memories.

Bold and clever Adaline always seemed to be one step ahead

of him. Her laughter mocking at times. Though she might be the only person who had ever laughed at him who made it feel as though she were laughing with him instead. Even with the laughter though, there seemed to be a lingering sorrow hidden behind her eyes. Though she had, of late, allowed him to see glimpses. Could he trust her now, as she seemed to trust him? Was he ready to defy his family's wishes, to risk everything for a happiness so uncertain?

And Millie. He did not know her voice, her eyes, only the sense that she understood him in ways no one else had. Was it love, or a trick of his wanting heart?

"Whatever you choose, Hugo, make sure it is your choice. Not Father's. Not Society's. If you pursue Miss Girard, you must be prepared to defend her when the next storm comes. If you do not love her, let her go. Spare her the pain of false hope. If you prefer the safety of your anonymous Millie, be certain she exists beyond the page before you destroy everything else you hold dear."

Hugo nodded, grateful and resentful in equal measure. He envied Arthur's certainty, his ability to see the world in stark lines, while Hugo's own heart was a chaotic tangle of *what ifs*. Then again, Arthur's world had never been challenged. Let alone his heart.

"And for the love of all that's holy, man, forgive yourself for our misguided actions. She apparently has."

He slapped Hugo's shoulder. "Now, if you'll excuse me, I am off to find more jovial company." Then he grinned at Hugo, and left him alone with his thoughts.

And the echo of the smile he had refused.

CHAPTER TWENTY-ONE

You've Got Mail

Dearest Mayhem,

I regret I must begin this letter with distressing news, but you were, in fact, mistaken about my abilities to make the best choices. Yet again, I listened to my hopeless heart instead of my logical mind and am the worse for it. Why can people not just be who they are? Why must they present one face to the world and keep their true nature hidden? And why must I fall for the deception every time? I have always considered myself educated and relatively intelligent. But perhaps I am nothing more than a simpleton after all. I cannot help but feel naïve in the worst sense of the word.

…

Confused and despairingly yours,
Millie

My dearest Millie,

Do not despair. You are the farthest thing from a simpleton. Do not attribute faults to yourself that rightly belong with others. Their failings are not yours, and seeing the best in people, believing them to be as good-hearted as you yourself are, is not a flaw but something to be admired and aspired to. I pray you do not allow the poor behavior of whatever rotten sod has hurt you to change your beautiful innate nature. Whoever this person is does not deserve you or your attention. And certainly not the affections of your hope*ful* (never hopeless) heart. My only word of advice is to perhaps proceed with caution… when a man reveals himself for who he truly is, believe him. Few people, I have found, can keep their true nature hidden for long.

Regarding your choices, perhaps I cannot speak with perfect knowledge on them. Choosing me with whom to correspond does show some lack of good judgment (and I hope you know I say this in jest with a poor attempt to bring some humor to the subject and a smile to your lips). However, in all sincerity, I can say without an inkling of a doubt, responding to your first letter was perhaps the single best decision I have ever made in my life. No matter the outcome, I will never regret that choice and will always consider it to be a shining moment in my life.

As are you. Always.
Mayhem

My dear Marquess,

You are mistaken in my lack of judgement. For sending you that first letter is one of the few choices in which I am confident. You are my best choice. Your letters, your friendship, your championship and support of me, have been a godsend to me. I will always be grateful for your kindness, friendship, and advice. And your ability to make me smile even on the darkest of days.

Thank you for your kind words. As always, they have cheered me greatly. And you are correct. This person showed me who he was the first moment our paths crossed, and I stupidly allowed myself to forget that. As they say, a leopard never changes its spots. I had forgotten that in the flurry of easy smiles and wicked jests. Until those smiles were suddenly, and without cause, no longer returned. I will not be so careless in the future.

...

With resolve and determination,
Your Marchioness

Hugo put down the newest letter from Millie, a frown furrowing his brow. With each letter he'd received, a suspicion had been growing in his mind. Even more so lately as he had grown to know Adaline Girard better. The similarities in their humor, their manner of speaking, their views on the world were remarkable. Still, that was not in and of itself proof that they were one and the same. But now, with her most recent letters...

He scanned the latest one again, the conviction growing. She had been upset. And he'd received that letter only days after the evening he'd spoken with her at the theater. The evening he'd failed to return her smile.

What if...

"What has put that sour expression on your face, Brother?" Arthur asked, sauntering into the library where Hugo sat near the fireplace. He glanced down at the letter in Hugo's hand and raised his brows as he dropped into the seat opposite him. "Another missive from your mystery Millie? Bad news?"

Hugo's frown deepened. "I…am not quite sure."

Would it be bad news if they were one and the same? In some ways, it might prove quite a relief. For as much as he hated to admit it, he had grown rather fond of Miss Girard. Perhaps more than just fond, as confounding as that thought was. And it was proving more and more difficult to reconcile his feelings for her with the feelings he knew of a surety he had for his Millie. A woman who for all intents and purposes only existed on paper. Which was admittedly a problem.

But if they were the same woman…

"I think," he said to Arthur, "there is at least a possibility that Miss Girard and Millie are the same woman."

Arthur gaped at him. "I…you…are you certain?"

Hugo snorted. "Of course not. I have never been more uncertain of anything in my life. But…the more I think of it, the more it fits."

Arthur cocked a brow. "Does it fit? Or do you just want it to fit?"

Hugo frowned at him. "What do you mean?"

Arthur just chuckled. "You know exactly what I mean, dear brother. If these women were one and the same, it would solve a great deal of problems for you."

"Would it? Or would it create even more?"

Now Arthur frowned. "What do you mean?"

"I would not have to choose between them, true. But the greatest problem with Millie has always been that she may be someone of whom the family would not approve. Someone I would not be allowed to marry, even if that were my choice. Right now, that is merely a possibility. But if she were, indeed, Miss Girard, that possibility would become a certainty. Mother and Father would never allow a match between us. They have told me repeatedly that they do not trust Miss Girard and her motives and would never support a match."

Arthur just shook his head. "Leave it to you to fall in love with not only one, but two…or possibly just one…of the only women on the planet our parents would deny their blessing to. Any other woman, they would be thrilled to see you wed to. But you—what are you doing?"

Hugo had stood and was striding toward the small writing desk in the corner. "I am doing what I should have done weeks ago."

"Hugo…"

"There is only one way to put all this speculation to rest once and for all. I must know."

Not only to ease his mind and heart, but also so he could begin to strategize if necessary.

He could not choose between Millie and Adaline. He didn't even know where to begin doing such a thing. If they were one and the same, that would solve a great deal of problems. And heartache. Though it would create a great deal more as well. If they were indeed two separate women…well, he would deal with that when he discovered the truth of it. And there was only one way to find out for sure.

They had begun to talk about it. It was time to ask in earnest.

He was already writing before Arthur made his way over to glance over Hugo's shoulder.

"You are suggesting you meet? Are you mad?"

Hugo chuckled at that. "Yes. Yes I am."

Arthur just shook his head. "What will you do if they are not the same woman?"

Hugo let out a deep sigh. "I do not know."

"Very well, what will you do if they are *not*. If Millie and Miss Girard are one and the same?"

Hugo shook his head with another chuckle, the sheer absurdity of the situation beginning to make his head spin. "I do not know."

But there was only one way to find out.

CHAPTER TWENTY-TWO
You've Got Mail

"**G**OOD MORNING, MISS," Thompson said, throwing open the curtains to allow sunlight into Adaline's chamber. Adaline mumbled a good morning but flipped over to bury her face in her pillows. The night had been late, and she had not slept well. Her mind had not stopped churning since the theater two nights past.

"This was delivered this morning for you, from Mrs. Harrow. Along with a note that she will call upon you this afternoon."

Adaline sat bolt upright in bed, all hint of sleepiness burned away in a rush of excitement. There was only one reason Lucy would send her a package.

She eagerly took the parcel from Thompson and dismissed her with thanks and then tore it open. Inside were several bits and bobs, mostly bits of ribbon and tassel for her to add to her drizzling box. But hidden amongst them all was a letter, a single peacock feather on the wax seal.

"Mayhem," she said.

She cracked the seal, anticipation curling in her chest, that quickly turned to utter shock.

My dearest Millie,

Forgive me for the forwardness of what you are about to read, but I find I do not have the restraint in this moment to proceed with more caution. I feel we have grown quite close over the last several months. It is a state of affairs I never could have anticipated, but one for which I only grow increasingly grateful. I cannot but believe that our connection would be even stronger if we were to finally meet.

I know we promised we would never do so. That we would keep all correspondence completely anonymous and be content with that.

However, I find I can no longer be satisfied with the limitations we have set. You are in my thoughts from the moment of waking to far into the night. And often upon closing my eyes as well.

I long to see you, face to face.

I swear to you, I have no expectations aside from discovering whether or not the connection we have upon paper will translate into real life. If upon meeting, you determine you cannot stomach my presence, I swear to you I will disappear into the ether, and you shall never hear from me again. My behavior will be guided by you in all things.

But I feel we have both come to a crossroads of late, one which neither of us can navigate until certain questions have been answered. Questions that I believe cannot be answered while we both remain in anonymity.

If you choose to decline my invitation, please know I will harbor no ill will. You are more than justified in proceeding with the utmost caution. And to be frank, if I were in your place, I would likely burn this letter rather than acquiesce to such a presumptuous request. So if that be your choice, I will abide by it and trouble you no more. We can resume our letters as though nothing has passed. Or you can be quit of me entirely. I will be guided by your wishes.

As for my wishes…

Let us meet. And perhaps then, the uncertainty which has plagued us will be resolved.

Yours always,
Mayhem

Adaline traced the elegant script with a trembling finger. Her near overwhelming excitement was matched by a sudden wave of anxiety. She pressed her lips together, wrestling with the enormity of what Mayhem asked. To meet was to shatter the illusion of safety their correspondence provided. And the outcome was not remotely assured. Yet the longing in Mayhem's words resonated with an ache she could not ignore.

She drew her shawl closer. Mayhem had been her secret for so long. Her confidant. Her escape from the judgements of society and the weight of her family's expectations. In his letters, she found humor, acceptance, and a reflection of her own soul that she had never dared show anyone.

Yet as she gazed out over the gardens, her thoughts wandered to Hugo—the man she least expected to occupy her mind, let alone her heart. He had thrust his way into her life as an enemy. His biting remarks and rampant conceit had been a source of constant irritation. And unexpected amusement.

Adaline had hated him then. And he, her. Or so she told herself. She had been angry, certainly. And with good cause. But in recent weeks, she had seen another side of him. One she wasn't sure he revealed to everyone. His own anger had faded, revealing flashes of genuine remorse. He had defended her from scandalous gossip, stood by her when others retreated. The memory of his hand, warm upon hers as she had wiped dirt from his face, sent a shiver through her.

But so did the words from Mayhem's letters. Words that had embedded themselves into her heart.

They both presented a mystery she ached to solve. With Mayhem, there was the safety of distance and anonymity. The comfort of familiarity along with the thrill of the unknown. And a touch of danger. He could be anyone. Someone entirely unsuitable. Or someone entirely perfect.

Hugo, on the other hand, felt far more dangerous, even though he was known to her. His flashing eyes and quick grin captivated her, despite her best efforts. His mere presence caused her heart to beat faster. Small touches of his hand only made her want more. And unlike with Mayhem, she didn't have to wonder if their physical attraction would match the intellectual.

Yet... Their families would certainly never approve. Even if she and Hugo had forgiven one another, the Brelsfords and Girards, as a whole, had not.

And...had they forgiven one another? She had thought so. Until he had looked right through her at the theater and refused to return her smile.

Then again, perhaps he had not seen her at all. She had been sitting a distance away, and she often found herself staring into space not actually seeing what—or who—was right in front of her. Though he had nodded. But perhaps he had been nodding at someone else. Or nodding in response to something someone had said. Or nodding just to nod. Or...

Good Heavens. She would never know unless she asked him. A prospect she did not enjoy pondering.

She let out a sigh. Assuming she had been mistaken about his near cut of her, and they were, in fact, still friends...Well then, her heart was divided over the possibilities a future with either man presented. A wild, exhilarating feeling, to be sure. But one tinged with dread. What if meeting Mayhem destroyed the magic? What if loving Hugo meant inviting further turmoil?

A small, furtive part of her wished they could be one and the same. Then she would not have to choose. But while they did remind her of each other, that simply couldn't be possible.

Could it?

A knock at the door startled her. Adaline hastily slid Mayhem's letter beneath her pillow as her cousin Lucy entered.

Adaline glanced at her in surprise. "It is not afternoon already, is it?" she asked, throwing a quick look out the window.

Lucy smiled. "No. But the shop was quiet enough this morning that I was able to step out for a bit. I thought perhaps I should check on you. That letter you are hiding under your pillow—" Adaline jerked in surprise, and Lucy just smiled before continuing, "had been shoved beneath my shop door in the dead of night. Which is unusual enough I thought something momentous may have occurred."

Adaline pulled the letter from its hiding place and held it to her chest. Lucy looked her over, her smile growing. Though there was a hint of concern in her eyes. "Judging by your expression, I am correct."

"He wants to meet," Adaline said, hardly believing the words though she'd read them over and over just a few minutes ago.

Lucy dropped beside her on the bed with an expulsion of air. "Well. That is momentous indeed."

She seemed at a loss for what to say for a few seconds before finally letting out a laugh. "What will you do?"

"I…" Adaline stopped, realizing she had been about to say that she would meet him. And perhaps there was her answer right there. The answer that had risen to her lips without conscious thought. Perhaps she had been thinking too much about the entire situation and needed to trust her instincts for a while.

She squared her shoulders and took a deep breath. "I will meet with him."

Lucy's eyes widened. Then she nodded slowly. "Are you certain? Be sure of it," she cautioned, before Adaline could answer. "Once you meet, there is no going back. If it does not go well, you've not only lost a cherished friend, correspondent though he may be, but depending on who he is…"

Adaline nodded. "I know."

"Let me speak frankly, and then I'll say no more about it," Lucy said.

Adaline nodded, already knowing what her cousin would say but recognizing she would feel better for having said it.

"This business of secret letters is dangerous. If anyone were to discover it, your reputation could be ruined. I am fairly certain your mother suspects already. And if this man is…I don't know, a rake, or a brigand, or a criminal, it will not just be your reputation in danger."

"Lucy, I know you worry, and I love you for it. But do you truly think that a man could correspond with a woman for so long, and not betray such nefarious leanings? Surely I would at least have some suspicions if he were a malcontent. And I have had none."

"I am glad of it, cousin. I merely wish to caution you. Men, at least certain men, are often terrifyingly talented when it comes to deceit."

"I know I needn't remind you of how you became acquainted with Lord Hugo Brelsford in the first place."

Adaline pursed her lips, then replied quietly. "No. But he's different now. It was a joke to him. That is not to say the entire affair doesn't still irk me. But, he was not the only one to blame. Or even the most at blame. Henry bears a great deal of that. And… I have decided to forgive him."

"Henry?"

Adaline gave her a wry smile. "Lord Hugo. I am still working on Henry."

Lucy raised her brows. "That is generous of you."

"I am feeling generous of late," Adaline said with a softer smile.

"Hmm, and does that have to do with a certain impetuous

young lord? Or a mysterious scribe?"

"Yes?" Adaline laughed. "I truly do not know. Perhaps both. Or neither."

"Just take care, cousin. I would not see you hurt. If Mayhem is not of our class, or worse, if he is unworthy, it will reflect on the whole family. And Lord Hugo… I greatly fear that it is his family, not ours, who may not approve. Their treatment of you has been icy at best. And frankly, your own family is little better toward Lord Hugo. Only with greater cause," she said with a sympathetic smile.

Adaline felt the sting of Lucy's words but knew she spoke nothing but the truth. And yet, she couldn't help the flicker of rebellion that ignited in her. She had, for the most part, been dutiful. Vocal in her discontent, perhaps. But dutiful.

Now her heart yearned for more.

Her thoughts churned. Duty warred with desire. Cautiousness with yearning.

She finally took a deep breath and let it out slowly. "I think it comes to this… when all is said and done, I will always wonder if I do not meet him. I do have a strange, unexplainable, and growing affection for Hugo Brelsford," she said with an exasperated half-smile. "But I will spend the rest of my life wondering what might have happened if I had met with Mayhem. I will see him in every face that I meet, wondering if it might be him. If it ends badly, I will weather whatever storm occurs. At least I will know. It is the not knowing, I think, that would hurt me far more."

Lucy regarded her for a moment and then nodded. "That, at least, I can understand. Well then, only one thing to do then. I have a few more minutes to spare if there is something you'd like to send with me."

She nodded at Adaline's writing desk with a smile, and Adaline hurried over to grab fresh paper and her quill.

To the Marquess of Mayhem,

I received your kind invitation, and I must confess I am flabbergasted. And intrigued. Confused. Excited. And a host of other emotions I have not quite identified yet. Above all, I am filled with curiosity and know I will be filled with regret if I do not accept your offer.

I will acquiesce to your request, my lord. Reveal the time and place you would like to meet, and I shall appear.

Yours,
Millie

She sealed the letter before her nerves failed and gave it to Lucy.

The reply came sooner than expected. Lucy arrived on her doorstep the very next afternoon and could scarce wait until they were alone before she pulled the letter from her reticule. Adaline tore open the envelope, her hands shaking.

My Dear Marchioness of Millinery Mischief,

I have seen fit to add to your title as, while I had hope, I had little expectation that you would truly deign to meet with me. Your agreement brings me both great joy, no small amount of trepidation, and a decided pride that I may have encouraged your rather shocking and ill-advised behavior. That you have seen fit to join me in an endeavor of extreme mischief will delight me for the rest of my days, no matter the outcome. Though I have no doubt the outcome will be wonderous, indeed.

As for where this illustrious event should take place, I pondered a great deal. And the perfect solution finally presented itself—the Duke and Duchess of Beaubrooke's annual masquerade ball this Friday. Maintaining the mystery of our identities during the festivities seems fitting. And, frankly, amusing.

Meet me near the portrait of the duchess in the conservatory. At midnight. As my seal is a peacock feather, wear a costume to match. Or, if the time is too short to procure such attire, incorporate a peacock plume as well as you can with the gown you have chosen. I shall do the same.

Until midnight Friday.

Yours always,
The Marquess of Mischief and Mayhem

Adaline pressed the letter to her heart, the thrill of anticipation mingling with dread. But Lucy was already thinking about the details.

"Hmm, a masquerade is actually a rather fine idea. If you don't like the look of him, you can always hide away and claim you did not attend."

"Yes, but he could do the same with me."

"Oh, never," Lucy scoffed. "Any man would be lucky to have you, a fact of which I am sure he is already aware. Though…Friday does not give us much time to incorporate peacock feathers into your costume." She frowned, chewing her lip. "It is lucky indeed that your gown is a deep blue. That will make it marginally easier."

She began muttering under her breath, something about ribbon and material. Adaline didn't bother asking her to enunciate. Lucy was lost in her own world, no doubt designing something spectacular for Adaline to wear.

Adaline frowned. "Oh. But… Where will I ever find peacock

feathers in only a few days' time?"

Lucy blinked, drawn from her internal thoughts. "I have a few left from the headdress I created for the Countess of Alanthew. And I may be able to get a few more. The Duchess of Whittsley has several of the creatures and will usually sell me a few." Lucy's eyes cleared, and she patted Adaline's hand. "Do not fear. I'm sure I can come up with something. A fan perhaps. Or a mask."

"I am in your debt," Adaline said, sincerely grateful not only for her cousin's loyalty, but also her talent. Left to her own devices, Adaline would have simply shoved a feather in her bun and called it good.

"Never. Though your brother will be," Lucy said with a smile. "I shall send him the bill."

Adaline laughed. Her brother would be happy to pay it. Well…perhaps happy was too strong of a word, especially if he knew the reason she needed such a thing. But under normal circumstances, he was happy to support whatever frippery she and her mother required. Particularly if it could advance her chances of making a match.

"Leave it to me," Lucy said, gathering her things to hurry out. "You shall be resplendent."

When she was alone once more, Adaline reread Mayhem's letter. Twice more. Then she clasped it to her chest with a sigh.

She would finally meet her Mayhem. Though…Hugo would likely be in attendance at the ball as well. The man went to every possible function he could, and simply everyone went to the Beaubrooke's masquerade. She and Hugo had taken to spending quite a lot of time together. But that didn't mean he expected or even wanted to be with her for the midnight unmasking. Especially after the way he treated her at the theater.

But what if he did? Could she rebuff him? The thought made her heart ache. Yet, she could do nothing but, if it came down to that. If she did not, she would miss her chance at finally discovering Mayhem's identity.

She belatedly realized Friday night may just prove the point at which she would have to choose between the two men. Yet still had no idea what choice she should—or wanted—to make.

And she was quickly running out of time to figure it out.

CHAPTER TWENTY-THREE

HUGO GLANCED OUTSIDE the diamond paned windows of his chamber, trying to calm the anxiety that gnawed at him. Outside, London's gaslit streets were already alive with lanterns and carriages filled with Society's revelers headed to the night's festivities, most heading toward the Beaubrooke's masquerade ball, no doubt.

Hugo lingered before his looking glass, savoring the last few moments of peace he had, even as his heart raced at how the night might end.

He knotted his cravat for what must have been the fourth time. Each attempt ended worse than the last as his mind continuously strayed toward a distant conservatory and who might await him in a few hours' time.

He had rehearsed this night in his imagination countless times since he'd received that first letter from Millie. Her wit and sincerity had shown through, even from the first. In her, he'd found a partner in discourse, a confidante, perhaps even a soulmate. Before Millie, he would have never believed a man could fall in love with a woman whom he'd never even seen. But perhaps it was the best way, after all.

With nothing between them but the pen and the page, they were able to be their true selves. And he had precious little opportunities for that it seemed. Everyone expected something from him. His parents expected obedience, maturity, dependability. They expected him to make a good match and provide them with grandchildren to spoil. Not bad or even unusual expectations. But expectations, nonetheless.

His friends expected him to always be the carefree gadabout. The jester. The mischievous scoundrel who avoided matrimony and responsibility at all costs. Society expected about the same and even forgave him for his foibles as long as at some point he buckled to their whims and did his duty.

But that was before Adaline. If Millie had been a pleasant surprise, Adaline had been a shocking monsoon that had come from nowhere and rearranged his entire view of the world. The man he was before she had entered his life was a far cry from who he was now. The hurt he had dealt her had changed him. Made him want to better himself. Prove that he was more than a wastrel. Ensure that he never wounded another person with his carelessness again.

They'd had their expectations of each other. In the beginning at least. She'd thought him nothing more than a puerile rogue. And he'd thought her a melodramatic harpy. But with each encounter, things had changed.

He never would have expected her forgiveness. He still wasn't entirely sure he had it. Yet their mutual bitterness had given way to camaraderie. Their rivalry had expanded to include laughter and the thrill of shared glances. Adaline challenged his every word with a sharp tongue and sharper mind. Her presence left him breathless and irritable by turns. And left him craving more, no matter which.

Though, as his affection grew, so did the obstacles. He never would have suspected his family would be so set against her. They wanted him to settle down. He'd have thought they'd be thrilled he was finally considering doing so, no matter who his choice. But it seemed it was not so.

And his prospects with Millie were likely even more dire. Unless she proved to be someone of such elevated station even his parents couldn't argue with their unusual beginnings. But if, as he suspected, Adaline and Millie were the same woman...well...it would of a surety make matters worse with his family. They would never believe she didn't know with whom she corresponded. If he were honest, the thought had crossed his mind more than once as well. After all, the first letter had come from her. If her motives were as nefarious as his family feared, their correspondence could have been a clever way to ingratiate herself with him.

But he couldn't, wouldn't believe that. He knew her too well now.

He hoped. Tonight he would find out for sure. A prospect that kept a continuous thread of dread-laced anticipation flowing through him.

He yanked on his cravat again and finally threw up his hands in exasperation and called for his valet.

Davies quickly entered Hugo's dressing room and fixed the mess that he'd made of his cravat. Once all was put to right's, Davies asked, "Shall I fetch the cape, sir?"

On the dressing table lay his mask, a domino of black leather embellished with a single peacock feather in the upper left corner. The mask covered most of his face, leaving only his mouth and chin free, its edges sweeping up to the line of his hair. Along with the emerald brocade cape that Davies helped fasten over one shoulder and under the other, the ensemble rather lent him the air of a highwayman or swashbuckling pirate. He smiled wryly at his own reflection, imagining Millie's, and Adaline's, reaction. Unsurprisingly, he thought they would react much the same.

Would Millie recognize him at all? He had no doubt Adaline would.

Hugo hesitated, his hand hovering over the mask. Each letter exchanged with Millie had been a revelation. Of her and of him. But always clever, intimate, sometimes teasing, always honest. And tonight, everything depended on whether Millie and Adaline were one and the same.

He pressed the mask to his face, securing it with the silk ribbons. A thrill of anticipation coursed through him, mingling with the customary nerves that attended such occasions. Would she see past the mask and know him? Would he, in turn, find the truth behind her own disguise? Would she even come?

Hugo stopped short, belatedly realizing she might decide not to attend at all. He gave his head a little shake. That was one possibility on which he could not dwell. He blew out a deep breath and continued on.

Downstairs, laughter and voices floated from the drawing room. The Brelsford family was in full pre-ball regalia. His father, distinguished as always in an embroidered tailcoat. His mother draped in crimson silk and a delicate filigree mask set with ruby crystals. Arthur lounged against the banister in a harlequin-patterned ensemble, his mask cocked rakishly to one side. Hugo's three sisters, all married, moved about with an energy he envied, their costumes a riot of color—gold for Mary, deep green for Elizabeth, and a soft lilac for Louise.

"Ah, Hugo, there you are!" cried Louise, her eyes dancing behind her gilded mask. "Come, let us see if our eligible brother is suitably attired for a night of mischief and matchmaking."

Mary laughed, fanning herself. "He looks quite dashing. Perhaps tonight he'll finally choose a bride and save us from Mother's constant reminders."

"Oh, hush girls. You look most distinguished," their mother said to Hugo, coming over to straighten his lapels with a pat. There was pride in her voice, but it could not quite mask a note of concern.

His father looked him over, then gave him a satisfied nod. "You are punctual tonight, Hugo. I trust you are prepared for a long evening of introductions and pleasantries."

Hugo forced a smile. "I am, Father."

His mother's lips pursed, her gaze drifting to the small clock on the mantelpiece. "You will remember, of course, the importance of making *new* acquaintances. The ball is an opportunity, after all. There are young ladies of excellent breeding and demeanor in attendance tonight."

He knew what she meant. Knew, too, the name she left unspoken.

Hugo stiffened. "Miss Girard is not—" But the words faltered on his tongue. What could he say? That her laughter was genuine, that he'd seen kindness in her eyes and heard vulnerability in her voice? That the ambition they thought they saw in her was merely a desire to be accepted? Wanted? That she had become precious to him, despite all the reasons she should not?

His mother touched his arm, her expression softening. "We only wish for your happiness, Hugo. A fortune-hunter has little interest in anyone's happiness but their own."

"Nor," his father added, "do we wish to see you wounded. By disappointment, or worse, by scandal."

Hugo looked away, jaw tight. "You do not know her as I do."

"Perhaps not." His father's voice was quiet. "Though consider that perhaps, with the absence of the affection you obviously carry for her, we may see the situation a bit more clearly."

Hugo longed to defend Adaline, but there was little he could say to change their minds. Their prejudice stemmed from her acceptance of his brother and her seeming transference of that interest to him. Even he could admit that it did appear suspicious.

Instead, he offered a nod. "I know, Father. And I do appreciate your concern. Even if I feel it is misplaced."

No more was said as the family piled into their carriages, his sisters in one with their husbands, Hugo and Arthur with their parents. London's night air was crisp outside the carriage windows. Gas lamps flickered in the dark, casting a hazy glow over the cobblestones, shadows shifting as the wheels turned.

Hugo gazed out the window, his thoughts straying to the woman whose words had enchanted him—whose laughter, wit, and kindness he longed to witness in person. Arthur nudged him, voice low. "Nervous?"

"Not at all," Hugo lied. "Just eager."

Arthur snorted. "Just remember, if you find her and she is not the woman you hope, you must be gracious. There's always another mystery waiting at a masquerade."

Hugo's lips pursed, unsure what exactly he hoped. He wanted Millie to be Adaline, needed her to be. He had rehearsed what he might say, how he might reveal himself. Or… not. Would she know him? Would he know her? Or would they remain strangers beneath their masks?

But if Adaline was indeed Millie…that presented another host of obstacles. Namely their families. And her latent hatred for him. Although that *had* seemed to wane of late. And at least it wasn't indifference. He could work with hate. Fine line between love, and all.

"Well, I for one am looking forward to this evening," Arthur said. "Masquerades are always great fun. And tonight promises more entertainment than most, doesn't it, Hugo?"

Hugo squinted at his brother in a one-eyed glare. "They are certainly always… unpredictable." This evening far more than most for certain.

His father's eyes narrowed shrewdly. "It is a chance for new beginnings. You are of an age to consider your future. One's choices might not always feel so monumental, but one misguided choice could lead to ruin."

Hugo bristled, then relented. "I am aware, Father."

His mother pressed on, more softly. "We do not doubt Miss Girard's charm, dear boy. And as a woman myself, I am fully aware that the lady in question may not have had much say in the match chosen for her by her family. It is her actions after the fact that give us cause for concern. If she indeed was as eager as the gossips made it seem, only to then transfer that eagerness to an attachment to you."

"And if that is not what occurred?" he asked.

"Is it not simpler to choose a woman of whom you will not need to ask such questions?"

His lips pursed, hating that she had a point.

"Be sensible, Hugo," his father said. "There are women with far less ambitious and volatile families who would suit you better."

He did not answer. He could not. In his mind, questions whirled. He already knew who would suit him to perfection. The problem is, there were two of them. Maybe. Could Adaline and Millie be one and the same? The idea filled him with dread and hope in equal measure.

If they were, he would have to take the secret of their correspondence these past months to the grave. His parents would never believe it was not all some scheme to catch a Brelsford boy. He wasn't entirely sure it wasn't exactly that himself. Though he was equally unsure if he cared. He was caught, well and truly. And happy to be so.

And if they were not, if they were two different women… He let out a sigh. There was no guarantee Millie would be any more acceptable to his parents. And if she was…what of Adaline?

He could do not but pray his instincts were correct and that they were, indeed, the same woman. The alternative would leave him with a choice he did not think he could make. He pressed his mask tighter against his face, glad it hid his confusion along with his features.

The carriage drew up before the Beaubrooke mansion, its columns awash in torchlight. Light spilled from tall windows while strains of music drifted out into the night. Servants in livery helped guests from their carriages and ushered them beneath a stone arch draped in garlands of greenery and white roses. Hugo descended last. He wouldn't have admitted it to Arthur, but yes, his nerves were fit for cracking.

What had he been thinking? He should have chosen a nice, quiet spot in a park. Under a willow tree or some other nice, secluded place. Away from the prying eyes of half of London. Where he would know her the moment she arrived because there would be no costumes or masks involved.

Well. No help for it now. He took a deep breath and followed his family.

Inside, the ballroom glittered. Men in domino masks and women in silks of every hue glided across the floor. The musicians played in the gallery above, the notes floating above the hum of conversation and laughter. Hugo's parents gave him one last knowing glance before melting into the throng.

He scanned the crowd, searching for Adaline. Or Millie. His gaze darted from mask to mask, from a lady in a ruby gown to another in silver feathers. Each could be Millie. Each could be Adaline. His heart thudded with every possibility.

A movement by the staircase caught his eye. A flash of peacock blue. His breath caught. The woman wore a mask feathered in emerald and sapphire, her gown trailing behind like the brilliant plumage of a peacock. He took a deep breath, then one step toward her, when another flash of color caught his eye. Another woman, this one in emerald green with a matching silk turban sporting an arrangement of jewels and peacock feathers on her head.

He frowned as he noticed just how many peacock feathers were in attendance this evening. One woman waved a fan with a stunning array of peacock feathers at her overheated cheeks. Another had a mask made entirely of the things, the feathers parting cleverly to feature the woman's eyes where the "eye" of the feather would normally be. Yet another wore them as a sort of cape, trailing from jeweled brooches at her shoulders.

And the gentlemen were just as decked out. Sporting everything from a single feather on a mask as he did, to a feather in a lapel, to an elaborate headdress full of them.

Hugo could not help it. He burst out laughing, drawing several startled glances. Arthur came to a stop beside him, glancing at him in question.

Hugo shook his head and then nodded to a few of the plumaged guests. "And here I thought I was so clever, choosing a relatively exotic bird to emulate. From the looks of things, every peacock in the country has been plucked bare. She could be anyone."

Arthur chuckled and tilted his head toward two gentlemen, both sporting feathers, conversing by a marble column. "No doubt the lady is thinking the same."

Arthur clapped Hugo on the shoulder. "Come, Brother. Let us dance. The hunt can wait. It's futile in any case with so many peacocks strutting about."

Hugo snorted and allowed himself to be drawn into the current of the ball. He danced first with Lady Catherine. She wore a gilded mask of swirled gold, nary a feather in sight. Her conversation, thankfully, was light and required little of his attention to follow. Hugo smiled and played his part. But his mind remained elsewhere. Arthur steered him toward partner after partner. Miss Marshburn. Miss Grey. Lady Anne. They were all witty, pleasant, and beautiful in their bejeweled masks. And none of them were who he searched for.

With each turn, Hugo's eyes flickered to the door, the stairs, the corners of the room...anywhere a peacock costume might appear. Well, the right peacock costume. For there were peacocks aplenty.

Arthur, sensing Hugo's distraction, murmured, "Patience, Brother."

"Easier said than done." Hugo laughed and shook his head. "She must be here. Somewhere."

"Well, if you simply cannot wait until midnight, you could always work your way through the possibilities instead of avoiding them entirely." He nodded toward a young woman in a deep green dress and resplendent peacock mask.

Hugo opened his mouth to object but snapped it shut again. He had been so focused on midnight and the agreed upon meeting in the conservatory, it simply hadn't occurred to him to try and find her beforehand. Actively, that is. Instead, he'd been skulking about and dancing with everyone *but* a peacock.

"Arthur..." He clapped his brother on the shoulder. "Why didn't you suggest that sooner?"

Arthur just laughed. "It didn't occur to me I'd need to. You truly are besotted, aren't you? It's beginning to interfere with your faculties."

Besotted? Very likely. But with whom? Both? "On second thought, perhaps I should just go home and drown myself in a bottle of brandy."

Arthur chuckled again, turned to murmur a few words to the peacock lady nearest them, and then drew her toward Hugo with a bow. "You could. But why would you want to leave such resplendent beauty?"

Hugo smiled at the woman and bowed. He knew instantly she was not Adaline. But that did not mean she was not Millie. Though he knew within moments of their dance beginning that she was not. Nor was the next lady. Nor the next.

Perhaps Millie had changed her mind after all. A possibility he refused to consider. Though the longer the night drew on without finding her, the more that thought took hold.

Where was the blasted woman? He was beginning to despair of ever finding her.

Chapter Twenty-Four

ADALINE STEPPED FROM her carriage with her heart pounding in her chest. The Beaubrooke mansion was bedecked in flowers and lantern-light, every surface glittering and inviting. The scent of honeysuckle and beeswax hung heavy in the air. And inside…

Adaline stopped short, causing her brother, who was escorting her, to look back, his brow drawn in confusion.

She shook her head and forced a smile, taking his arm again. Then she looked around, bemused, as he led her farther into the ballroom. Where no fewer than a dozen men and women were milling about sporting peacock feathers. Well, that explained the difficulty Lucy had had in procuring feathers for Adaline's costume.

She bit her lip to keep from laughing out loud. Though she must have made some sound because Henry glanced down at her, eyebrow raised in question.

"I am just surprised at how many peacocks are attending this evening," she said. "I had meant to be one myself, but due to a severe shortage of peacocks feathers, Lucy and I needed to change our plans a bit."

"Ah," Henry said. "Well, you are still the loveliest one here. The peahen is quite a handsome bird." He lifted her hand and kissed the back, and a rush of warm affection for her brother hit her. Oh, he aggravated her to no end, and his overprotective tendencies would drive her mad. But he could be sweet when the occasion demanded.

"Go on with you," she said to him. "You don't need to waste your evening at my side. Mother is perfectly capable of chaperoning."

"Mother has already disappeared into the crowd and likely won't be seen again for the rest of the evening," Henry said, his eyes narrowing.

Adaline rolled hers. "Go on, Henry. It's a masquerade! We're meant to have a little scandalous fun."

He snorted and bowed his head in her direction. "Very well. But I shall be close if you need me. Perhaps you can befriend another peacock or two," he said with a chuckle.

She smiled in return, intending to do just that. She would find her Mayhem if she had to dance with every peacock in the room.

Speaking of another befeathered fowl…

"Miss Girard, how lovely to see you," Miss Archard said, coming to stand beside her, soft white feathers capping her head and trailing down her neck. Small brilliants were sprinkled throughout the headpiece, looking almost like sparkling drops of water on a swan's neck. Her mask glittered with black jewels that highlighted her smiling blue eyes.

Adaline gave her a polite smile, wishing the masks they wore concealed their identities as much as everyone pretended they did. But she had no trouble recognizing the Brelsfords' cousin.

"Miss Archard. You make a lovely swan," Adaline said, her smile much more genuine. The young woman's costume was truly beautiful. Even the delicate swirls and patterns on her white gown had been embroidered to resemble feathers.

"Thank you, Miss Girard. And may I return the compliment? You are quite the most resplendent peacock in attendance. And the most clever."

Adaline laughed and brushed a hand down her gown. Lucy had only one solitary peacock feather remaining in her stock and had been unable to procure more. She was, however, able to obtain the emerald green feathers that the female of the species often sported on their necks, along with enough soft brown peahen feathers to create a short cape of sorts that complemented the cream silk gown she wore. The result was quite effective.

A spray of green tipped brown feathers rested at the crown of her head that resembled the plumes on a peahen's head. The green feathers from the peahen's neck, Lucy had used to create Adaline's mask. That, along with a three-stranded emerald choker helped create the illusion of the green feathers of the peahen's long neck.

The brown feathered cape hugged her shoulders, trailing down longer in the back, while the cream of her gown was reminiscent of the cream feathers of a peahen's chest. Overall, Adaline thought the look both lovely and accurate.

And just in case Mayhem wasn't quite as clever as he had seemed in his letters, they had added what was apparently the last peacock feather in London at the apex of the plumes on her headdress. A bit more colorful than a peahen might sport, but she was willing to sacrifice a bit of the accuracy of her costume to err on the side of caution.

"I'm not sure I should take credit for the uniqueness of my costume," Adaline said. "I fear it was less cleverness and more an unexpected lack of peacock feathers that necessitated the change from peacock to peahen. If it were not for that, I would have been merely another blue and green peafowl in this increasingly large muster." She nodded toward yet another peacock making her way into the ballroom.

Miss Archard flashed a brilliant smile. "I confess, I was almost one of the flock myself. But my cousin Hugo stepped in and insisted that I choose another costume."

"Did he?" Adaline asked with surprise. "I wouldn't have taken him for such a fashion maven."

Miss Archard giggled. "I think it was less concern for me and more a desire to not be outshined. He is wearing peacock feathers as well and likely didn't want the competition."

Adaline's gaze flashed to Miss Archard's. Now *that* was too big a coincidence, surely. Her heart thundered as her eyes darted about the room again, seeking him. Mayhem, she would not know on sight. But Lord Hugo Brelsford...*him* she'd know no matter how many feathers he covered himself in.

That Hugo should be sporting the very same feathers Mayhem had chosen for them to wear would, on any other night, be enough proof for her to declare that they were indeed one and the same. Her pulse thundered in her veins at the thought, though whether in exhilaration or panic she could not be sure.

But tonight...

She paused as a striking pair of peacocked feathered dancers swished past her. Tonight, there were simply too many peacocks to be certain. Or so the logical part of her brain said. But her traitorous heart hadn't stopped skipping about since the moment she'd walked into the room knowing Mayhem...and possibly Hugo...waited for her within. And it had only worsened in the last few moments.

Was Hugo Mayhem? And what would she do if he was?

Miss Archard laughed quietly beside her. "Speak of the devil..."

Adaline's head jerked toward the man who had just come to a stop beside them.

Hugo.

Devastatingly handsome in his coat and tails, a rakish cloak in brilliant emerald green slung about one shoulder. And peacock feathers adorning the mask that covered half his face.

His eyes raked over her as a slow smile spread across his lips. The heat from that glance made Adaline's breath catch in her throat.

His gaze shifted to Miss Archard. "Amelia. I am glad to see you took my advice after all. You not only make a very lovely swan, you have saved yourself from joining the ever-growing flock." He ran a hand over the feather at the corner of his mask. "I have danced with no fewer than six peacocks this evening."

Then he turned to Adaline, his eyes going molten again as he took her in. "I have not yet, however, danced with any peahens." He gave her a gallant bow and held out his hand. "If you would do me the honor?"

Adaline bit her lip, trying, and failing, to keep her stomach from flip-flopping as she hesitantly slipped her hand into Hugo's. Was it because this man might indeed be her very own Mayhem? Or was it simply because it was Hugo himself that was causing her blood to race? She truly did not know.

But as terrified—or exhilarated, she really wasn't sure—as she was, it was far past time to find out.

HUGO HELD HIS breath until Adaline took his hand. He could almost see the same confusion warring in her eyes that raged in his own mind. But the excitement was there as well. The heightened color in her cheeks. The hitch in her breath. It was as though they both stood on a precipice and were just waiting for the other person to jump off first.

He took her hand and led her to the dance floor. They could jump together.

The first notes of the country dance rang out, and they came together and twirled apart, performing the steps of the dance in silence for the first few moments despite the dance giving them ample opportunity to speak.

The feathers of her cape tickled his fingers during one of their turns, and he let a small smile peep through. A peahen. Clever woman. Exactly the sort of thing Millie would do.

His heart hammered in his chest. It *had* to be her. He was nearly sure of it.

But...

There was that small chance that it was, indeed, simply a

coincidence. And if it was, betraying Millie to a woman who once professed to hate the very air he breathed would not be a wise choice. Though, he didn't think she would actually do anything to harm him. Now, at least. A few months ago, of a surety. She would have burned his house down with him in it and danced on his grave. But things had changed between them now.

Still, he needed to proceed with caution. Just in case. Though the way she eyed him with equal confusion and speculation made him all the more sure she *was* Millie.

"I am surprised you wish to dance with me, Lord Hugo. The last we met, I believe you made your displeasure with me quite clear. Unless I am mistaken…"

He winced, knowing she referred to when she had smiled at him…and he had failed to return the gesture.

"I must apologize for my ill manners that evening, Miss Girard. I'm afraid I allowed too many voices to clutter my own mind. I am sorry for any hurt my actions may have caused you."

She regarded him speculatively, as if she were trying to decide if he were being truthful. He had, at least, nodded at her that evening, avoiding giving her the cut direct. But only just. He deserved her ire.

She blew out a breath. "I cannot pretend I was not affronted. However, I suppose I have been guilty of listening to the wrong voices myself on occasion. Presuming it does happen again," she said, raising her brows, "I accept your apology, my lord."

He gave her his most charming smile. "I am very glad to hear it. Are you enjoying your evening thus far, Miss Girard?" he asked.

"Very much, Lord Hugo," she said, seeming much more relaxed in his presence now that they had cleared the air over their previous confrontation. "You?"

"Very much. Though much more so now."

Her eyes narrowed as she regarded him, but she didn't say anything for a moment. Neither did he.

Inwardly, he cursed himself. This was ridiculous. They were

obviously both suspicious of something. And all logic told him what that *something* was. Yet…if he asked outright, and she wasn't Millie… No. He couldn't risk it just yet.

"Your costume is quite clever. Joining in with the apparent theme for the evening," he said, waving vaguely at the other peacocks in the room, "while still being unique. And quite lovely as well."

"Thank you." Her eyes narrowed further, as though she were trying to ascertain the true meaning behind his compliment.

He chuckled. "You needn't be so suspicious every time I pay you a compliment."

"Well, it happens so rarely…"

Hugo cocked an eyebrow, and Adaline flashed him a wry smile. "My apologies, Lord Hugo. Old habits, I suppose."

Her eyes strayed to the feather that curled around the left eye of his mask. "Your feather is quite lovely as well."

"Thank you." This was getting them nowhere. Time to be a little less subtle. "I thought myself quite debonair until I arrived and found myself lost in a sea of peacocks. I had thought to be unique, as peacock feathers are not the easiest to come by."

She snorted gently though her gaze sharpened on him. "Yes. Though you'd never know that by the display tonight."

He followed her glance around the room and chuckled. "Well, you are correct in that. It seems everyone is sporting at least one peacock feather."

"Or an approximation of one," she said, nodding toward a woman with a full faux spray of peacock feathers sprouting from her turban. They seemed to have been made from ostrich feathers and painted to resemble those of a peacock. Clever that.

"Hmm, yes, a bit of a miscalculation on my part."

Her eyes flashed back to his. "Miscalculation?"

The steps of the dance took them apart for a few moments, though their eyes never left each other, even as they wove between the other dancers.

"Yes," he said once they came back together. "I had hoped to stand out tonight."

Her gaze sharpened. "You wish that every night."

"True," he said with a wolfish grin. "But tonight is special."

Her steps faltered. "Is it?"

"Hmm, yes." When they came together, hands pressed against each other, he leaned closer and lowered his voice. "I had hoped to attract the attention of someone in particular with my peacock plumes."

Her face drained of color aside from two bright pink spots high on her cheeks.

"Who?" she asked, her voice barely audible.

The music ended—a good thing as Miss Girard had stopped dancing entirely—and everyone politely clapped.

Hugo held out his hand to escort her from the floor. She took it, her fingers tightening on his after a few steps.

"Who, Lord Hugo?" she asked again, her voice more strained.

He led them to one of the refreshment tables that was a bit less trafficked than the others and handed her a glass of ratafia.

"Drink this," he said. "You look like you need it."

"Lord Hugo," she bit out. "Will you answer my question or not?"

He let a slow smile spread across his lips, more sure than ever that she was who he had thought. Hoped.

"No one of your acquaintance, I am sure," he answered, deliberately drawing out her suspense. He leaned in again, enjoying the hitch in her breath at his proximity. "I was to meet a young woman tonight, who I would know by her peacock feathers." He chuckled. "A futile plan, as it turns out, with so many peacocks *milling* about. As I said, a miscalculation on my part."

He watched her as he spoke, his eyes not missing a single twitch, nor the dawning realization in her eyes. He kept chattering, waiting for her to say something first. There was still the slightest chance it was not she, though that chance grew more and more slim with each passing second.

Perhaps she needed a stronger nudge.

"I am normally quite fond of a bit of mayhem, but I confess, so many peacocks at one ball—"

"It can't be!" she blurted out. Then her eyes darted about, belatedly realizing her outburst had drawn attention.

"What can't be?" he asked, ignoring everyone else. All his attention was now completely focused on her. The rest of the world be damned.

Say it, he mentally urged her. *Say it.*

She stared at him. He could almost see her thoughts warring with each other in her mind. She opened her mouth...and then shook her head and turned to go.

And that...he could not allow.

"Millie," he said, taking a step toward her.

She froze, and so did he.

He waited, his pulse thundering in his ears.

Then she rounded on him, her face frozen in shock. He wasn't sure yet if that shock was good or bad.

"Mayhem?" she whispered. Or at least he thought that was what she whispered. It was so quiet he couldn't actually hear. "I...I thought..." she whispered a little louder.

He raised a brow. "What did you think?"

She stepped closer, her eyes boring into his before they narrowed. Though he wasn't sure if it was in suspicion or confusion. Perhaps both. "You...you're... Mayhem?"

He let out a breath, his smile spreading again to finally hear that name from her lips. "In the flesh. And you're Millie."

"I..." She let out a choked sound that was half laugh, half pure disbelief. "I think I may need to sit down."

He laughed again. "I understand the sentiment. Drink your punch," he said with a nod to the glass in her hand. He took a healthy swig from his own glass, his head spinning.

He had been right! A jolt of pure excitement flowed through him. Followed closely by a spike of anxiety. This would present some problems. Several problems. Several significant problems.

But it solved a rather important one as well. The relief that flooded him that the two women he was pretty sure he was in love with were one and the same nearly made his knees buckle.

He let out another deep breath. She, however, still hadn't spoken, and he looked her over. "Are you well?"

"Yes. No." She blinked up at him. "I do not know."

That drew another smile to his lips. "Are you surprised?"

"Yes." Then she let out a sharp laugh. "And no." Her gaze met his again. "You?"

"Yes and no," he said, his lips twitching. "How do you feel about…" he waved a hand between them, "this surprising yet not surprising revelation?"

"I…" She stopped and blinked again. Then she laughed and let out a deep sigh. "I truly do not know."

His chuckle echoed hers. "Now that I understand completely." He drained his glass and then held out his hand. "Shall we dance again? It will give us the chance to talk. With a few less prying ears."

He glanced around at a few of the other guests who had started to mill closer to them. Trying to eavesdrop, no doubt.

She hesitated only a moment and then placed her hand in his. "A second dance? It will only fuel the gossip."

He laughed again. "I think we are past that at this point."

She gave him a wry smile. "True enough, May…my lord." She snorted softly. "I do not know what to call you."

He leaned in so only she could hear him as they took their positions on the dance floor. "Call me Hugo."

❧ ⸙ ❧

CHAPTER TWENTY-FIVE

ADALINE'S BREATH CAUGHT in her throat at Lord Hugo's...Hugo's...request. She couldn't possibly call him by his Christian name. Could she? Certainly not in public. Though, she had been doing so in her own mind for quite some time now. And she couldn't call him Mayhem.

Mayhem.

She couldn't believe he was actually standing there before her. Dancing with her. And he was *Hugo.* Now *that* she truly couldn't believe. Though...she'd hoped...in the quiet corners of her mind she wouldn't acknowledge even to herself. She had hoped.

Now that she knew his identity, she could admit it. The exhilaration racing through her confirmed that much. She knew if he had not turned out to be Mayhem, a part of her would have been disappointed. A very large part. And it would have presented a choice she wasn't sure she could make.

Now... It certainly simplified matters. Well. Some matters. Others had just become vastly more complicated.

Not to mention, trying to reconcile a person she trusted implicitly with a person she trusted not at all—or not much—was making her head spin.

But if she had to pinpoint an emotion, she was...happy.

She thought.

Hugo watched her, amusement flitting across his face along with what she could only describe as triumph. Her eyes narrowed.

"Did you know?" she asked.

His brows raised. "Did I know what? Who you were?"

She nodded with a sharp jerk of her head, and he shook his. "No. I hoped," he said with a slow smile that spread like a ray of warm sunshine through her veins. "And lately, I've suspected. But no. I didn't know for certain until just a few moments ago."

He'd hoped? Her heart did a happy little flutter that she did her best to ignore.

"What do you mean, you suspected?" she asked, focusing on that surprising revelation. "For how long?"

He shrugged. "Not very. There were things you said that reminded me of Millie. Or things Millie wrote about circumstances in which I was involved that sounded far too familiar for it to be a coincidence. But I couldn't be certain. Not until this evening when I saw you standing there, magnificent in your peahen feathers."

"Oh," she said faintly. She should say more. There were hundreds of thoughts cascading in a riotous jumble through her mind. But she wasn't sure she could grab a hold of any long enough to formulate an articulate response.

Mayhem was Hugo. Hugo was Mayhem.

For a moment, the world spun, the truth finally, fully setting in. The orchestra's lilting strains faded, replaced by the roar of her pulse. Her Marquess of Mayhem was really Lord Hugo Brelsford. Her adversary in countless verbal duels, the man she increasingly loved to hate—or maybe just loved.

The thought stunned her. The letters that had soothed her loneliness and challenged her soul had been his all along. Joy, confusion, and a sharp-edged uncertainty warred within her. Did he feel the same? Was it possible he had known? Had he played her for a fool?

He watched her expectantly. And suddenly, she could no

longer bear the press of curious eyes and swirling questions. Adaline turned on her heel and wove her way through the crowd, skirts swishing in her wake. She made her way down a quiet corridor, passing portraits of solemn-faced ancestors and other partygoers taking advantage of the night of anonymous revelry, until she finally slipped into the dim sanctuary of the library. The heavy door closed behind her with a muffled thud, and she leaned against it, letting out a long shuddering breath.

Heavy brocaded drapes were parted to allow the full moonlight to filter through floor-to-ceiling windows. Adaline pressed her hand to her chest, steadying her breath as she breathed in the scent of leather and parchment. She finally pushed away from the door and wandered between the shelves, fingertips trailing over the gilded spines. Her mind was a chaotic tumble.

Had their written exchanges been truly anonymous? Had Hugo known all along that she was Millie? He said not. But he didn't seem surprised to discover the truth. Though perhaps he had just been better at putting the puzzle together than she. That was a thought she did not enjoy though she couldn't help an amused smile.

She took another deep breath, her thoughts spiraling. Each question gnawed at the fragile hope blooming in her heart. Hope…or hurt? She still wasn't sure. Both perhaps. Anxiety certainly. What did all this mean for them now? There was probably no need to continue corresponding.

The thought saddened her. Though she and Hugo had been seeing each other more and more frequently, she would miss the letters from Mayhem.

The handle turned, and Adaline whirled, her gaze meeting Hugo's as he slipped into the library and closed the door behind him. He paused, probably waiting to see if she would launch a book at his head. The idea had merit. Her hand hovered over a particularly hefty tome…just in case.

"Miss Girard," he said, his voice low and measured as if he were trying not to spook her. Too late. "We need to speak."

"I know," she said. A thousand thoughts fought to escape all at once, her mouth opening and closing as she tried to find the exact right thing to say. Which was an impossibility she couldn't quite deal with just then. She let her breath out in a rush and turned to flee again.

"Miss Girard..." Hugo reached out, grasping her hand. "Adaline."

The sound of her name on his lips stopped her. She slowly looked up at him.

"Please don't run from me," he said, his voice low and gravelly.

He gently pulled her to him, his thumb rubbing gentle circles on her hand. The heat of him, even through the material of their gloves, sent a shiver through her. Not for the first time that evening, she wished she could feel his skin against hers.

"Why?" she whispered finally, her voice trembling. "Why did you not tell me?"

"I didn't know. I swear to you. Not for certain. Not until tonight." Hugo's jaw tensed. "I must ask as well. Did you know? Before this evening?"

"Of course not! Or...not for certain, at least. I had begun to suspect...though I didn't truly believe..." She shook her head. "No. I did not know." She searched his eyes, desperate for truth. "Were the letters a jest to you? Another elaborate game?"

He shook his head, dark hair falling across his brow. "Never. I swear it." His thumb brushed the back of her hand again, and she drew in a shuddering breath. "The letters were my refuge. They were..." His voice faltered. "They were everything. *You* were everything."

She shook her head, though she could not stop a small smile from peeking through.

"Oh yes," he said, his lips pulling into a half-grin. "I stalked that hat shop like a madman, waiting for the next letter. I wanted to share everything with Millie. And then...I ran into you there. And then again in the marketplace. And the park. And the more time we spent together, the more time I wanted to spend with you. Yet I never stopped longing for Millie. I did not know, I swear it. But I couldn't help but hope you could be—"

"But…" Adaline pulled her hand away, hugging it to her chest. She took a step back, her spine pressed to a bookshelf. "But you have always despised me."

Hugo chuckled quietly. "Have I?"

"Yes," Adaline said, voice rising with emotion. "All those arguments, all those… battles—"

"Were as much entertainment for me as they were for you. And do not try to deny it."

She opened her mouth to do just that but could not. He was right. She enjoyed every moment of their verbal sparring.

"I never despised you, Adaline. Yes, I argued. Yes, I sparred with you. And yes, I will admit to a certain degree of…"

"Hate?"

His lips twitched. "Frustration. Our association did not begin in the best light. And I am at fault for occasionally responding to your justified anger poorly. But no, I never despised you. I might have harbored a few ill-advised, pre-conceived notions," he said with a sheepish grin. "But even in the beginning, I admired you. Your wit, your courage. I enjoyed our battles. As did you."

She couldn't stop the soft smile that stole across her lips. "Yes. I did." She sucked in a deep breath and let it out slowly. Her uncertainty warred with the longing she had tried so hard to hide. The man who stood before her was no longer just the enemy she had loved to hate, nor solely the confidante she had adored in letters. He was both. Finally standing before her. Heartbreakingly and beautifully real.

Hugo reached out, cupping her cheek in his palm. "I swear to you, Adaline, I did not know. Everything I've ever written to you was honest. More honest than I've ever been with anyone. I fell in love with you through those letters."

Adaline sucked in a gasp, and Hugo smiled softly, caressing her face with his thumb.

"That was something I didn't want to admit, even to myself until this very moment," he said with a quiet chuckle. Then he sighed. "I've never been the best when dealing with emotions, I fear. Millie changed that. It seems it is easier to be honest with oneself when conversing anonymously."

She smiled in agreement, having often felt the same thing. "There is no reason to lie when the person with whom you are corresponding does not know who you are."

Hugo nodded. "Precisely. I not only got to know you better, I began to know myself as well. And your letters…there was never any judgement. Only understanding. I've never had that before. With anyone. I've never felt so connected to someone. So accepted."

She nodded and looked down for a moment, trying to maintain her composure though her emotions threatened to overflow. "I felt much the same about Mayhem. You," she said, glancing back up at him a bit shyly. It would take some getting used to, equating the two men in her mind.

"I fell in love with Millie through those letters," he said, and she closed her eyes, leaning into his touch despite herself. "And the more time I spent with Adaline, the more I began to love her, too."

Her eyes flew open, and he smiled down at her, his thumb moving to sweep just under her bottom lip.

"You have no idea how relieved I am to find that Millie and Adaline are one and the same."

Adaline burst out laughing and then slapped a hand over her mouth to muffle the sound. "Oh, I have an idea," she said, her voice still choked with laughter. "For I feel much the same about Mayhem and Hugo."

She wiped tears of mirth from her eyes and let out a shuddering sigh. "Do you have any idea the torment I've gone through the last several days? Wondering who you were? Wondering what I would do if you were *not* Mayhem? And what I would do if you were?" She laughed again and pressed her back against the bookshelf, her legs suddenly feeling less than steady.

"Oh yes," he said, his lips pulling into that half-grin that made her heart skip a beat. "I am very well acquainted with that torment."

"It is as though I have been living two lives," she whispered. "One with *you*, in the open. Fighting with you, then conversing, then growing surprisingly more fond," she said with a smile that he echoed. "And then one in private. One just for me. And my marquess. Where I discovered hope and kindness and a camaraderie I thought never to find, only to uncover it in a stranger's letters. I suppose I am now finding it difficult to marry the two."

Hugo pressed his forehead to hers, his voice deep and husky. "We were strangers, and yet not. I have longed for you in both worlds, hardly daring to hope they might become one."

She let out a shaky breath, her heart racing. "And now that we know…what now? I do not know what I am to you."

He smiled, a glimmer of hope shining in his eyes. "You are everything, Adaline. You always have been. Enemy, friend, confidante…beloved."

For a moment, silence hung between them, charged and electric. Hugo's hand traced a gentle path along her cheek, and she opened her eyes to find his gaze aflame with hunger and longing. Much the same as he likely saw in hers.

"And what am I to you now?" he asked.

She smiled gently. "Enemy. Friend. Confidante." Her eyes searched his, her heart pounding as she uttered the last word. "Beloved."

The smile he gave her took her breath away.

Slowly, he bent his head, giving her time to back away if she chose. Instead, she rose up on her toes, meeting his lips. It was tentative at first. A gentle brush of his lips against hers. Then with a groan, he deepened the kiss, unleashing all the passion and uncertainty that was flooding through them both.

Adaline melted into the kiss. Her arms wound around his neck, her fingers threading through his hair. The months of secret longing and exhilarating encounters, the hours spent cherishing his letters and anticipating their face-to-face confrontations, all coalesced in this single, breathless moment.

It overwhelmed her. Her knees buckled, but Hugo held her fast, his arms wrapping tighter about her and pulling her close.

For long moments, the world beyond the library ceased to exist.

At last, she pulled away to drag in a shuddering breath. Hugo laughed softly, his fingers lingering on her cheek as he rested his forehead against hers, their ragged breath mingling.

"I will miss Mayhem's letters," she finally said.

Hugo barked out a laugh and pressed another lingering kiss to her lips. "Oh, I shall still write. I would miss Millie too much as well."

She smiled, her happiness nearly overwhelming her. "Promise?"

He nodded and kissed her again. "Yes, I promise. As long as you promise me," he whispered, "that you will never run from me again. Whatever may happen in the future, we will deal with it together."

She nodded. "I promise."

"Good. Now that that's settled…"

He dragged her back to him, and she laughed as his lips captured hers once more.

Chapter Twenty-Six

Hugo's heart pounded to the point of pain. So much happiness flooded through his body, he wasn't sure how to contain it. How could one person feel such exhilaration without shouting it to the world?

He wrenched his lips from hers with a ragged breath. "Marry me," he ground out.

She blinked up at him, eyes still dazed. "What?"

Perhaps that had been a little too abrupt. He cupped her beautiful face in his hands, his heart overflowing. "Marry me."

A hesitant smile spread over her kiss-swollen lips. "You wish to marry me?"

"More than I've ever wanted anything. And that is saying a lot. I'm quite a greedy glutton."

Her soft, husky laugh made things tighten low in his belly. It would be a miracle if he was able to walk out of this library.

"Well, that I can believe easily enough. The gluttony, that is," she said with a teasing glint in her eye. "You do seem the greedy sort."

"Only where you are concerned," he chuckled.

God, he loved this woman. Though, he hadn't told her yet. Not in so many words. "I really am an unforgivable dolt."

"True," she said, startling another laugh out of him. "Though only the dolt part. On occasion, perhaps," she continued.

"Certainly not the unforgivable part. For I forgave you long ago. I'm not even confident when." She frowned slightly, her eyes going distant with her thoughts.

"I will strive every day to be worthy of that forgiveness," Hugo said quietly, his heart aching at the hurt he'd done her so many months ago. "Though you are far more charitable than I. I'm not certain I will ever forgive myself."

"Hmm." She reached up to caress his cheek. "You are far harsher on yourself than you ever are on others. You should be kinder to the man I love."

Her admission rocked him to his foundations. "You love me?"

She nodded. "A truly staggering amount. It's a bit embarrassing, really."

He chuckled and shook his head. "I was just about to confess my own embarrassingly staggering amount of love for you."

"Hmm," she murmured again with a sly smile. "Yet I said it first."

"I was unaware we were in competition."

"Aren't we always?"

"I suppose we are." He flashed her a delighted grin. "I suppose I shall just have to say it better then."

"I don't see how—"

"I love you," he said, pressing an ardent kiss to her lips. "I have loved you since the moment you nearly struck me with that ribbon in the hat shop." He trailed his lips over her temple, her cheeks, and then down the column of her neck. "I have loved you from the very first letter you sent."

His hands skimmed up her sides, barely brushing the flesh beneath. A fine tremor ran through her, and he smiled against the soft skin beneath her ear. "I have loved every word you've written, every word you've spoken. The teasing ones, the angry ones, the mocking ones." He punctuated each example with another kiss along her neck and collarbone until she was gripping his arms to keep herself upright. "The passionate ones," he nearly growled in her ear.

A quiet gasp escaped her throat, and he kissed her again, his mouth moving over hers with a fervor that was almost frantic. He could not get enough of her. He did not think he'd *ever* get enough of her.

"I love you so much it nearly overwhelms me. It is… uncontainable. Exhilarating. And terrifying. And if it ever stops, I am very afraid I might cease to exist altogether."

He pulled back so he could look into her eyes. Eyes that were suspiciously bright, though the smile she gave him nearly stole his breath.

She dragged in a jagged breath, exhaling with a sharp laugh. "Very well. You win."

Hugo chuckled and pulled her into an embrace. He loved the feel of her in his arms. He'd hold her all day if she'd let him. "And what is my prize then?" he asked.

She tilted her head back, her cheeks flushing pink. "I do not consider it much of a prize. But if you truly want me, then…I shall marry you."

⇥⟫⟨⇤

ADALINE'S HEART THUNDERED in her chest. Had she really just agreed to marry him? This didn't feel real. Even with her lips still swollen from his kisses, her skin still tingling from his touch, it felt like a dream. And she was terrified she'd wake.

"You have made me the happiest man alive, my love," he said, caressing her cheek.

She raised a brow. "Are you certain of that? We do have a tendency to argue. Over everything."

"Ah, but we both enjoy that," he said, waving that away.

"And if we stop enjoying it?"

He shrugged. "We shall find other, more enjoyable, ways to pass our time." He leaned in closer, his lips hovering near her ear. "Perhaps there are a few ideas in those books you love to read."

She gasped and slapped at his arm. "That was of the utmost secrecy, my lord, never to be uttered aloud."

"My apologies," he said with a chuckle. "Though the idea itself has merit, you must admit."

"I suppose," she teased. "Though perhaps we should check your sketchbook instead."

Hugo beamed at her. "We can do both, dearest. And shall." His smile faded into an impatient grimace. "As soon as the vicar gives us his blessing."

Her brow furrowed, some of her happiness waning. "A vicar might be the only one who will give us his blessing," she said. "Our families will likely not."

Hugo rubbed her upper arms, pulling her to him for a quick kiss on her forehead. "We shall make them. I will not let anyone stand in our way."

"Oh?" She raised her brows. "You cannot simply bully your way past their prejudices."

"Can I not?" He raised his own brows. "I can be rather stubborn, as I am sure you well know by now. And charming as well, as I am certain you know."

Adaline rolled her eyes, drawing a chuckle from Hugo.

He gave her arms a gentle squeeze. "We will convince them. Our families both desire us to wed. We are both from good households—"

"You are the son of a duke."

"A second son," he reminded her. "And your father might not have been titled, but he was a very well-respected member of Parliament. As your brother is set to be when he is elected to your father's seat. He has been assured by the landholders in his borough of the position, has he not?"

"Yes, but…"

Hugo smiled. "Well then. My family should have no objections to you based upon your bloodlines."

"No. But they shall object to me all the same, will they not?"

Hugo frowned, unable to refute her. "It is true they fear that you had set your sights on Edward and then decided upon me when he was unavailable."

She shook her head, vehemently. "But that simply isn't true. I hadn't heard a word of any supposed proposal until I returned to town days after the conversation occurred. And I would not have accepted even if I had been consulted."

Ha! That confirmed his suspicions about her supposed reaction. She hadn't known anything about her brother's actions. "I know, dearest," he said, trying to soothe her. "My family will accept the truth eventually."

She sighed. "Even if they do, mine will certainly object to you," she continued. "My brother would rather see you bleeding on the end of his rapier than wed to me. He feels you purposely humiliated him. And...he is not wrong," she said, glancing up at him. "Though he bears a large amount of blame for exacerbating the situation."

Hugo let out a sigh and pulled her back into his arms. "I know. But they will get used to the idea. If we can not only forgive each other but fall in love, surely they can put aside their grudges."

Adaline laughed quietly. "You have more faith in them than I, my lord."

"Hugo." He took her chin in his fingers and tilted her face up to meet his gaze. "I would like to hear my name on your lips. Adaline." He kissed her and then whispered, "Millie."

Adaline shivered in his arms, her entire body coursing with warmth and desire.

"I love you, Hugo." She reached up on her tiptoes to brush a soft, barely-there kiss to his lips. "My Mayhem," she added, her voice hardly more than a whisper.

He crushed her to him, and she clung to him desperately, their lips moving feverishly together.

When they finally broke apart, she was ready to burn down the world if it stood in their way.

Hugo took a deep, shuddering breath and then squared his shoulders. "Come, love. Let us go face our dragons."

Chapter Twenty-Seven

H UGO HAD NEVER considered himself a coward. Quite the opposite, truth be told. But at this precise moment, he was not too proud to admit, (to himself, at least), that his nerves were failing him. His family would not be pleased. And that was likely gilding the lily somewhat. He took a deep breath, steeling himself for what lay ahead.

He had prolonged it as long as he could, hoping to give his family time to recover from the previous night's revelries before he caused the inevitable uproar.

Late afternoon light spilled into the sitting room as he entered, casting delicate patterns on the pale blue silk wallpaper. His father stood by the fireplace, gesturing animatedly as he recounted the day's news to Hugo's mother, whose sharp eyes caught Hugo the moment he entered. Arthur lounged in a window seat, a book forgotten beside him.

"Hugo," his mother said, voice laced with surprise. "I am surprised to see you so early. You disappeared from the masquerade. I confess, I hadn't been sure you'd made it home at all."

Hugo smiled and clasped his hands behind his back. "I have news. Good news. At least I believe it to be. If you have a moment?"

His father's eyes narrowed, but he gestured to a chair. "Do you now? Well, come along then. Don't keep us waiting."

Hugo took another breath. Well. Here went nothing. "I have asked for a lady's hand, and she has accepted. I intend to marry."

A hush fell, interrupted only by the rhythmic ticking of the mantel clock. Lady Haltham's lips parted in surprise, but pleased surprise. His father's shoulders relaxed, suspicion momentarily dissolved. Arthur looked stunned. Then his eyes widened slightly, obviously realizing the identity of the lady in question. Thankfully, he snapped his mouth shut, settling back in his seat to watch the oncoming disaster unfold.

"Splendid!" his mother exclaimed. "At last, Hugo! Who is the fortunate young lady?"

Hugo hesitated, glancing at Arthur, who raised a brow, his face alight with amusement. The moment stretched taut. Hugo straightened to his full height, back ramrod straight.

"Miss Adaline Girard," he said.

For a heartbeat, his parents stared at him, faces frozen. Then, his mother's smile collapsed. His father let out a grumbling cough, as if he couldn't get his rejection out fast enough and choked on it instead.

"Adaline Girard?" his mother repeated, her voice thin.

"What foolishness is this?" his father sputtered.

His mother shook her head. "You cannot mean the same girl who started all the trouble with Edward earlier this year?"

"*I* started all the trouble with Edward earlier this year, Mother. Adaline had nothing to do with it."

His father set down his glass with a sharp clink. "Oh, yes, she did, Hugo. You may have made the remarks, but you made them in jest, and she accepted the supposed proposal and spread it about in order to use public pressure to bring it to pass."

"Her brother is the one who started the rumors," Hugo argued. "She cannot be held accountable for the sins of another. She had no knowledge of it until after the fact."

"Or so she may have told you," his mother argued.

"Yes. She did. And I believe her."

His father snorted. "Oh, come now."

Hugo continued, ignoring him. "Even if I did not, what happened in the past has no bearing on our present. I know there is some animosity between our families—"

"*Some* animosity? Her brother challenged you to a duel!" his mother said. "And not a mere form of etiquette. He wanted you dead!"

"I remember," Hugo said. "And it likely wouldn't have been to the death. Only to first blood." Then he shrugged. "He didn't mean it."

Arthur laughed in his corner, then choked it off when both their parents shot him irritated looks.

"She is well-born," Hugo replied, "not titled, I know. But her family is reputable—"

"Her family may be reputable," his mother interjected, "but she herself is a social climber. How can you simply dismiss the fact that she—whether she knew at first or not—would have likely accepted a marriage proposal from your own brother? And what then? When she realized she couldn't have him, she obviously set her sights on you."

Hugo's jaw tightened. "That isn't what happened, Mother."

"That is exactly what happened," his father insisted. "And what will happen if this match falls through as well? Hmm? Will she be after Arthur next?"

Everyone glanced in Arthur's direction, and he immediately threw his hands in the air in mock surrender. "Leave me out of this. I am a mere spectator. Thank you."

"Hear the boy out," Duchess Catherine said. "He obviously has feelings for this girl. He at least deserves to make his case."

Hugo gave his grandmother a grateful smile, then turned back to his parents. "I know this is difficult to accept. But I promise you, I did not enter into this blindly. She did not make overtures toward me. In fact, it was I who instigated our friendship. I, who sought her out, not the other way around. It was many weeks before she stopped seeing me as an enemy who would bring about her downfall. As she was more than justified in doing, considering the damage my thoughtless jest wrought. It took great effort on my part, and extraordinary forgiveness on hers, before she saw me as a friend. And then more."

"Or so she would have you believe," his father said, fixing Hugo with a stern gaze. "How can you be so certain? She is clever, obviously. And charming, as I remember. But it would be naïve to believe she seeks anything but your name and fortune."

"Even if that were true, how would that make her different than any other woman you have thrown at me over the last year? Not one of them know me or have even bothered trying to do so. They, or at least their families, see our name and our bank account, and that is all they need to know. So at the very least, be honest about the reasoning behind your rejection. But I assure you, that is not the case here. Adaline would not marry unless for love."

His parents glanced at each other, but neither of their expressions softened. They were not swayed.

Hugo let out a deep sigh, anxiety and disappointment pressing upon him. He had known this would not go well. But he had still held out some hope. Hope that was rapidly dwindling. He hadn't wanted to betray their secret. But perhaps knowing the truth would sway his parents.

"I know her motives are pure because she loved me before she ever knew my name."

His father snorted again, his mother making a slightly more feminine version of the sound, her eyes narrowing. "How is that even possible?"

Hugo gritted his teeth, his jaw popping, before he answered. "We corresponded for months. Anonymously."

His mother gasped. His father looked at him as if he'd gone mad. And Arthur had never looked so entertained in his life. Hugo glared at him before turning his attention back to his parents.

"She found a letter that I had misplaced, one I had written to Grandmother." He nodded at her, and she gave him an encouraging smile. "She did not reveal any identifying information in the letter. I had no inkling of her true identity. Nor she of mine. But I found the letter to be clever. Amusing. I was intrigued. And so I wrote back, sending it through the same channel as the one which delivered mine to me. And…we simply continued. I found her mind keen, her heart true. We shared our fears and hopes, we found our minds and hearts aligned in nearly every way. And she did this without any knowledge of my identity."

His mother shook her head, lips pursed. "That you know of. You may hope. Assume. But you cannot be sure, truly sure, that she did not know. Whether she did or not, the simple fact that she engaged in such activity with a man to whom she is not engaged or related is highly improper. And *this* is the woman you wish us to welcome into our home? Our family?"

Yes. He'd known that wouldn't work in their favor. Which is why he wouldn't have betrayed their secret unless it was absolutely necessary. But they had to understand their connection. How deeply it went.

"Anonymous letters?" His father shook his head. "How reckless. How can anything good come of such secrecy? It reeks of deception." His father pressed on, voice rising, "You are besotted, Hugo. You see virtue where there may be none. We cannot sanction this match. For your own good."

"Think of what people will say," his mother added. "The whole of society knows of the rancor between our families. A match between you would do nothing but invite curiosity, questions that you may not want to answer. And if the truth were ever discovered…"

"You speak of reputation as if it outweighs happiness," Hugo said, trying to keep his anger, and fear, in check. He had known this wouldn't be easy, but it was going a good sight worse than he'd anticipated.

"Adaline is not what you believe," he insisted. "She is kind, wonderful. Better than most in our acquaintance, frankly. She is the woman I choose. I will have no other."

His mother's voice trembled with emotion. "We only wish to spare you pain. Think carefully, Hugo. How can we ever trust her?"

"*I* trust her," Hugo replied, voice steady. "That should be enough."

His father stood, his frame rigid. "If you persist in this folly, you do so without our blessing. You will not have our permission, nor our support. We cannot—will not—see the Haltham name tied to such scandal."

Hugo's vision blurred, anger clawing at his gut. "There will be no scandal as long as you do not betray the secrets I have confided in you. Only those of us in this room and Adaline herself know of our correspondence. Just as only those in our family and hers know what truly transpired between us when I made that damnable joke months ago."

His father's face remained stony, though his mother's softened a degree. "Hugo," she said gently, taking his hand. "We are only trying to protect you."

"I know, Mother," he said, giving her hand a squeeze. "But I do not need your protection. I need your blessing to marry the woman I love."

His mother's face softened, but his father let out a deep sigh. "And that, I'm afraid, we cannot do."

Arthur stirred from his seat, concern etching his features. The silence grew heavy, suffocating. At last, Hugo turned away. "If you cannot accept Adaline, then you cannot accept me. I will not live without her."

With that, he strode from the room, the familiar corridors of Haltham House seeming suddenly foreign and cold. Outside, dusk was falling. Hugo paused on the steps, breath curling in the chill air. He closed his eyes, fighting the tremor of doubt that gnawed at his resolve. He had never gone against his parents' wishes before. He'd never needed to. And he did not regret doing so now. But he did mourn the rift that now existed between them.

The door opened behind him, and Arthur emerged, his coat hastily thrown over his shoulders.

"Hugo, wait."

Arthur stopped at his side. "I'm sorry. I tried to intervene, but you know how Father is when he's set on something. I know how you care for her. And she's obviously extraordinary to put up with you."

Hugo chuckled. "That she is."

Arthur looked up at the flickering lamps lining the square, his voice low. "What will you do now? They will not relent easily. You know how Father is. If you marry her, they may cut you off. Are you prepared for that?"

Hugo's gaze drifted to the horizon, where the last rays of sunlight struggled against the gathering gloom. "I will not give her up. I would, of course, prefer to remain in our parents' good graces," he said with a wry smile before sobering. "But I'll marry her without their permission if I must. If she'll have me."

Arthur smiled and clapped him on the shoulder. "Glad to hear it. I like her. And for what it's worth, I am certain they'll come around. Eventually. I do think they genuinely want your happiness. They just need to be convinced Miss Girard is not what they think. And until then, I will help you, whatever you need. You have my word."

Hugo clasped his brother's hand, warm affection for him soothing some of the sting of his parents' rejection. "Thank you, Arthur. That means more than you know."

Arthur gave him a nod and then turned his gaze to the road, pulling his coat tighter about him. "Well then. What now?"

Hugo turned his gaze to the horizon as well, his mind swimming with possible plans. Though only one truly mattered just then.

"I am going to claim my lady."

CHAPTER TWENTY-EIGHT

ADALINE PAUSED BEFORE the family dining room doors, her heart in her throat. Faint laughter drifted from within. It sounded like her brother Henry from the low, measured tones. Her mother's honied voice followed, not yet sharp with worry. Oh, but it would be. Though…maybe her family would surprise her and greet her news with enthusiasm. Wishful thinking, but one could hope.

She took a deep breath and steeled her spine, then pushed open the door. Conversation ceased. Her mother paused, her teacup halfway to her lips. Henry looked up but continued to shovel eggs into his mouth.

"Adaline!" her mother said with a welcoming smile. "You are awake at last. Did you enjoy yourself last night? I'm afraid I was so tired when we left, we didn't speak more than three words to each other."

Adaline met her gaze. "Yes, I did. Very much. In fact…" She faltered, then pressed on, voice trembling but clear. "In fact, something quite wonderful happened."

"Oh?" her mother said, eyes alight with curiosity as she sipped her tea. Her brother had gone back to his breakfast, likely assuming the women were about to embark on a bit of morning gossip.

"Yes." She'd thought to perhaps preface her announcement

with a bit of explanation or an anecdote to ease into it but finally decided to just come directly to the point. And pray for the best. She cleared her throat. "A gentleman of my acquaintance asked for my hand last night. And I accepted him. I am to be married."

Two pairs of eyes stared at her in abject shock. Henry had frozen mid-bite, his toast crumbling between his teeth. Her mother was the first to recover, setting her teacup down with a clatter.

"Adaline! Well, this is wonderful news! It is, isn't it?" she asked, her brow suddenly furrowing. "Nothing untoward occurred to spur this sudden proposal, has it? You haven't been compromised, have you?"

"No, Mother," Adaline said with a nervous laugh. "Everything occurred quite properly."

Not the exact truth, but what they didn't know wouldn't hurt them.

Her brother did not look convinced. "Not entirely proper, or this supposed gentleman would have asked *me* for your hand before deigning to ask you."

Getting his permission first wasn't strictly necessary, especially as she was past her majority, but her brother always had been a bit old-fashioned. And overzealous when it came to what he considered his duty to her. Though now did not seem a prudent time to point that out.

"Henry, I assure you he meant no disrespect. The proposal itself was sudden. Perhaps we could blame the ambiance of the masquerade," she said with a little chuckle. That no one else echoed.

She cleared her throat again. "I assure you, our attachment has actually been quite long in the making. He is truly everything I have always hoped for in a husband."

"That is wonderful, Adaline," her mother said with a loving smile. Though her eyes sharpened, not missing the fact that Adaline had yet to divulge her new fiancé's identity.

"Who is this paragon of virtue?" her brother asked dryly.

"One of the gentlemen I have selected, I hope."

Here went nothing...

Adaline swallowed. "Lord Hugo Brelsford."

The effect was instantaneous. Henry muttered a curse, his eyes narrowing dangerously. Her mother gasped, paling beneath her coiffure. The name hung in the air like a clap of thunder, heralding imminent disaster.

"You cannot mean it," Henry barked. "After everything that man did to make a spectacle of you, and this family?"

Adaline's hands clasped together, trembling. She forced herself to meet her brother's gaze. "He regrets it, Henry. It was a mistake. He meant the offer as a jest, one he did not think anyone would believe. It... was merely a prank that went a little too far. It was foolish, yes, but it was not meant to wound so deeply. Nor at all."

Henry's voice was cold. "A prank? He humiliated you. The entire ton spoke of it for weeks. He used you to amuse himself."

"No! That isn't true. Stop exaggerating, Henry. You bear just as much blame as he, as it was you who took him at his word and spread the news before even verifying anything with the duke or Lord Lockhaven."

Henry sputtered but couldn't argue the truth.

Adaline continued before he could try. "While I'll admit the gossip did do some harm, it did not do so permanently. Society moved on to the next scandal as they always do. Hugo never meant for any of it to happen."

"You cannot know that for certain," her mother said, her voice strained. She seemed to be trying to contain her emotions so they might have a calm and rational conversation. But it was with obvious difficulty.

"But I do, Mother. We have spoken of it at length. I'll admit, when we first met in person, there was a great deal of animosity on both sides. But we have moved past that and found that we have much in common. We truly enjoy one another's company. He is a good man."

Her brother snorted. "A good man would not have acted as he did."

Adaline pursed her lips. Pointing out the same could be said for Henry and his actions would not help her case, though it was difficult to keep from saying so. "He agrees. Which is why he has done nothing but try to make amends and better himself since the day it happened."

"He is very likely just telling you what you want to hear," Henry muttered.

Adaline threw her hands up. "To what purpose? Marrying me brings him nothing. A good dowry, perhaps. But he has wealth. He doesn't need mine."

"That you know of," Henry said. "He might be the son of a duke, but he's a second son. One, who by all accounts, is fond of unruly pastimes that most certainly include gambling and other revelry. You cannot know the state of his financial affairs for certain."

Adaline shook her head and folded her arms, trying to rein in her anger. Losing her composure would not help her now.

"I know he is who he presents himself to be." She hadn't wanted to divulge their secret, but it might be the only way to get her family to understand. "We have been writing to each other for many months, anonymously. Neither of us knew who the other was. And in so doing, we were able to truly be ourselves. To become familiar with each other in a deeper way than would have ever been possible with only brief public meetings in person. I know his heart."

"You know nothing." Her mother rose, making a visible effort to control her emotions. "My child, I love you and have never wanted anything but your security and happiness. But I fear you have been misled. All these months, you have been corresponding in secret? With an unknown man who could have been anyone? Have you no thought for the consequences to such actions? I can only guess at the content of these letters. How can you be sure that they were, indeed, anonymous? That he didn't know your identity the entire time? Perhaps even shared your letters with others for their own amusement. Did you never think of such a thing? The gossip, the scandal, that could once again come of it, not just for you but for the entire family?"

"Of course, I thought about the consequences, Mother." She just hadn't deemed them worth discontinuing something which had brought her such joy. Though again, pointing that out seemed detrimental to her cause.

"And yet you acted recklessly anyway," her brother cut in, his booming voice making her flinch.

"Hugo would never harm me in such a way," Adaline insisted.

Henry threw up his hands. "He already has!"

Adaline's cheeks burned. That was the one argument she could not truly refute. "This is different. His letters were never meant to be shared. Our letters *were* truly anonymous. And... they were initiated by me."

The general uproar at that statement made Adaline's ears ring. She closed her eyes for a brief second, praying for strength. "It is not so bad as it sounds. I found a letter, unsigned, written to his grandmother. No names were included, so I had no inkling of whom the letter might have been from. However, I did recognize the footman who had dropped it when I saw him again, and I returned the letter to him to give to his master. And... included one of my own."

Her mother gasped. "Adaline." She stared at Adaline for a solid ten seconds, her mind seemingly unable to process what she had just been told. Adaline forged ahead, hoping for the best.

"We continued our correspondence, leaving the letters for each other at a secret designated location." She didn't know if her family would feel better or worse knowing that Lucy had been instrumental in their scheme. Either way, Adaline had every intention of protecting her cousin's involvement.

"Even without the letters," she continued, "we have grown closer in person as well. Yes, we started as enemies due to his past actions. But he regrets them bitterly. It was those very actions that spurred his change. He wanted to ensure he never did such a thing again and has done much to make amends. And yes, through our association and through the letters, I feel I truly know his heart. He is a good man, I swear it. And…I love him," she said, hardly daring to say the words aloud. "I wish to marry him."

Her brother's expression darkened. "I love you, Sister, but you have always had a tendency to over-romanticize things. You have been reading the words of a scoundrel. He has been and always will be reckless. If he truly cared, if he were truly honorable and wished to do right by you and this family, why did he not come here, like a gentleman, and ask for your hand?"

Adaline fought the urge to shriek out her frustration. Instead, she took a deep breath and spoke as calmly as she could manage. "He intends to. Once I have spoken with you. It…happened rather suddenly. And I thought the news would be better coming from me. Considering the good possibility you'd have shot him on sight before he had a chance to speak."

Her brother's eyes narrowed further. "He should never have broached the subject with you before speaking to me first."

"Oh, Henry," their mother said. "While it is an honorable tradition, it is not strictly necessary to ask permission of one's guardian first. I seem to remember your father proposing to me before speaking to my father," her mother said with a fond smile. "And I had not yet reached my majority at the time. Unlike your sister."

Henry glanced at her, startled, and then grumbled. "Yes well…this is different. Lord Hugo should have made his intentions honorable from the start."

"He didn't *have* any intentions toward me other than steering clear of my ire, and me of his," Adaline insisted. "Until…things changed. And do not ask me when or why they did so because neither of us could tell you. They just…did. And now that they have, we are happy and wish to marry. Can you not be happy for us?"

Her mother seemed to be wavering, but Henry's scowl did not bode well. He looked moments from storming out, though he didn't actually have any legal authority to stop her from acting as she wished. Truly, neither did her mother. She did not legally need their permission to wed. But she wanted it. Both because she loved and respected them, and because it would make her life a good sight easier if she were not cut off from them emotionally and financially.

"I wish nothing more than to secure your future, Ada," her brother said.

"And my happiness?" she asked, brow raised.

"That would be preferable, yes. But I fear that you will not find that with Lord Hugo. You insist he has changed. That you know his mind through his letters. All I see is another example of how little care he has for you and your reputation. No true gentleman would have engaged in such a campaign with you, no matter who initiated it. That he did so does not speak well of his character, or his honorable intentions."

Adaline frowned, another shard of misgiving piercing her resolve.

Had she been a fool? She had hoped that telling them of the letters would prove to her family that their feelings were real. That they did indeed know and love each other. Instead, it seemed to have only made matters worse. Perhaps they should have waited. Maybe they did need to know each other better. They had made some questionable choices, she could admit that. Were they on the verge of making another?

Doubts pressed in, cold and suffocating.

But only for the briefest of moments. No. She straightened, pushing all uncertainties aside. She was not mistaken. Not this time.

"I understand your fears, Henry. Truly. And if it had only been the words on the page I had fallen in love with, then perhaps I might be swayed by your fears. But it isn't his written words alone that have won my heart. We have grown closer with every meeting as well. I've seen for myself the type of person he truly is."

Henry snorted. "Oh? And what type of man is that?"

Adaline glared at him. "A man who helped me, though he knew I hated him. He showed me compassion when I had given him nothing but scorn. He's a man who is kind to children, who obviously loves his nieces and nephews. Who plays with them and truly enjoys their company, which is a far sight better than I can say for most men of my acquaintance."

Henry had the grace to look a little sheepish, knowing well enough that he was one of those men. Though his jaw was still set in that stubborn way of his.

"He is a man who is witty and amusing and compassionate, who has gone out of his way to put me at ease and make me laugh when he had no reason to do so," Adaline continued before turning to her mother. "I know he is not perfect, Mother. But neither am I. But I know in my heart he is a good man. He has done nothing but strive to make me happy. I love him. I wish to marry him. And so," she said, looking back at Henry, "I ask for your blessing."

Her brother's face remained stony, though he did seem to be wavering. A little, perhaps. "Please," she added, her voice cracking.

Henry's eyes crinkled with regret. "I am sorry, Adaline. You may not understand or appreciate my actions now. But I assure you, I think only of you and your best interests. I will not allow you to wed a man who cannot be trusted with your reputation, much less your heart. You say he has changed. But all I see is a man whose behavior has remained distressingly consistent. His choices repeatedly put you and your reputation at risk."

Adaline's hands shook. "You cannot mean to judge him based on a few mistakes—"

"A pattern, more like," Henry interjected. "You cannot hope to change him, Ada. He will only bring you more heartbreak."

"Henry…" their mother began. But Henry shook his head.

"I am sorry. But I'm afraid my answer is no." His steady gaze met Adaline's and her heart dropped. There was not an ounce of vacillation in his countenance.

"I may not be able to stop you from marrying this man," he said, his voice hard as steel. "But my approval of your spouse *is* required for you to access your trust. And your dowry. If you choose to go ahead with this marriage, you will do so without a shilling from this family." He turned to leave, then paused. Adaline watched him warily. Finally, he sighed. "I am sorry, Ada. Truly."

"No, you're not," she said, swallowing hard to keep the emotions that were choking her from spilling over.

"I am. I'm sorry for your pain. But I hope you understand that we are simply trying to prevent you from a lifetime of worse."

He bent to kiss her cheek and then escorted their mother from the room.

Adaline dropped into a chair and leaned her head against her hand.

His words had battered her. She knew they feared for her. And she was honest enough to admit that were she in their shoes, she'd likely feel much the same. If she did not bow to their wishes, she could lose them. Or at least lose their trust. Respect. Support. And that was no small thing for a woman. However. If she did acquiesce… it meant losing Hugo.

And that, she feared, was the one thing from which her heart would never recover.

Chapter Twenty-Nine

You've Got Mail

My dearest ~~Mil~~ Adaline,

How strange to be addressing a letter to a name other than Millie. I shall miss that, I think. Though should I try a thousand years, properly conveying my happiness that you and she are one and the same would prove an impossibility. Perhaps you shall remain Millie in our private moments, if only for nostalgia's sake.

I am considerably less happy that I have no news from you in three days. My wretched misery grows by the second, and I fear your silence is the unfortunate consequence of your family's reaction to our news. If their ire was similar to my own family's…well, suffice it to say, my anxiety to see you knows no bounds.

I must pray that Mrs. Harrow will once again act as an intermediary on my behalf and deliver this letter to you. I have attempted several times now to deliver a missive to your home. Each time, my messenger has returned with the letter undelivered. And when I attempted to call and ascertain for myself your condition, I was denied entry and told no one in the family was at home, though I knew that to be a lie.

If Mrs. Harrow refuses, I may have to resort to hiding in the bushes or throwing rocks at your window. Actions I will gladly undertake take if necessary. But it will be exceedingly simpler if Mrs. Harrow is amenable one last time.

My darling, I have not yet had the time to properly convey the strength of my love for you. Though had I a hundred lifetimes, it would not be enough. I love you to distraction. It's an odd feeling, love. One would think one falls in love and that is an end to it. Instead, this feeling for you grows, doubles, trebles, every day. Every minute. Until I cannot function for thoughts of you are all that fill my head. My family fears I have gone quite mad, and I cannot fault them as they are likely correct. I am mad. And you are the only cure. This situation in which we currently find ourselves is untenable. It cannot continue.

To that end, I have formulated a plan. I have told no one, not even Arthur, as the danger is too great. I must see you, my love. We must be together. And we must not allow the prejudices of our families nor anyone else to stand in the way of our happiness. For I will be honest, my love. I have no wish to continue through this life without you. I can only pray that you feel the same. That somewhere along the way, you have also stopped seeing me as your greatest enemy and by some miracle now view me as your dearest love. As I do you.

If you feel as I do, I beg of you, meet me tonight at midnight. In front of Mrs. Harrow's shop. And we shall make our own plans for our future. Our families be hanged. Let us go where they cannot touch us. Where our decisions are our own, our happiness in our own hands. Come with me, my love.

I know this may seem sudden. Rash. Foolish. I do realize I am possibly—or entirely—dicked in the nob. If you'll pardon the vulgarity (and I know you will as you have forgiven me far worse). I fear I cannot be otherwise but entirely mad, such is my fear of losing you.

Meet me, I beg of you. I shall await you until the sun rises.

Always faithfully and forever yours,
The Marquess of Mayhem

Postscript. I shall likely wait until long after the sun rises, such is my desire to steal you away. But I do feel obliged to mention that it will be considerably easier to run off to Gretna Green if we leave under the cover of darkness. Should you be so inclined.

H.

Adaline reread the letter thrice more, then lowered it, her smile growing as she read the postscript one last time.

"Cheeky, foolish man," she murmured, though her body trembled with a nearly overwhelming mix of excitement, anticipation, and sheer, unadulterated happiness.

"Well?" Lucy asked. "What did he say?"

Adaline glanced up. "My family, it seems, has been keeping Hugo from me. He has tried to call and write several times, all to no avail."

Lucy nodded. "I thought as much when he arrived at my door begging me to deliver this to you," she said, waving at the letter. "But what did he say? Something has put that bloom back in your cheeks."

"I..." Adaline let out a nervous laugh. "I suppose I have a decision to make."

✦ ✦ ✦

CHAPTER THIRTY

Hugo paced in front of the Harrows' shop, not caring if he looked like a disturbed madman. It wasn't far from the truth. If he had to wait any longer… He looked at his pocket watch again. Three minutes until midnight. Exactly a minute and a half since the last time he had looked.

He took a deep breath, his gloved hands clenching into fists as he forced himself to slowly release it. She would be there. She would come. He knew it. Hoped it. Prayed for it? He hadn't ever considered himself an overly faithful man, but if praying would help in this moment, he was game to give it a try.

A rustling from beyond the corner drew his attention. His head snapped up, his gaze fixed on the cobbled street just out of his sight. Every muscle in his body tensed in expectation. And dread.

Finally, a figure appeared—a slight figure in a dark cloak, skirts hitched above serviceable boots as she strode toward him. The face beneath the hood was half-shadowed, but he knew the curve of her cheek, the determined set of her shoulders.

The tension drained from his body, leaving him nearly shaking with relief. He hurried toward her, and she stopped short, breathless, trembling as much as he. For a moment, neither spoke. And then he let his lips spread in a slow smile, and she flung herself into his arms.

"You came," he murmured, voice raw as he held her tight.

"How could I resist a request from my Mayhem?" she said, her voice unsteady. A sheen of tears glimmered in her eyes, but her smile warmed him to his soul.

The world narrowed to the press of her body against his, her hands clutching his lapels. One small tug was all it took, and his lips brushed hers. Her quiet gasp made him pull back. Their gazes locked. Their breath mingled in the cold night air. And then she wrapped her arms about his neck, drawing him back to her with a quiet sob as she crushed her mouth to his. He tightened his arms about her, shielding her from the world, as he lost himself in the feel of her soft lips.

He didn't know if it was minutes or hours later when they finally broke apart, dragging in ragged breaths. He rested his forehead against hers.

"Are you certain?" he asked, voice low. "There will be no turning back."

She pulled away enough to meet his eyes, a playful smile on her slightly swollen lips. "Are you trying to dissuade me, my lord?"

"I should." He smiled and shook his head, brushing his thumb across her cheek. "If I were a better man, I would. Then again, if I were a better man, I would never have proposed such a scheme."

She pressed her fingers to his lips, stopping his words. "There is no better man, Hugo."

He chuckled and pressed a kiss to her fingers. "Now I know for certain you are in no state of mind to be making such monumental decisions. I should return you to your family immediately."

Adaline scoffed and slapped him lightly on the shoulder. "You will do no such thing. Besides, if you had not broached the idea, I would have." She retrieved her satchel from where she had dropped it, and he took it from her, brows raised.

"Is that so?"

"Yes." She stepped closer and placed her hands on his cheeks.

"I am finished with setting aside my happiness in favor of everyone else's."

"And I will make you happy?" he asked, hardly daring to hope she truly meant what she said.

Her gently amused smile soothed the last bit of doubt from his mind. "Despite all odds and both of our attempts to thwart just such an occurrence, yes. You vex me, undeniably. Frustrate me. At times infuriate me."

He chuckled, and she pressed a quick kiss to his jawline, sending his heart racing. "And yet still, I come away from each encounter with you with my heart soaring and a smile upon my lips."

He pulled her closer and kissed the lips that smiled for him. She rose on her toes, deepening it with a tiny moan that brought an answering one from his own throat.

The horse pawed at the ground and shook his head with a snort that brought the reality of their situation crashing back.

Hugo pulled away reluctantly. "As much as I would love to explore all the many ways I plan on making you happy," he said with a wicked grin, "we shall never get the chance if we do not make haste whilst the world yet sleeps."

"Well then, my lord. Let us depart."

He quickly stowed her satchel. "My lady," he said, taking her hand to help her into the curricle. Once he'd settled in beside her, he gave her one last questioning glance.

"Second thoughts, my lord?" she asked with a teasing grin.

He chuckled. "Never." The sturdy chestnut gelding shook his mane when Hugo flicked the reins, and the carriage lurched forward, rattling over the rutted lane. Adaline's hand found his in the dark, her grip steadying him.

"Are we going all the way to Scotland in your gig?" she asked, her tone implying more than her words her skepticism at traveling for several days in such a light vehicle. "And will your family not notice the gig and horse are missing?"

"Eventually," he conceded with a chuckle. "But the gig isn't used much. I'm sure my family will simply assume I have returned to my previous habits and will return eventually. And no, we will only be going a few hours up the road to the next post inn. We will need a fresh horse by then in any case. We can rent a sturdier conveyance with fresh horses at the inn, and I will pay someone to return this handsome gentleman and the gig. After a measured delay, that is. With luck, we shall be well on our way before either of our families have realized we are gone."

"You have thought of everything."

"I have. I am quite proud of myself, truth be told. I have absconded with a beautiful lady, and no one is the wiser."

She laughed, as he'd intended, and snuggled into him. "The Marquess of Mayhem, indeed. You are certainly living up to the name."

He wrapped his arm around her shoulders, drawing her into his warmth. "I must prove my worth to my Millie, mustn't I? Give her a reason to follow me into mischief."

She shook her head, though her smile did not fade. "You have nothing to prove to me, my lord. And I hope my being here now proves I will follow you anywhere."

He met her eyes, his throat tightening at the way she gazed up at him. He nodded and swallowed hard against the emotion. Then pressed a gentle kiss to her lips.

Then another, his blood pounding when she melted against him.

He pulled her closer, their lips moving feverishly together. For a moment, nothing else existed but the two of them. He forgot where they were, what they were doing. Everything but the feel of her in his arms. The soft sweetness of her lips giving way to his. He had dreamt of holding her so since the moment he'd read her first letter. Since the moment she'd berated him in that hat shop. Even through the anger and the mistrust and the doubts, he had always been drawn to her. Intrigued by her. Captivated.

And the feeling had only grown more intense the better he'd

gotten to know her.

Now? Now, he was willing follow her over a cliff, just to be there to try and cushion her fall.

How he ever got lucky enough to have her fall in love with him as well, he'd never know. But he'd never stop trying to prove that he deserved her.

His hand moved from her shoulder, up the slender column of her neck to tangle in her hair. He cupped the back of her head, angling her so he could explore her mouth more fully. She wrapped one arm about his neck, pressing her body against his. The hand that was trapped between their bodies, she laid on his thigh, and he groaned, sorely tempted to—

The horse snorted and tossed his head, and the curricle's wheel bounced hard over a large rock on the side of the road. Adaline gasped, and Hugo scrambled for the reins he had dropped.

"My apologies," he said with a sheepish chuckle once he'd guided the horse back to the smoother middle of the road. "I must have been distracted."

He fixed a heated gaze on her, fire rushing through his veins at the slow smile she gave him. God, but the woman was perfection.

"It is I who should apologize," she said. "I shall try to keep my hands to myself."

"Perish the thought!" he said, flashing a properly horrified look at her. He wrapped his arm back around her and drew her as tight to his side as he could. "You shall sit right here and do whatever wicked things you would like to do to me. And I shall endeavor to keep the horse on the path whilst you do."

She laughed and shook her head, keeping her hands firmly tucked inside her cloak. But she did not move away. He would accept that as a consolation. For now. Once they got to the inn however…perhaps they would stop to rest for the night.

His body tightened at the thought, even as he knew it wasn't possible. They needed to put as much distance between them and

London before daybreak as they could. It might be afternoon or even evening before his family would think to wonder where he was. But Adaline, he had no doubt, would be missed much more quickly.

If they weren't wedded and bedded by the time their families caught up to them, it was very likely they'd never be permitted to see each other again.

Or…he'd be staring down the dangerous end of a pistol held by her brother at tomorrow's dawn.

They rode in companionable silence for a few moments, though Hugo kept an anxious eye on the gathering clouds obscuring the moon. A few drops began hitting the hood of the curricle. Not a huge concern, as long as the rain stayed light. And didn't last long.

Adaline did not complain, but he couldn't miss her slight shivering with her body tucked up against his. He wrapped his arm more firmly about her.

"I do wish we could have taken my family's carriage. It would have been much more comfortable and kept us fully shielded from the elements. But my family would certainly have noticed it missing."

"Hmm, no doubt," she said. "Especially as it would have required four horses compared to the one you've taken."

He chuckled. "True." Then he sighed, bemused at how his life had changed. "This may be the first time when I am not relishing choosing subterfuge over safety."

Adaline snorted softly. "Spoken like the agent of mischief you are." She patted him sympathetically. "No worries. I have no doubt you will be back to your devil-may-care ways soon. But in this instance, it cannot be helped."

"Hmm, true," he said, pressing a kiss to her temple.

Thankfully, the post inn was only another hour or two up the road. With luck, they could rent a post chaise and horses and be on their way. The need for a postillion was unfortunate. But the benefit of the enclosed chaise for both privacy and protection from the weather outweighed the drawbacks of hiring a driver for the duration of their trip.

"How did you make your escape?" he asked, both to help pass the time and because he was genuinely curious. Her family was surely far more concerned with her whereabouts in the dark hours of the night than his were of him.

Adaline gave him a wicked little grin that had him wanting to both applaud and pull her on his lap to kiss her senseless.

"I feigned a headache. Locked myself in my room, and then when everyone was occupied for the night, I snuck down the back stairs and out one of the back doors we never use. I left a note for my maid. She will inform my family, of course. But I do hope if she discovers me gone before morning that she gives us a little time before she sounds the alarm."

"Hmm yes," he murmured, wishing he could spur the horse a little faster.

But the rain was coming harder, beginning to lash down at the hood of his gig. If it didn't let up, the road would soon be a quagmire of unpassable mud.

Within a quarter hour, with his view of the road ahead obscured by sheets of unrelenting rain, Hugo slowed. The gelding tossed his head, displeased. Puddles pooled in the ruts, mud splashed up, and the wheels threatened to slide.

"Hold tight, love," Hugo said. "Hopefully this will pass soon."

Adaline, her hair curling damp at her brow, smiled. "I am perfectly well. Do not fret about me." Her attempt at nonchalance was belied by the chattering of her teeth.

Hugo appreciated her trying to assuage his worries, but his concern only deepened. The horse's gait faltered, and the carriage jolted dangerously. Adaline shivered, though she tried to mask it. He pressed his lips together, weighing the risk of continuing versus the need for shelter. The inn was still at least an hour up the road. Likely longer, given the current conditions.

Hugo's jaw set. "We must stop. I will not endanger you, nor the horse."

"Is that safe?" Adaline asked, her brow creasing in a frown. "They may be searching for us even now."

"It cannot be helped," he replied, his concern for her wellbeing overshadowing his fear of being discovered. He scanned the landscape, searching for any sign of refuge. The main road narrowed, then diverged. A rough track seemed to cut through the woods up ahead. Narrow, but well-traveled and wide enough for the horse and gig to pass safely. And at least the trees would shelter them from the worst of the rain.

He turned the gig, guiding it gingerly off the main lane.

The rain intensified, thunder rumbling in the distance. The track twisted between ancient trees, roots snaking across the path. Adaline braced herself against the bumps and jolts as best she could, though they were both being bounced about until their teeth rattled.

At last, there was a break in the trees, and an outline of a building appeared in a small clearing. A cottage, from what he could tell. Long abandoned, its stone walls streaked with moss and ivy, its sagging roof hunched low over shuttered windows. Hugo exhaled in relief.

He drew the gig to a halt, leapt down, and helped Adaline to the ground. The horse whickered, stamping restlessly.

"Wait here," he bid Adaline, pushing open the cottage door so he could quickly inspect it before she went inside.

The door hinges protested, obviously unused to being opened. A good sign. They were sorely in need of those. Inside, the air was stale and musty, cobwebs swathing the corners. And everything was covered with a thick layer of dust. There was no bed. No furniture at all aside from a dilapidated table and a broken basket near the hearth with a few moth-eaten blankets. Rough, but serviceable. They would do.

He went back out to fetch Adaline, his heart jumping when he didn't immediately see her or the horse and gig. But a noise around the back led him to a small lean-to where she had improvised some shelter for the animal. She was stroking the gelding's neck, murmuring reassurances to him, but paused to smile at Hugo when he appeared.

His heart swelled at the sight of her. There she stood, sodden, shivering. Yet not a word of complaint passing her lips though he deserved a thorough tongue-lashing for stealing her from her warm bed in the dead of night to lead her directly into a storm.

He pulled her to him, his hands trying to rub some warmth back into her arms. He gave her a swift kiss, then turned her toward the cottage.

"Go inside while I tend to the horse. There are some blankets by the hearth. I'll see what I can find for firewood."

Hugo settled the horse and returned to her as quickly as possible, his arms laden with firewood he'd scavenged from beneath the eaves.

Adaline raised a dented tinderbox with a triumphant smile. "I found this in the corner."

"Excellent," Hugo exclaimed, praying their good luck held out. "That is fortunate, indeed."

He knelt before the hearth, coaxing flame from brittle twigs and shavings while Adaline removed her sodden cloak, draping it over the table to dry.

Hugo breathed another sigh of relief when the flame caught, greedily jumping to the logs he fed into the hearth. In a few moments, they had a crackling fire casting welcome warmth into the cottage.

He removed his greatcoat, hanging it from a hook near the door, and then reached out, catching Adaline's hand to draw her down beside him so she could get warm. She leaned against him with a surprisingly contented sigh and held her hands out to the flames. Then she hesitated, glancing at her sodden gown.

"We must dry our clothing," she said, glancing up at him, her cheeks flushing. "Or we'll catch our death of cold."

She pulled away from him and slowly stood, her gaze locking with his. His heart thundered, his mouth drying out completely when she reached up and began undoing the fastenings of her gown.

Chapter Thirty-One

Adaline's hands trembled as she undid the laces and pins that held her dress in place. Yes, they needed to dry their clothing. But that was just a convenient excuse. They were alone. Really and truly alone. On their way to be wed. And she had been dreaming about what this moment would be like for months. She would not squander the opportunity. Not when he was standing before, his hungry eyes devouring her as much as hers were likely doing to him.

"Adaline," he said, his voice gruff with an emotion she couldn't quite name. But that made a delicious shiver run through her.

She didn't answer, but merely pulled the last pin holding her gown to her stays and let it fall.

Hugo watched in rapt wonder as her gown puddled at her feet, leaving her in her petticoat, stays, and chemise. With every layer of clothing that she removed, she grew more bold. More confident. It was difficult not to when the man of her desires stared at her as if she were Aphrodite herself disrobing before him.

When she stood in nothing but her chemise, she moved toward him. Then lifted her hands to push his coat from his shoulders. She pulled his cravat from his throat, smiling when he swallowed hard. Her fingers trembled only slightly as she worked at the buttons of his waistcoat, her eyes never leaving his.

She pushed it from his shoulders, along with the braces that held his trousers up. When she began to tug his shirt from his waistband, he stopped her, his hands encompassing hers.

"Are you certain?"

She smiled up at him, tamping down on the nervousness that threatened to undermine the confidence she'd found. "We travel to be wed, do we not?"

"As quickly as I can manage," Hugo said with a smile.

"Then a few days will make no difference." She shrugged. "Merely traveling alone with you, not to mention spending the night alone in this cottage, is enough to ruin me. Even if you were never to lay a finger on me." She pulled at the cotton fabric of his shirt, biting her lip when her hand came in contact with the bare skin of his stomach.

He sucked in a hissing breath, the sound making things tighten low in her belly. She untucked the rest of his shirt and skimmed her hands up his bare chest beneath it.

"If we are to be damned no matter our actions tonight, there is no reason not to do what we most desire," she said, trailing kisses up his chest as she lifted his shirt and helped him remove it.

Hugo sucked in a ragged breath and crushed her to him. He was done objecting, it seemed. His mouth worked over hers until she moaned against his lips. He ground his hips against her, and she gasped at the hard length she could feel rubbing against her core.

Lucy had revealed some of the secrets of the marriage bed to her. Far more than her mother had ever divulged. Adaline was an educated and curious woman who enjoyed reading novels that were considered scandalous by most. And Lucy had been helpful in answering some of the questions Adaline had had over the years. She knew the basics. Knew what occurred between a man and woman when they lay together in the dark.

But knowing it, and feeling it, she was discovering, were two entirely different things. Nothing could have prepared her for the sheer sensations that were cascading through her. The utter bliss of his mouth licking and nipping and kissing its way across her exposed skin. The fire that would follow the wake of his hands as they skimmed across her skin and caressed parts of her she had scarce dared touch herself.

She whimpered, desperate for more, as his teeth grazed a trail down her neck.

He picked her up, wrapping her legs around his waist as he carried her to the hearth, and the makeshift bed she had created of the old blankets. He gripped her hips, and she gasped, tightening her legs around him so she could press herself closer. She had never felt such a sensation. Such hardness against her softness. Even when she'd hesitantly touched herself, the sensation had never come close to what she was experiencing now. And she wanted more.

He groaned as she writhed against him and kissed her again, sinking to his knees until he could press her to the pallet, his mouth and hands stroking her into a frenzy. Her blood raced, igniting every nerve ending in her body.

He sucked at her nipple through her chemise, and she struggled for breath.

"If you want me to stop, at any time, you need only say so," he said, his hand massaging her other breast, rolling the nipple between his fingers.

She flung her head back, her body twisting under the delicious torture his mouth and hands were inflicting.

"Do not stop," she begged. "I…I do not know what I want. I don't know what to do. But…" He rocked against her again and she moaned. "Please. Do not stop."

He sucked her earlobe into his mouth. "I want to see every inch of you trembling for me," he breathed into her ear.

She choked out a breathy laugh. "I believe you already are."

The heated smile he gave her set her on fire. "Oh. I think I can do better than that."

He stood to unbutton his trousers, and her mouth went dry

as she stared at the expanse of muscle he revealed. And the evidence of his desire for her. She'd heard of it. Read of it. Seeing it was another thing entirely. And feeling it… She trembled again, her body already aching for him in ways she didn't quite understand. Yet.

She grabbed the hem of her chemise and pulled it over her head, leaving her kneeling in front of him, wearing nothing at all.

His eyes widened as he took her in. "You are so beautiful," he said, his gravelly voice sending another shiver through her.

He leaned back over her, pulling her with him onto her side and hitching her thigh over his leg. She pressed against him again and let out a strangled gasp when the hard length of him nudged at her entrance. He kept her at bay, not letting her get too close, though every instinct she had screamed for him. Her body arched against his, trying to bring as much flesh into contact as possible.

"Not yet," her murmured against her lips. "Your first time, you will likely feel some pain. I want you to feel pleasure first."

More than this? Was that even possible?

He chuckled, and she realized she'd said that aloud. But before she could be embarrassed, his mouth left her breast and trailed down her body, settling near the apex of her thighs. His hands slid up her legs, pushing them farther apart, gripping her hips to keep them still when she squirmed beneath him. His tongue circled, once, twice, before slipping inside. Her hips left the bed and he licked her in long, sure strokes, holding her hips against him so she couldn't escape, tormenting her with every touch of his mouth until she came apart.

He sat up, hauling her back beneath him and kissed her until she whimpered. The taste of her on his lips made her quiver beneath him while he continued to drive her mad.

"Hugo," she said, clutching at him.

"Easy, love," he said, kneeling between her thighs. "Are you certain?" he asked again.

"Yes. Please."

Perhaps she should have thought about it longer. Perhaps she should be more prudent, wait until they were actually wed. But she didn't want to wait anymore. She was tired of waiting.

This man had slowly become everything to her. First her enemy, then a cautious friend, now…a lover. Soon, God willing, her husband.

She'd left her home, willingly put her future in his safekeeping. Perhaps it was a mistake. But for her, it was too late now. She fully intended upon marrying him. But if something were to go awry… Whether they walked away from each other or continued on to Gretna Green, she wanted this moment with him. She wanted something she could hold onto for the rest of her life. Whether this was the start of a lifetime of happiness, or a small moment of beautiful bliss that could sustain her through a dark future without him, she needed this moment with him.

When he finally pressed himself home, she sucked in a gasp at the pinch of pain. He murmured to her, sweet words of love and encouragement she didn't quite hear above the pounding of her heart. He kissed her and stroked her, rebuilding that heat that threatened to consume her.

And when it finally did, when that overwhelming sensation finally crested into another explosion that made her head spin and her heart shatter, she held onto him. Her anchor in the darkness. Her safe haven. Her enemy. Her friend. Her confidante.

"Beloved," he whispered, pressing a kiss to her lips so sweet, it brought tears to her eyes.

She didn't know if she'd spoken the other words aloud or if, as always, he just knew her mind enough to know what she was thinking. How she felt. It didn't matter at the end of it. All that mattered was him. This moment.

"Beloved," she whispered back, wrapping her arms about him as she drifted off into sweet oblivion.

CHAPTER THIRTY-TWO

HUGO COULDN'T STOP smiling as he came back inside the cottage and was greeted by an equally happy and adorably rumpled Adaline. The sun had barely risen, and the horse and gig were ready to resume their journey. It had thankfully stopped raining and while there was still a great deal of mud about, the conditions had improved considerably. Once they were back on the main road, he hoped they would make good time.

Adaline's cloak, he was happy to note, was almost completely dry and toasty warm from its position nearest the fire during the night. He wrapped it about her shoulders, taking the opportunity to pull her close and press a lingering kiss to her lips.

A throaty little hum escaped her throat, and she nestled closer, wrapping her arms about his waist.

"Must we leave already?" she murmured, pressing a kiss to the hollow of his throat.

He chuckled, the sound low and gravelly. A delicious little tremor ran through her and she burrowed even closer to his chest. "Oh, if ever I were to be tempted to climb back into bed, it would be now. In fact, I shall probably berate myself for this moment for the rest of the day." He sighed and lifted her chin with his finger. "But unfortunately, we have already lingered too long. We must be on our way before—"

A muffled shout and rapidly approaching horse hooves had

Hugo spinning toward the door and shoving Adaline behind him. He pulled a pistol from beneath his cloak and aimed it at the door.

"Hugo," Adaline gasped.

Before he could say anything, the door flew open and Henry burst in. He came to a sudden halt, freezing at the sight of Hugo. And his pistol.

The moment Hugo realized who had come through the door, he immediately aimed the gun toward the ceiling, then tucked it back in his waistband. But he kept Adaline firmly behind him, backing them slowly away from her irate brother.

The moment Henry saw Adaline clinging to Hugo—and the crumpled bedding in front of the hearth—unmitigated chaos broke out. His shouting drew in the others. Arthur, their parents, even Adaline's mother and his own grandmother had ventured in.

It didn't take long for them to all ascertain what had occurred there the night before. Hugo and Adaline watched in horrified bemusement as everyone began shouting at once. Her family were shrieking at him, his at her, then they turned on each other.

Arthur seemed to be trying to calm the situation. Henry, on the other hand, stood with his nose less than an inch from Arthur's spitting accusations and threats while their mothers stood, only slightly more civilized, bellowing their wrath at each other. Hugo's father seemed at a total loss as to what to do, and his grandmother was in the corner...laughing, if he wasn't mistaken.

Adaline crept out from behind Hugo, her gaze bouncing between them all, her mouth open in astonishment. Then her eyes narrowed with pure anger, and she strode forward, dodging his attempt to draw her back.

"That is *enough!*" she shouted above the uproar.

The stunned silence was immediate, and everyone turned to stare at Adaline.

"What is going on in here," her mother said, pushing her way into the already crowded cottage…and coming to an abrupt stop at the sight with which she was greeted. "Adaline," she breathed, bringing a trembling hand to her mouth. "What have you done?"

Adaline squared her shoulders, but Hugo had had enough.

"She has done nothing," he said, his words clipped and furious. He took her hand and drew her back to his side. He would have liked to have planted himself firmly in front of her, but he knew she wouldn't stand for that. And she had as much right to confront their families as he did. Though he wouldn't hesitate to throw himself in front of her if anyone showed any signs of violence.

"If there is any blame to be laid, it is at my feet. Not hers."

"No," Adaline murmured, but he stood more firmly. He would not allow anyone to disparage her, no matter who it was.

"You have ruined her," her mother cried.

"He has done nothing of the sort," Adaline protested.

Another chorus of collective arguments broke out, the volume growing until his grandmother banged her cane against the ground, drawing everyone's attention.

"Jumping to conclusions never helped anyone," she said. "Perhaps we should ascertain the truth of the matter before we pick out our dueling weapons."

Her amusement-tinged gaze flashed to Henry, who hadn't taken *his* furious gaze off Hugo.

"The truth is of little consequence in these matters," Mrs. Girard said. "They spent the entire night alone. Even if he slept with the horse, she is still ruined."

His grandmother remained unfazed. "She is only compromised if he will not marry her. And considering where we have found them, I do not think that is an issue. Is it?" she asked Hugo.

"Of course not," he said, squeezing Adaline's hand. "We are traveling to Gretna Green so that we can be married immediately." He did not say *were* because he still fully intended on getting Adaline over the border and making her his wife as soon as humanly possible.

Though the uproar that followed his announcement did not bode well.

"But the scandal, Adaline!" her mother said, wringing her hands.

"It will die down soon enough," Adaline said, trying to placate her, "as long as we are wed. We are far from the first couple to elope."

"I see. And was this the plan all along?" his father asked. "We wouldn't give permission and so you concocted this scheme to wed my son? Did it even matter which one?"

"Father!" Hugo's fists clenched, his anger burning through him so hotly, he shook with the force of it.

"How dare you?" Mrs. Girard sputtered.

"He will wed her or face me in a duel!" Henry shouted.

"No one is dueling," both of their mothers said, turning to each other in surprise at their momentary agreement…that rapidly devolved into another shouting match over who was trying to ruin who.

Arthur seemed to be the lone voice of reason, attempting to interject that if they truly loved each other, they should be allowed to be together.

His grandmother stood solidly in the middle of the fray, her eyes narrowed as the insults flew around her, the voices mingling until Hugo could hardly tell who was shouting what at whom.

"If he doesn't marry her, she'll be ruined!"

"If he does marry her, he'll be cut off!"

"She should be sent to a convent!"

"Convents do not exist anymore!"

"More's the pity!"

"This is your fault!"

"He'll not get a penny of her dowry!"

"She'll not get a penny of his inheritance!"

"You crafted this scheme!"

"I will see you at dawn, sir!"

"If everyone could calm down, perhaps—"

"He is a brigand!"

"She is a schemer!"

"I shall call the constable!"

"I will appeal to the queen!"

Adaline stepped closer to Hugo, burying her face against his chest, and he wrapped his arm around her shoulders, pulling her against him. She gazed up at him, her eyes filling with tears. The sight threatened to rend his already breaking heart beyond repair.

"I do not care what they threaten," he said. "Let them cut me off. We will be fine. I will happily live in this cottage with you if we must."

"Hugo…"

"I do not care what they do to me," he insisted, his hand cupping her cheek.

She leaned her face into her hand, then turned it to kiss his palm. "But I do."

He gently brushed a tear from her cheek and kissed her forehead, and she gave him a sorrow-laden smile.

"I love you," she whispered.

And then she stepped away.

His arms dropped to his side, his heart cracking wide open as she took another step, her eyes never leaving his.

He lifted his hand to reach for her. "Adaline," he said, his voice cracking.

But she turned away. "Enough," she said. Her voice was quiet but somehow broke through the bedlam around them. "Enough."

Everyone stared at her, but she focused on Hugo's parents. "I am not a schemer. I would never use Hugo in that way. And I would never deny myself the chance for happiness just to tie my name to yours. But I can see that I will never be able to convince you of that. To prove to you how much I love him." Her voice cracked again, and she closed her eyes for a brief second, sucking in a trembling breath. "I will not allow him to suffer for the sin of loving me."

She glanced back at him with that sad smile that would forever be burned into his heart. "I love him too much for that."

She looked back at his parents. "No one but those of us in this room know what has transpired this night. If no one reveals the secret, there will be no scandal tied to your name."

"No, Adaline," her mother said. "You are still compromised."

Adaline shook her head. "Says who? As far as anyone is aware, we both spent the night peacefully in our own beds. And no one will know different unless someone in this room betrays us."

His father straightened. "You have my word."

Adaline nodded once and turned to the door.

"Adaline," Hugo said again, hoping she would return to his side. Though…he did not know what he would do if she did. He couldn't fight them all off. Though he would die trying if he thought it was what she wanted.

She took a deep shuddering breath. "I will meet you outside," she said to her family.

Her mother looked as though she would protest again, but Adaline looked at her sadly. "Allow me to say goodbye."

Her mother's brow furrowed, lips pinched at her daughter's distress. But she nodded and turned to go, brushing past Hugo's parents and brother.

His father nodded at him. "Say your goodbyes then. I must get your mother and grandmother home and out of the cold. I expect you to be just behind us."

He didn't wait for Hugo's agreement before gesturing for everyone else to leave, obviously expecting total obedience from his son. The thought rankled. He had never had a reason to outright disobey his father before.

But he did now.

His grandmother pinned him with a look on her way out that steeled the resolve that had already begun to settle in him.

He would not lose the woman he loved.

"I will await you both in the carriage," her mother said, not without sympathy. Her eyes crinkled with what looked like regret when she glanced once more at Adaline before leaving.

Finally, only her brother remained, obviously loathe to leave them alone together again. Good. Hugo didn't want him to leave.

Adaline took a step away, but Hugo grasped her hand, keeping her at his side.

"Hugo," she said, her voice cracking again. "I'm so sorry. But I—"

"No," he said, shaking his head. "I will not lose you."

He pulled her to him and wrapped his arm around her shoulders, drawing her close. She didn't fight him. If she had, he would have let her go. Instead, she wrapped her arms about his waist and held him with all her might.

Hugo crushed her to him and kissed the top of her head. Then he pinned her brother with the full force of his fervent gaze.

"Girard," he said. "This is your doing. I know you do not wish to admit so, and I will take responsibility for the blame I bear. I mocked you. I played on your weaknesses and exploited them for my amusement. And I bitterly regret it. But what occurred afterward? This animosity between our families? It is largely of your own making."

Henry bristled. But...he did not argue. His eyes shifted to his sister for a moment, and then back to Hugo.

"You could fix this," Hugo said, his voice deep with emotion. "All of it. Own your part in this. Take responsibility, as I have done. Your family's objection to me is the humiliation I caused them. Caused Adaline. The damage that embarrassment did to her future. I cannot undo what has been done. Though I have made amends as best as I can, and I will continue to do so for the rest of my days if need be.

"But there would have been no humiliation without your scheming or misunderstanding, whichever you want to call it. And my family's fears of Adaline and her motives only exist because of the tales you told. I will not lose the woman I love because you do not wish to take responsibility for the part you played. Fix this. If you love your sister, fix this."

Henry's jaw clenched, perhaps working around words he did not want to say. Could not say. Didn't know how to say.

"I will beg if I must," Hugo said, his own voice cracking under the weight of his imminent loss. "Help us."

"Henry," Adaline said, her quiet voice drawing his gaze. "I love him. Please."

Henry stared at his sister and swallowed hard before tearing his eyes from her and bowing his head. He kept his gaze on the ground, too many emotions chasing across his face for Hugo to identify them all. Though there was one he recognized. One he had seen on his own face more than once over the last few months.

Shame.

Henry finally sucked in a deep breath and let it out slowly before slowly nodding. He looked back at his sister, his eyes suspiciously bright.

"Very well."

Adaline startled and pushed away from Hugo.

"Henry?" she asked.

"He is right," he said, though his lips puckered a bit as he let the admission slip. Then he let out a loud and exhausted sigh. "He is right." He gave his sister a tight smile. "I...will make things right."

Adaline's breath left her in a rush, and she threw herself into her brother's arms. "Thank you," she said, kissing him on the cheek before letting him go to return to Hugo.

The sudden rush of relief—and disbelief—that hit Hugo was enough to make his head spin. He held onto Adaline, letting her anchor him until he felt steady once more.

He nodded at Henry. "Thank you," he said, his voice gruff.

Henry nodded in return, then took another deep breath. "Go," he said, startling them both again.

"What?" Adaline asked.

"You mean to do right by my sister, do you not?" Henry

asked, pinning Hugo with a fierce stare. "You mean to marry her?"

Hugo nodded, wrapping his arm more tightly around Adaline. "As soon as we can manage."

Henry gave him a sharp jerk of his head. "Then go. I will cover for you. Your family has already left. And I will deal with Mother," he said to Adaline. "I cannot promise your family will not follow again, Brelsford. But I will do my best to keep them from your trail. Hopefully my confession eases your path somewhat." He jerked his head toward the door again. "Go."

Hugo looked down at Adaline, making sure she was still with him. The brilliant smile she aimed at him nearly brought him to his knees. She went to give Henry one last hug while Hugo quickly gathered their things and threw her cloak around her shoulders. Then he clasped her hand in his, gave Henry one last nod, and hurried out the door to his gig.

"Adaline?" her mother said, hanging her head from her carriage as Adaline and Hugo quickly got into his gig. "Where are you going? Henry, what is going on? They—"

"Be still, Mother," Henry said. "All is well. I will explain."

Hugo snapped the reins and guided the horse back through the woods and onto the main road. Adaline snuggled against his side, fairly radiating happiness. He pressed a kiss to her temple.

"I can hardly believe this is real. It is, isn't it?" she asked.

"Oh, my love." Hugo cupped her face in his free hand and kissed her until his heart ached. "Yes. It's real. Though I will not rest easy until you are my wife in truth. If you'll still have me."

She raised her brows. "You must ask?"

"It seems prudent under the circumstances."

She laughed and shook her head. He loved that sound. The sound of her happiness. Perhaps more than any other sound on earth.

"My Millie," he whispered, kissing her again. "Will you be my wife?"

Adaline leaned forward, bringing her lips back to his. Again and again. "My brilliant, mad, resourceful Mayhem," she said, laughing again. "Yes. A thousand times yes. On one condition."

His eyes widened. "And what is that?"

"That you keep writing to me."

Hugo laughed. "Always, my love."

About the Author

USA Today bestselling author Michelle McLean is a jeans and t-shirt kind of girl who is addicted to chocolate and Goldfish crackers and spent most of her formative years with her nose in a book. She has degrees in history and English and is thrilled that she sort of gets to use them.

Her love of historical romance began in the pages of a Victoria Holt novel. A love that is entirely to blame for both her degrees and her current career. Her days are spent working in her local high school library and writing…or avoiding deadlines by fixating on a variety of hobbies or, if really desperate, cleaning something.

She currently resides in PA with her husband and two kids, the world's most spoiled dog, and a cat who absolutely rules the house. She also writes contemporary romance as Kira Archer. Her novel Truly, Madly, Sweetly, written as Kira Archer, was adapted as a Hallmark Original movie in 2018.

Social Media Links:
Newsletter: landing.mailerlite.com/webforms/landing/b6c0h6
Website: michellemcleanbooks.com
Instagram: michellemcleanbooks
Facebook: michelle.m.mclean
Tiktok: @authormichellemclean
Pinterest: michellemcleanbooks
Amazon: amazon.com/stores/Michelle-McLean/author/B0041OFZSS
Bookbub: bookbub.com/authors/michelle-mclean